Praise for Thomas Kies

Random Road
The First Geneva Chase Crime Reporter Mystery

A *Library Journal* Book of the Month

"Kies's debut mystery introduces a reporter with a compelling voice, a damaged woman who recounts her own bittersweet story as she hunts down clues. This suspenseful story will appeal to readers who enjoy hard-nosed investigative reporters such as Brad Parks's Carter Ross."

—*Library Journal*, Starred Review

"Kies tells a taut, fast-paced tale, imbuing each character with memorable, compelling traits that help readers connect with them."

—*Booklist*

"Kies's fiction debut lays the groundwork for an entertaining series."

—*Kirkus Reviews*

Darkness Lane
The Second Geneva Chase Crime Reporter Mystery

"Multiple m_____ _____ ____ ____ key components in Geneva's ul____ ____ _____ The flawed but dedicated heroi__ ____ ___ __ ___ _y with a compassion that compels readers to root for b___, ice and redemption."

—*Kirkus Reviews*

"Kies neatly balances breathless action with Geneva Chase's introspection and sleuthing savvy."

—*Publishers Weekly*

"There's a solid thriller here—the key is sex trafficking—but the real pleasure is watching Geneva work. Cheer her on as she wrestles with that vodka bottle and trembles with fear as she confronts the monster behind the child-slavery ring. She's also pretty good at standing up to a newspaper publisher about to screw the help into the ground."

—Don Crinklaw, *Booklist*

Graveyard Bay
The Third Geneva Chase Crime Reporter Mystery

"Journalism may be changing, but investigative reporters like Geneva Chase will always find the truth. *Graveyard Bay* is a tense, razor-sharp hunt for some genuinely terrifying criminals, set in a vivid and believable New England winter."

—Joseph Finder, *New York Times*
bestselling author of *Judgment*

"When it comes to gritty, real-life plots, believable characters, and on-point descriptions of both people and place, Thomas Kies can't be beat."

—*New York Journal of Books*

Also by Thomas Kies

The Geneva Chase Crime Reporter Mysteries
Random Road
Darkness Lane
Graveyard Bay

SHADOW HILL

SHADOW HILL

A GENEVA CHASE CRIME REPORTER MYSTERY

THOMAS KIES

Poisoned Pen
PRESS

Published by Poisoned Pen Press, an imprint of Sourcebooks
P.O. Box 4410, Naperville, Illinois 60567-4410
(630) 961-3900
sourcebooks.com

Library of Congress Cataloging-in-Publication Data

Names: Kies, Thomas, author.
Title: Shadow Hill / Thomas Kies.
Description: Naperville, Illinois : Poisoned Pen Press, [2021] | Series: A
   Geneva Chase crime reporter mystery ; 4
Identifiers: LCCN 2020031818 (print) | LCCN 2020031819
   (ebook) | (trade paperback) | (epub) | ISBN
   9781464214424 (pdf)
Subjects: GSAFD: Mystery fiction.
Classification: LCC PS3611.I3993 S53 2021 (print) | LCC PS3611.I3993
   (ebook) | DDC 813/.6--dc23
LC record available at https://lccn.loc.gov/2020031818
LC ebook record available at https://lccn.loc.gov/2020031819

Printed and bound in the United States of America.
SB 10 9 8 7 6 5 4 3 2 1

Chapter One

Bleach.

The smell is all that's left behind when the cleanup crew in the hazmat suits have scraped up the blood, brain tissue, and skull fragments. All the evidence of two violent deaths was wiped away.

Except for that lingering smell of bleach.

"My father didn't kill himself." Eric Cutter whispered, shaking his head, his eyes wide. Ever since we'd entered the house, he'd kept his voice low. As if he didn't want to awaken any ghosts. "And he sure as hell didn't kill our mother."

His wife, Olivia, nodded silently in agreement, stealing nervous glances in the direction of the kitchen where her in-laws had violently died.

The heat in the house was off, and there was a February chill in the air. I involuntarily shivered in the damp living room.

Standing next to me, Nathaniel Rubin, owner of the agency for whom I'd just started freelancing, wore a wool overcoat over his trademark blue button-down shirt, red bow tie, black slacks, and black sport coat. He gripped the handle of his scuffed, leather valise that held the police report. Nathaniel was tall, was in his forties, and had a full head of prematurely silver hair. His thin, clean-shaven face reminded me a little of an eagle with his prominent nose and his wide eyes, unblinking behind wire-frame glasses.

It was Sunday afternoon. On Friday, when Nathaniel had emailed me about this meeting, I'd looked the tony Sheffield shoreline address up online. Situated on the edge of Long Island Sound, the house had been put up for sale about a month before Morris and Julia Cutter died. The mansion's price tag was slightly under eleven million dollars.

Modest for that waterfront neighborhood.

The home was constructed primarily of fieldstone and wood, both inside and out, giving it the dark, cold feel of a medieval castle. It was intensified by the multiple stone fireplaces, thick-beamed ceilings, and stained-glass windows throughout the nine-bedroom home. Nestled in a quiet cul-de-sac, at the end of a long, tree-lined drive, the home was surrounded by seven acres of rolling lawn and had a stunning view of the water. Of course, it came with a swimming pool and a tennis court. Both were closed for the winter.

The website said that the house had been built in the thirties, but it felt much older than that to me, like it had been there for centuries. But whether it had been constructed during the Great Depression or during the Reagan years, it smelled like every other house there on the shoreline. It reeked of money.

And now, bleach.

That afternoon, before Eric and Olivia had arrived in their seventy-thousand-dollar BMW Series 6 sedan, Nathaniel and I waited in the front bucket seats of my road-salt-encrusted, muddy, ten-year-old Sebring, discussing the police report and looking through some of the photos. It appeared that the cops had done everything by the book. They'd locked down the house and treated it like a crime scene, looked for prints, taken photos, shot video, talked to the neighbors, family, and friends. There were no signs of a forced entry, no signs of a struggle.

They concluded that Morris Cutter had come up behind his wife, shot her once in the head, then put the gun to his right temple and pulled the trigger.

Murder-suicide, case closed.

When it happened, I was still the *Sheffield Post* crime reporter. The media, including my own newspaper, had a field day with it. The deaths of Morris and Julia Cutter were a huge deal. To the world, they had it all. Morris had recently retired from his high-profile position as CEO with Continental Petroleum & Gas, and the couple had the money and the time to do anything they wanted.

And yet Morris Cutter killed his wife and himself.

You never really know what bugs are crawling around in someone's head, do you?

As we sat in the car, motor running, heater cranked up high, Nathaniel lifted his eyes from the police report and spoke to me from around the peppermint Life Saver he had in his mouth. He confirmed what I was thinking. "The cops were very thorough. They didn't want to make any mistakes."

I nodded. "I get the feeling that we don't want to either."

Morris Cutter had been a philanthropist, well known in the community, and Julia Cutter had served on the boards of the town's hospital and library. Both were known as being generous. For days after their bodies were found, the story was front page news both locally and in New York, where Morris had worked. Conspiracy theories and dark rumors were rampant. It was difficult to grasp that someone so wealthy and successful could murder his wife and then blow his own brains out on the kitchen floor of his multimillion-dollar mansion.

It had to have been a double murder. Or at least that was the street gossip.

Fingers were pointed at rival oil companies and oil-rich countries like Saudi Arabia, Venezuela, and Russia. Blame was leveled at climate activists. Even Morris's own family found itself on the wrong end of murder theories.

The Sheffield cops had wanted to get the investigation right, and so did we.

When I saw the Beamer drive up, I quickly pulled down my visor and checked myself out in the mirror.

My name is Geneva Chase, and I'm a freelance journalist formerly with the *Sheffield Post* and a half dozen other media outlets. Around Christmas, I had a job offer to be a full-time "researcher" at Lodestar Analytics, owned by Nathaniel Rubin. I didn't like the idea of being tied down to a single company again, so I agreed to work for him in a freelance capacity, which would allow me to work for other media outlets as well. That way I could work on the stories and jobs I wanted and walk away from the stinkers.

I'm crowding forty, and yes, I'm concerned about my appearance. What girl isn't? I wanted to make sure my blond hair was in place, the liner accenting my blue eyes hadn't smudged, and lipstick wasn't smeared on my front teeth. I try to ignore the encroaching lines and wrinkles around the eyes and mouth that high-priced cosmetics have done well to camouflage.

I could see Nathaniel's bemused expression in my peripheral vision. "Girl's got to look good for the clients, boss."

He smiled. "Time to meet the aggrieved children."

———

"I don't care what the goddamned cops say." Eric said, his voice low and tense.

We stood in the living room on thick, wine-colored carpeting.

In strategic areas of the expansive room were white fabric couches, upholstered wingback chairs, and coffee tables replete with stacks of books. All of it was covered in opaque plastic to keep ambient dust from settling on expensive surfaces.

Jutting out of the wall to our right was one of the home's massive stone fireplaces, cold and empty. Framed paintings of ships on rolling oceans hung on plaster walls. A single brass lamp, from one of the end tables near the foyer where we'd entered, served as our illumination. The only other light came from the dim February sunlight creeping through gaps in the closed curtains of the bay windows overlooking the front lawn.

An antique grandfather clock stood silent sentinel against the wall. The pendulum was still. No one had set the heavy brass counterweights. In this house, time had stopped.

The house was much like that fireplace in the living room. Cold and empty.

To me, it felt like the life had been sucked out of it.

I was certain that at some point, the home had been filled with laughter, lively conversations, warm, crackling fires, and the scents of delicious meals.

But at that moment, it was a house of ghosts.

Nathaniel glanced at me with an expectant expression.

I took a breath before I started. This was the very first street assignment that he'd given me since I'd started freelancing for Lodestar Analytics, a commercial research and intelligence firm based in New York, and I desperately wanted to impress my new boss.

I'd even dressed up. I was wearing a knee-length wool skirt and a conservative long-sleeved top under a black ankle-length coat. Oh, and heels. I hate heels. I'm tall enough without them, plus they hurt my feet.

I began by asking, "Can you think of anyone who would want to harm your parents?"

Eric's chin jutted and his eyes narrowed. "Too many to name. Competitors, politicians, crazy environmentalists, you name it. You know that he used to run an oil company?"

I nodded. "I do. Did he ever get death threats?"

"All the time. While he was CEO, the company paid for around-the-clock security."

"But not after he retired?"

"No. The company didn't seem to think he needed it anymore. Neither did Dad. Although he kept a gun with him most of the time."

Is that what he killed your mother and himself with?

I didn't ask that question but tucked it away as something I'd want an answer to.

I glanced at Nathaniel, waiting to see if he was going to jump in at any time. When it became obvious that he wasn't, I asked the hard question. "After he retired, what was your father's state of mind?"

Eric shot me an evil look. "You mean was he depressed?"

I nodded silently.

"He'd been looking forward to retirement for years. He said he wanted to travel just to enjoy the sights. Not have to worry about business or politics. He wanted to write a history of the business. The Cutter family started CP&G before World War II. Dad was looking forward to having time to do that." His expression softened. "Believe me, he wasn't depressed."

"Were your mother and father having any problems?"

"With their marriage?" He folded his arms. "Solid as a rock. They loved each other. Every marriage should be as good."

Olivia clearly grimaced.

I continued. "Can you walk me through the day your parents died?"

In his early thirties, Eric personified the patrician son of a successful and powerful executive. Well-groomed black hair slicked back away from his forehead, clean-shaven face, perfect teeth, soft hands, manicured nails. He wore black designer jeans and a black Moncler puffer jacket over a white turtleneck sweater. "It was New Year's Day, and Mom and Dad were supposed to come over to our house for brunch."

I had my reporter's notebook out. "Where do you live?"

Olivia answered. "Ridgefield, 17 Goodwin Circle, it's about twenty minutes from here." Her chestnut hair was shoulder length and swept back in layers. I couldn't help but marvel at how perfect her cheekbones and skin were.

Money will do that for you.

Her wide brown eyes glanced at the kitchen doorway again. *The kitchen. Where it happened.*

I turned to Eric and repeated back to him what he'd just told me. "Your folks were supposed to come to your house for brunch."

He took a breath. "Right. They were supposed to show up at eleven, but when it got to be nearly noon, I tried calling them. Dad's never late for anything. I tried their landline, I tried their cell phones, all I got was voicemail."

Olivia glanced at her husband. "It wasn't like them at all. When we'd talked to them on New Year's Eve, they were really excited about coming to see the baby."

I smiled. "You have a baby?"

She gave me a proud grin. "A little girl, six months old; her name's Amelia."

"Such a cute age."

Like I know.

I've never had children of my own. As close as I've come was when my fiancé died and I became legal guardian of his daughter, Caroline, now fifteen years old and a roller-coaster ride of attitude and mood swings. "Who's watching Amelia now?"

"Maria, our live-in nanny."

Nice address, live-in nanny, expensive car; we've established that everyone involved so far is stinkin' rich.

"You couldn't reach your parents by phone."

"I got worried and drove over here to make sure they were okay," Eric said. "When I got here, I saw Dad's car was in the drive. I figured they had to be home unless they took Mom's car, which Dad never does. So, now I'm really freaking out, and I knocked on the door, but there wasn't any answer."

"Was the door locked?"

"Yes. I used my spare key to let myself in."

I glanced back at the front doorway, a solid combination of oak and stained glass. I noticed there was a square box with a keypad on the wall next to it. "Was the alarm on?"

Eric shook his head. "No. I immediately thought that was odd. They were religious about keeping it on, even when they were home."

"Anyone else that you know has a spare key and knows the alarm code?"

He thought a moment, shaking his head. "My sister, Lisa, does. I don't know. Can't think of anyone else."

"Your sister. Was she in town on New Year's Day?"

He shook his head. "No, she lives in DC. Doesn't get up here much anymore. She was up over Christmas to see Amelia"

"How would you describe her relationship with your parents?"

"She was okay with Mom. Lisa and Dad didn't get along at all."

"Why's that?"

He stared at the empty fireplace with an expression of belligerence. "She's a meteorologist for NASA. Believes in this global-warming bullshit. She claimed that Dad and his company were ruining the earth."

Olivia said, "While she was at our place on Christmas, she

told us that if things didn't change, by the time Amelia is grown up, the human race will barely be able to survive. The earth could be a wasteland."

Eric's face was crimson. "Who would say something like that on Christmas? In our own home?"

I needed to get the subject back on track. Recalling that the house had been up for sale, I asked, "How about the Realtor? Does the agency have a key and access to the alarm code?"

"It's listed with the Pullman Realty Group in New Canaan. I guess it's possible. After what happened, we took the house off the market until we can get all of this settled."

Something else I'll check on.

"So, you unlock the door and come in."

"I came through the front door and called out to them. When I didn't hear anything, I really got worried. I walked through the foyer and the living room." He waved his hand in the air. "And then I went into the kitchen."

He stopped talking. Eric blinked, once, twice, tears pooling in his eyes; then in a voice that cracked under the emotion, he said, "That's where I found them."

Olivia put her arm around her husband's waist and pulled him close.

Eric had his hand over his face when he sobbed, "That's where some son of a bitch shot my parents and left them on the floor to die like animals."

Chapter Two

Nathaniel and I didn't see any reason why Eric or Olivia needed to come into the kitchen with us. Not that there was much to see. The cops had come and gone. So had the cleaning crew in their hazmat suits.

While the bodies were gone and the blood, brain tissue, and skull fragments had been removed, the memories remained.

Nathaniel flipped on the lights. The spacious kitchen was spotless. The stainless-steel appliances shone like mirrors. The marble floors gleamed in the overhead track lighting. The granite countertops were wiped clean.

While the kitchen was modern, it had an old-time feel like the rest of the house. The ornately carved oak table and matching chairs appeared to be antiques. The walls were red brick. Heavy wooden beams accented the ceiling. There was yet another fireplace on one wall.

Nathaniel took the crime scene photos and the police report out of his briefcase and placed them neatly on the kitchen island. I admired how connected Nathaniel must be. What he managed to get was a copy of the complete case file, not the sanitized, abbreviated crap that the police had fed to us reporters.

The first photo I looked at was a professionally done portrait of Morris and Julia Cutter while they were still alive. They'd posed in front of one of their magnificent fireplaces. I knew from the stories I wrote that he was sixty years old at the time of death. Standing, with one hand in his pocket and a hand on his wife's shoulder, Morris had salt-and-pepper hair and a receding hairline, and wore tortoise-shell eyeglasses and a white shirt with the collar unbuttoned, under a black blazer. He appeared very dignified.

Julia, age fifty-two, was seated in a wingback chair, both hands in her lap, wearing a burgundy top under a white blazer. Her auburn hair was layered, ending at the nape of her neck, complete with a cute set of bangs. Her brown eyes sparkled, and she appeared much younger than her actual age.

Both were attractive as they smiled into the camera.

Then I turned my attention to the rest of the photographs. They were of the crime scene, including the two bodies taken from every imaginable angle, as well as blood spatters and other evidence the police found pertinent.

In the pictures of Julia, she appeared to be kneeling, crumpled in a heap on the floor in front of the counter next to the stove. Her head and right shoulder rested against the blood-streaked cupboard door, her legs doubled up under her, arms hanging limp.

Close-up photos showed that Julia had been shot in the left part of her forehead, near her temple, at point-blank range.

I glanced at the freshly painted cupboard against which she'd slumped. "After she was shot, she must have just dropped where she'd been standing."

Nathaniel agreed. "Most likely dead before she hit the floor."

The other body in the photos was Morris Cutter. He was on his side, sprawled on the floor, gun in his right hand, entrance wound in the right temple, exit wound in the left. His head rested in a small puddle of dried blood.

Nathaniel popped another Life Saver into his mouth and observed, "From the amount of blood on the floor, Morris most likely died quickly as well."

The police postulated that Morris had come up quietly behind his wife while she was preparing a breakfast casserole for the New Year's Day brunch. She must have heard him and started to turn around, and he shot her once. The bullet entered her skull just above her left eye.

Then he put the gun tight to his own head and pulled the trigger.

Murder-suicide.

Except that's not what his son and daughter-in-law insisted.

I glanced around the kitchen again, not knowing what I was looking for. "Most obvious question, was he right-handed?"

Nathaniel smiled at me. "Yes."

"Was the gun registered to Morris Cutter?"

"No, but it wouldn't have to be if he bought it outside of Connecticut. It was a 9mm M&P Shield Smith & Wesson. It's thin and lightweight, very good for concealed carry. Perfect for a woman because it fits well in smaller hands."

I frowned. "Do you think they were shot by a woman?"

Nathaniel shook his head and answered in a slightly testy voice. "That's not what I said." He picked up one of the photos showing a close-up of the weapon. "This particular Smith & Wesson doesn't have a thumb safety."

"Doesn't that make it dangerous to carry?"

"Not really. But the real value of no thumb safety is the ease of use. Just aim and pull the trigger."

"Did he own other weapons?"

"A whole gun cabinet full. Morris Cutter was originally from Oklahoma. He liked his guns. He kept them under lock and key, unloaded. The cabinet was locked when the police arrived."

I studied the spot where Julia had been shot. "Was the break-fast casserole in the oven when they died?"

He consulted the report. "No, apparently Julia had just started putting it together. The oven was on when the police got here, but the casserole was still on the counter."

I nodded.

"Point of information, Julia's blood was spattered over it."

My stomach twisted. "Thanks. I think that's a little too much information."

Nathaniel looked up from the photos. "Okay, let's say for a moment that it *is* a double homicide. What does the MO tell us?"

My teeth scraped my bottom lip as I glanced around the spotless kitchen. "It tells me that if it was a double homicide, whoever the killer was, he or she didn't do it to make a state-ment. It wasn't a revenge killing or a warning. It was most likely someone close to them who doesn't want to be caught up in a murder investigation. Someone who may have a key to the house and knows the alarm code."

Nathaniel nodded. "Or someone they let into the house. The Cutters most likely knew their killer. It was someone they were comfortable enough with that the killer could get close to them."

I tapped the top of the counter with my fingertips. "If...if it's a double homicide, how difficult do you suppose it would be to stage two murders to look like a murder-suicide?"

Looking back at the photos, Nathaniel had his glasses perched halfway down his aquiline nose. He took them off and glanced around the room. "Not impossible, but certainly difficult. The killer would have to have all the pieces in place to make a single shot to Mrs. Cutter's head, and then, in almost a single motion, bring the barrel of the gun over and shoot Mr. Cutter."

"Was an autopsy done?"

He consulted the report. "In Connecticut, autopsies are done on all gunshot victims."

"Do we have the report?"

Nathaniel looked up at me. "Of course. The ME established they each died of a single gunshot."

"The police are certain this was a murder-suicide."

He nodded. "That's their conclusion."

"Did Morris have gunpowder residue on his hands?"

"Trace amounts."

I glanced around the room again, marveling at the size of the refrigerator and the stove. "I don't suppose this house is wired for video surveillance?"

Nathaniel slowly shook his head. "According to the police report, Morris had around-the-clock armed security up until he retired. After he retired, his company stopped paying for them. The house has an alarm system. Maybe that's all they thought they needed."

I sighed. "I'm out of questions for now."

"Ready to go back in and face the Cutters?"

We put the reports and the photos back into Nathaniel's briefcase, then walked back into the living room where Eric and Olivia were patiently waiting. The young man asked, "Have you seen everything you need to?"

"Almost," I answered. "Did your father have a home office or a study?"

"A library. When he was home, if he did any work, it was there."

He walked us down a short, carpeted hallway and opened a door, flipping on a light as he did.

I felt my jaw drop. The room oozed with old-world charm.

There was a massive antique maple desk pressed against the wall adjacent to a bank of floor-to-ceiling windows that looked out over the gray surface of Long Island Sound. Sitting at that desk, you'd have an unparalleled view of the waves lapping on the shore and the boats cutting through the water.

Not that there was a lot to look at on that dreary February afternoon. Through the glass, it was easy to see the cold rain as it drizzled onto the ice and snow in the yard. Long Island Sound was the color of coal ash under a heavy cloud cover.

The desk and curtained windows were impressive, but not as impressive as the bookshelves that were also floor to ceiling, twenty-feet high, filled with hundreds, maybe thousands of books.

To our left was another large stone fireplace. Two wingback chairs and end tables were placed so that the occupants could stare into the flames, talk politics, and sip snifters of expensive brandy.

There were no paintings or photographs hung on the walls. Instead, there were hunting and fishing trophies. The heads of two deer silently stared at us accusingly through glass eyes. Just below them, fish, all of them saltwater, I thought, were also mounted on the wall. I'm no expert in game fish, but they looked like tuna, and the grandest of all, a blue marlin. It must have been ten feet long.

Dead things. It was the one thing about the room that I immediately despised.

I turned and saw Nathaniel standing silently in the doorway. His face was dispassionate, like a chess player studying the board as he casually glanced around the room.

When I focused back on Eric, who was gazing out the window, I noticed a six-foot-tall teak cabinet tucked away in the shadows in the corner. "What a beautiful library." I said, ignoring the dead things on the walls.

Eric nodded. "Dad loved this room."

I pointed toward the cabinet. "What's that?"

He faced where I pointed. "That's Dad's gun cabinet."

I already knew the answer to my question. "He kept it locked?"

He nodded. "It was locked the day he died."

"Can I see?"

Eric looked apologetic. "After the police checked it out, we emptied it and sold the guns. I don't like them. I never have. I take after my mom like that. Dad tried teaching me how to shoot, but I didn't take to it like my sister did. She's a crack shot."

"How many weapons did he have?"

He thought for a moment, doing a mental inventory. "A couple of hunting rifles. A shotgun. Three or four handguns. Our estate attorney has the complete inventory."

I motioned toward the trophies on the wall. "Your dad was a hunter?"

"He used to be." Eric glanced up at the trophy wall. "He'd been more into fishing over the last twenty years or so." He walked over to the desk and picked up a framed photo, holding it out, showing it to me. "This is Dad pulling in that blue marlin there on the wall aboard the company fishing boat."

As he put the photo back, his eyebrows furrowed and he appeared confused.

"Something wrong?"

He studied the desktop.

From where I stood, I could see a widescreen computer monitor and keyboard and a clutter of stacked folders and books.

"Yeah, something's missing. Dad's laptop isn't here."

"Your father used both a laptop and a desktop computer?"

"The laptop was exclusively for the book he was working on. He was writing about the history of the company."

I came up beside him. On the desk was another framed photo of three dirt-covered, shirtless young men in overalls standing in front of an oil rig. They were smiling and slick with black spatters of oil. I pointed. "Is your father in this picture?"

"He's the one in the middle. That was back in the seventies when my grandfather still owned the company. Gramps had Dad and my uncle start at the bottom working as roughnecks. Dad said it was a real character-builder. It made him a better man. It made him a better leader."

"Who are the other two men?"

"Uncle David and Uncle Parker."

I glanced at Eric, who was staring at the photo. I wondered if he wished he could have been one of the men in the photo. I was certain that Morris Cutter had never made his son prove himself by working his way up the corporate ladder. Nathaniel had told me that Eric Cutter made his money by investing in real estate, mostly in Manhattan and parts of New Jersey.

It made me wonder what Eric's relationship had been with his father.

There was a third photo of a young Morris and Julia Cutter with a little boy and girl standing in front of them. I pointed to it. "Is this you and your sister?"

For the first time that day, Eric smiled. "I think I was about eight at the time and Lisa was six. That was taken at the CP&G hunting lodge up on Juniper Lake in the Catskills."

"Looks nice."

"It's a place they used to take politicians and businesspeople to." He nodded toward the photo. "We were up there every summer when we were little kids. The company sold the lodge the year this picture was taken."

Hearing what he said about his sister being a crack shot, I recalled again that Nathaniel had made a point of saying the murder weapon was perfect for a smaller hand.

"Why did the company sell it?"

Eric looked up at me. "It was the year Lisa wandered away from the lodge. Mom and Dad were frantic. She was missing for hours. The state police came, and they were about to call in a helicopter when the owner of a neighboring lodge drove up. Turns out Lisa had seen another little girl by the lake, they made friends, and Lisa went off to play with her. Just before dark, the little girl's father saw them in the yard and knew something was wrong."

Nathaniel spoke up. "That must have been scary."

Eric answered. "Enough that we never went up there again."

Off to one side of the desk was a stack of books. I read the titles out loud. *"The Path to Power, Three Days in Moscow, Churchill, Presidents of War."*

Eric explained. "Dad devoured books. He loved history. He loved biographies of powerful men."

Then I picked up something that surprised me, *The Uninhabitable Earth—Life after Warming.* I held it up. "I wouldn't have expected this to be on Morris Cutter's bookshelf."

According to the book jacket, it was "a terrifying, apocalyptic description of what the earth will look like if we keep pumping carbon into the atmosphere".

He rubbed his face. "Most likely something my sister gave him."

"Tell me about the missing laptop."

"I suppose it could be still in his office in New York."

"He had an office in the city? I thought he was retired."

Eric answered with a small grin. "CEO *emeritus.* He still went into the city a few days a week to offer advice when it was needed. Truth be told, he might have missed the hustle and bustle a little bit. Plus, he was working on his book. By being in the city, he had access to company archives and records."

That made me curious.

Eric said that his father had looked forward to retiring, and yet he continued to keep an office in the city.

He motioned to an empty place on the top of the desk. "When he was home, this is where he worked. He kept all of his notes on that laptop. He never plugged it into the internet. He said he didn't want to take any chance that some hacker could get into his laptop and delete or steal his notes. If he used the internet, he did it on the desktop computer."

When he went silent, I glanced up at him.

Still staring at the desk, he said, "I just can't imagine he would have left it in New York over the holidays."

"Did your father use a calendar or an appointment book, or did he keep all of that on his phone?"

Eric sat down at the desk and started going through the drawers. "He was too old-school to use a phone for much more than making calls. He had an old-fashioned leather-bound appointment book."

I watched as he fruitlessly opened the drawers, searched them, then shoved them shut. Exasperated, he looked up at me. "Son of a bitch. That's not here either."

Chapter Three

The plan was for me to drop Nathaniel off at the South Sheffield Train Station so he could hop a Metro-North back to the city, where he could work from his home office overlooking the East River. Nathaniel didn't own a car. I'm not certain he even knew how to drive. I guessed that made him a typical New Yorker.

Leaving the circular driveway of the Cutter mansion, we were silent—the only sound was the slapping of the intermittent wipers clearing away the droplets of cold rain and the hissing of the tires on the wet road. Since October, the weather had been abnormally cold. But for the last few days, a warm front from the south had forced temperatures into the low forties, melting much of the snow and ice. That afternoon, we drove on pavement slick from the precipitation, headlights from the other vehicles glistening on the highway as they passed.

Nathaniel cleared his throat. "So, are you ready to take this on?"

According to its website, Lodestar Analytics conducts open-source investigations and provides research and strategic advice for businesses, law firms, and investors as well as for political inquiries, such as opposition research. Lodestar employs a diverse range of experts including scientists, retired FBI agents, private detectives, and journalists.

In January, Nathaniel had done his best to lure me away from the crime beat on the *Sheffield Post*. That newspaper was going through a messy sale to a media conglomerate looking to make higher profits by slashing costs. The newspaper's owner, Ben Sumner, had a change of heart when he discovered that an urban mall was being built in town, meaning buckets of advertising dollars he hadn't known about when he signed the contracts. He wanted out of the sale and to keep the newspaper.

Galley Media, the communication network that wanted to purchase the *Sheffield Post* said a deal's a deal. No backsies.

The whole hot mess would eventually end up in court.

Caught in the unsettling crossfire, I was thrilled when Nathaniel offered me a position as "researcher/analyst" for Lodestar. But I know some of his work involved digging up dirt on political candidates or their families. That had an evil odor.

At the end of the day, I had to look at myself in the mirror, and I never want to be ashamed about the work that I do. So, I decided to freelance instead. That way I could always tell Nathaniel no if he handed me an assignment that smelled bad.

For the first couple of weeks, he'd had me doing background checks on possible corporate executive hires and investigating the profitability and viability of companies that were going onto the market. It was mostly brainless work I did on my laptop from my kitchen table.

Not terribly exciting, but it paid well. I'd already splurged and bought four new tires for the Sebring to replace the dangerous slicks I'd been riding around on for six months.

Plus, I'd done a couple of simple assignments for Ben at the

Post just to keep my hand in the game and help him out until he hired another reporter for the cop shop.

But the thought of being on the street again, doing a full-blown investigation made my heart race. I answered Nathaniel's question. "Oh, I'm more than ready to take this on, boss. But the cops have already closed this case. Any physical evidence that they might have missed has been scrubbed from the house by the cleaning crew. I'm not sure there's anything more to find."

He smiled as he gazed out at the traffic ahead of us. "It doesn't matter, does it? We're being paid to look into it one way or another."

"No matter the outcome?"

"We still get paid." His eyes blinked at me, owl-like, from behind his glasses, and he offered a sly smile.

I nodded in silence.

He added, "But, just so you know, the company gets a sizable bonus if you find verifiable evidence that it was a double homicide."

"Does that include finding out who the killer is? *If* there is one?" I threw extra emphasis on the word "if."

Nathaniel shook his head. "They just want us to prove it was a double homicide. Do that much and our job is done. Let the cops reopen the case. By the way, if the company gets a bonus, you get a bonus." He dragged a finger across the dust on my dashboard. "Maybe enough to put a down payment on another vehicle."

I glanced at Nathaniel who was crunching on one of his damned hard candies.

Upon mention of the bonus, I wanted to ask how much, but I didn't. I didn't want it to taint my investigation.

How much did I really know about Nathaniel? I knew he'd been a kickass journalist for some of the biggest media outlets in the country. I knew he was the sole owner of Lodestar Analytics. I knew he wasn't married. But other than that?

Nothing.

I didn't know what kind of a man he was. Both John Stillwater and Shana Neese, two people I admired greatly, vouched for him. But when the two of them were working on a sex trafficking case together, even their own moral compasses stopped pointing true north. They weren't above breaking the law.

I had a feeling that Nathaniel wasn't either.

I was blunt. "Are you telling me that you want me to gather evidence that it was a double homicide?"

He turned and stared at me, his expression aghast. "I'm telling you to find the truth. But that being said, let's go at this investigation with the mindset that both Julia and Morris Cutter were murdered by an unknown assailant."

That didn't make me any more comfortable.

I turned right on East Avenue. "Who's signing the checks? The kids? CP&G?"

I pulled up in front of the two-story glass facade of the train station, tucked in between a Gym Source and a Citibank. Nathaniel reached behind him, pulled his valise and overcoat into the front seat, and opened the door.

Before he got out, he answered. "CP&G doesn't want this investigation reopened. They hate that kind of press. The money's coming from the Cutter estate. Eric is the executor, but he doesn't want to be involved with the day to day. The checks and any decisions we need made are coming from the estate attorney. He says he knows you, by the way. His name is Frank Mancini."

———

That was a sizzling lightning bolt from the past I hadn't seen coming. Frank Mancini was a tall, incredibly good-looking attorney with chocolate-brown eyes, Mediterranean olive skin, and a closely cropped George Clooney beard. He spent enough time in the gym to have the body of a man half his age, and he was articulate, intelligent, successful, and funny.

And good in the sack. When we were seeing each other, our cute code word for sex was *dessert*. Because it was sinfully good, but without the hip-padding calories.

If he sounds like he was too good to be true, he was.

Frank Mancini was married. And not to me.

He and I had an affair that he barely kept secret from his wife for nearly two years. Back then I was drinking heavily, and that made the shame of being an adulteress all the easier to bear. Spending the holidays alone, the sneaking around, staring at his wedding ring when we were in bed in a hotel room together.

After I broke it off, we stayed in touch by phone and text—just friends. Up until last October, then we both drifted off, losing touch, lost in our own lives. I hadn't talked with him in months.

The thought of seeing him again was both exhilarating and scary as hell. I had no intention of renewing our affair. But still, my heart thumped hard when Nathaniel dropped the bomb that we might be working together.

Before I went home, I stopped off at DaVinci's for their take-out meatballs and angel hair pasta, glancing longingly over at Al's Liquors across the street. Before Christmas, I would have gone in and picked up a bottle of vodka, hidden it in my bag, and snuck it into the house.

Don't get me wrong, I have a half a bottle tucked away in my panty drawer at the house. But I haven't had a drink since the holidays. Not even for New Year's. I'd made a terrible mistake after knocking back a couple of stiff ones in a bar just before Christmas and nearly gotten myself killed.

I'd been sober before. I needed do it again.

Working for Nathaniel, I was starting over. I'd made so many mistakes in my life.

If I worked hard at it, maybe this time I could get things right and get my life on track.

———

Tucker met me at the front door with his tail wagging so hard his little butt wriggled. He was seven pounds of brown and gray fur with two shiny eyes and a tongue that lolled out of the side of his mouth. I went into the kitchen and placed the plastic bag with the containers of Italian food on the counter, took off my coat and hung it in the closet, then swept the Yorkie up into my arms.

"Hey, baby," I whispered, Tucker's tongue reaching out and touching my cheek. "Have you been outside yet? Where's Caroline?"

As if to answer me, she came down the stairs, followed by her best friend, Jessica Oberon. Then to my surprise, they were both followed by a young man in jeans, Nikes, and a West Sheffield High School Warriors sweatshirt.

Caroline sounded chipper. "Hey, Genie. Welcome home."

Jessica followed suit. "Hey, Genie."

For years, Jessica Oberon had called me Miss Chase, but I'd never been comfortable with it. It made me sound old. Ditto on calling me "ma'am."

The young man, sporting shaggy black hair, a lip ring, and a sparse tuft of fur on his chin, chimed in. "Hi, Genie. It's nice to meet you."

Caroline had a boy…up in her room?

Anger flashed. "Young man, you don't know me well enough to call me by my first name. I'm Miss Chase to you. And, by the way, just who *are* you?"

He was tall for his age, not as tall as me yet, but certainly in growth mode. He blushed and glanced nervously at Caroline who wore the expression of someone who had just tasted tuna that'd gone bad. "I'm really sorry, Miss Chase. I'm Tyler."

"Got a last name?"

He apologized again. "I'm sorry. Greenwood. I'm Tyler Greenwood."

Sounds like some kind of half-assed country-western singer.

Still frowning, Caroline explained, "Tyler just moved here with his mother. They're from upstate New York." She turned to face him. "Which part?"

He flashed me an embarrassed grin. "Finger Lakes. Wine country."

I took a breath to try to let go some of the anger. "So, what have you guys been up to?"

Caroline couldn't manage a smile, only clenched teeth. "We were talking about putting a Dungeons and Dragons club together."

"Dungeons and Dragons. I thought that game died in the eighties."

Jessica spoke up. "All of sudden D&D is hot. Nerd culture is cool."

Hot, cool…who can keep up?

There was a short, awkward silence. Then Tyler mumbled, "I'd better get going."

Jessica was chewing at her lower lip. "Me too."

They both headed for the closet to get their coats.

"Jessica, tell both your moms I said hi." Then I turned and headed into the kitchen.

I got some plates down out of the cupboard and heard muffled conversation coming from the front door. At one point, I thought I heard Caroline say, "I'm sorry."

When Caroline came into the kitchen, there was fire in her eyes. "What the hell, Genie?"

I gave her a look. "Excuse me?"

"What the hell? You embarrassed me in front of my friends."

My anger creeped back in. "You had a boy up in your room."

"Yeah? And Jessica was up there with us. What do you think was going on? We were having a threesome?"

I took the containers of pasta, bread, and salad out of the plastic DaVinci's bag. "How do you even know what that is?"

"We get Netflix, Genie. And I'm fifteen, not twelve."

She was going to be sixteen next month. What the hell was *that* going to be like? "No boys in your room."

I had my back turned, but I could almost hear her rolling her eyes. "You're not my mother."

She'd only said that twice before. Each time was like a knife to the chest.

Caroline Bell's mother had died when she was eleven from breast cancer. Her father was killed in a car crash when she was thirteen. Kevin Bell had been my fiancé at the time. He'd made me promise that I would look after Caroline if anything ever happened to him.

Then it did.

I stood with my hands on my hips. "You're right. I'm not your mother. I never said that I was. It doesn't mean I don't love you. I promised your father that I'd watch out for you, and damn it, that's what I'm going to do." I felt the tears welling hot in my eyes.

She stood staring at me for a moment.

I knew she had regretted saying the "you're not my mother" thing, but I also knew she wasn't going to apologize for it. She was every bit as stubborn as her father had been.

The silence was an angry spirit hanging in the air. So, like an idiot, I threw another log on the fire. "My house, my rules; no boys in your room."

I saw the defiance in her eyes. The same look I saw in Kevin's eyes when he was angry. "This is my *father's* house. The only reason you're living here is because he's dead."

I gazed at her wide-eyed. Both of us were wordless.

Finally, she said, "I'll eat dinner in my fucking room."

Chapter Four

Emotional stress is a trigger for me. It's when my urge to drink is strongest.

The photographs of the Cutter crime scene had been disturbing. In my long career as a journalist, not the worst thing I've seen, but looking at dead bodies is not my idea of a party.

Discovering that I'd be working with Frank Mancini made my nerves jangle, both in a good and a bad way. After all, while I was seeing him, he was the best of times and the worst of times.

Then the shock of seeing that boy come down the stairs and then having the bitch session with Caroline had just sucked all the energy out of me.

No wonder I never wanted to be someone's parent.

Nestled in my bed, all I wanted right then was a big tumbler of vodka over a couple of ice cubes. I knew there was that bottle in the dresser.

But I didn't. Instead, I read well into the night. I'd downloaded a copy of the book I'd found on Morris Cutter's desk about climate change onto my smartphone. It's a terrifying account of what will happen to the earth if we don't stop pumping crap into our atmosphere. Famine, droughts, hurricanes, wildfires, major cities inundated by rising oceans. It wasn't sleep-inducing.

I only found slumber after taking an Ambien.

In the morning, I got up, choked down a hot cup of coffee, went for a run down by the harbor, and then took a nice, hot shower. While toweling off, I told myself how nice it was not to have a mind-blowing hangover.

Downstairs, Caroline and I had a silent breakfast together. She ate a bowl of Cheerios, and I had coffee and yogurt. I made sure Caroline had money for lunch and drove her to school. Still sullen, she didn't say a word until she opened the car door to get out. "What time will you be home tonight?"

She'd surprised me. There didn't seem to be any anger there. Just an innocent question in a temperate voice. It was hard to keep up with her mood swings.

They almost never corresponded with my own.

By nature, I'm suspicious. It makes me a good journalist. My first thought was that she really wanted to know when she had to get Tyler Greenwood dressed and out of her room before I came home and raised hell.

But I gave her the benefit of the doubt. "I don't know for sure. I have to go into the city. I'll call you if I'm going to be late."

"No sweat. I'll catch a ride home with one of Jessica's moms. And we have plenty of spaghetti left over from last night."

Translation: No hurry, Genie.

Before she closed the door, I asked, "Hey, are we okay?"

She glanced down at the ground for a moment then looked back at me, a slight grin playing on her lips. "Yeah, we're okay."

I watched as she got out, slung her backpack over her shoulder, and headed for the front steps of the high school, mingling with the young throng. Caroline was filling out and growing up. Real boobs and a real attitude to go with them. With her long blond hair and the blue eyes that she inherited from her father, she was going to melt some hearts.

I just don't want you to make the same mistakes I made when I was your age.

———

I started my investigation by stopping off at the Sheffield Police Department and talking to Assistant Chief of Police Mike Dillon. Mike is tall and thin with a handsome face that's all angles with highly defined cheekbones and a strong chin. He has a slightly receding hairline, and the predatory brown eyes of a wolf. While I was the full-time crime reporter for the *Sheffield Post*, he and I'd had our ups and downs. That's the nature of a journalist's relationship with the local police department.

On a more personal level, however, Mike and I had at one time been friends with occasional benefits. It had happened after Kevin died. We'd both just lost significant others, Mike due to divorce, and me from the death of Caroline's dad. We'd found solace in each other's arms. But eventually, Mike wanted more of a commitment and I didn't. I needed space.

Mike gave it to me. In spades. Last December, he kicked me to the curb and started a relationship with a younger woman.

It was okay. I figured sooner or later she'd break his heart.

When I walked through the doorway of the police building into the foyer, the middle-aged woman sitting at a desk behind a sliding glass window looked up at me in confusion. "Genie? What are you doing here? Did you go back to work for the *Post*?"

I smiled at her. "No, Dot. I'm here to talk to Mike. Is he in?"

She blinked and picked up the receiver to her phone. I watched as Dot McKinley cupped her hand over the phone and carried on a brief conversation. When she hung up the phone, she glanced up at me. "I'll buzz you in. You know where his office is."

I understood her confusion. For several years, I was in that foyer nearly every morning collecting the file of incident reports from the previous night. It would be where I'd start my day working the cop shop. I hadn't been inside that building since mid-January, when I resigned from the newspaper and went freelance.

Mike was standing in the doorway of his office waiting for me as I came up the hall. He had a huge grin on his face, and as he came forward, he wrapped me in his arms. "Genie Chase, I can't begin to tell you how much I miss you being on the crime beat."

I hugged him back, wondering what had caused this sudden burst of physical affection. "You do? When I was working the beat, you always thought I was a royal pain in the ass."

"Come in, come in, sit down."

I slipped off my coat and folded it over the back of one of his plastic chairs. Then I sat in the other, and he took a seat behind his desk. As always, it was stacked high with folders and reports.

He slid his laptop to one side so he could see me better. "Well, there's an even bigger pain in the ass working for the newspaper now."

"Who is it?"

When he said the name, he almost spat it out. "Colby Jones."

I tried to keep my poker face on, but hearing the name rattled me. He and I had worked together while I was at the *Boston Globe*. Colby Jones was a good investigative reporter but had zero empathy. Plus, the boy was a hard drinker. On a good night, he could put me under the table, and that says a lot.

And he was witness to the kind of stupid behavior that got me fired from the Globe.

The last thing I wanted was for Jones to be telling everyone in this town what a party girl I used to be.

Mike looked at me expectantly. "Do you know him?"

I sighed. "Yeah, I know him. Well enough to say I'm sorry for what you're going through."

"He's kind of a dick. Anyway, what can I do for you?"

I leaned forward, my hands in my lap. "I'm not sure that I've told you, but I'm freelancing with a company called Lodestar Analytics."

Mike sat back and squinted at me. "Isn't that the company that digs up dirt on political candidates?"

"It's called open-source research."

"Is your boss Nathaniel Rubin?"

I nodded.

"He must have some clout. Chief Angelo gave him copies of the full case report for the Morris and Julia Cutter investigation. What's the story? We closed that."

I sat back. "We've been hired by the estate to take another look."

He cocked his head. "Nothing to see. It's open and shut."

"Then this will be quick and painless. There seems to be a laptop and an appointment book belonging to Morris Cutter missing from the Cutter residence. Did you take them for evidence? I didn't see anything about it in your report."

He furrowed his brows. "I'll look at the case file again, but that's not ringing a bell. Cutter's son never said anything about them being missing."

I shrugged. "He only thought about it when we were going through his father's desk."

The normally confident expression on Mike's face faltered for a second. "Great." His voice dripped with sarcasm.

"Does that mean you're going to reopen the case?"

He took a heavy breath. "It means I'm going to have to take another look at it."

"Any chance at all that it could have been a double homicide?"

"Our investigation was very thorough." This time, he sounded official. "No forced entry, no struggle."

"Did Morris Cutter leave a note?"

He eyed me suspiciously. "No. We think he shot his wife in the heat of the moment. Then, regretting what he'd done, he killed himself."

I took a deep breath. It made as much sense as anything else. I had to wonder what could have caused that kind of action. "Any advice you can give me?"

He folded his arms in front of his chest. "Yeah, don't waste your time."

I gave him a warm smile, hoping to soften his tone. "C'mon, Mike. Any players I should watch out for?"

He eyed me for a moment, and then his demeanor thawed. "Yeah, the guy who replaced Morris Cutter as CEO, he obviously didn't like his predecessor at all. And some of Cutter's family would have just as soon killed him as look at him. Especially the nephew."

I would remember that, the nephew. I raised an eyebrow and gave him a grin. "Got it."

"But, like I said before, you're wasting your time."

It sounded like he was ready for me to go away. As I stood up, I said, "So, around the holidays, you mentioned that you and I might grab dinner some night. That was way back around Christmas. I don't recall getting a phone call. Did you change your mind?"

His face flushed crimson. "Yeah, well, that was when I told Vicki that I thought our relationship wasn't working out. That our age difference was causing too much drama. Christ, I thought she was going to have a nervous breakdown."

Vicki Smith was the owner of her own successful real estate

agency. She was petite, very attractive, and looked great in her television commercials and on her billboards. The problem was that she was easily a dozen years younger than Mike, she'd never had kids, and her biological clock was ticking away.

"You're still seeing her?"

His lips twisted into a weird combination of a half-smile and a grimace.

"And you're getting it regular." My snide comment came out of me as an angry growl.

Mike frowned.

I put my coat on, then came around the side of the desk and put my hand on his shoulder. "You know she wants babies. Those eggs she's carrying around have a sell-by date, Mike. I hope you're using protection, big daddy."

Meow.

Chapter Five

I took the Metro-North train from South Sheffield into Manhattan, idly watching from my window seat the dreary urban landscape slide by. This time of year, at the end of winter, everything is a shade of gray—the roads, the buildings, even the sky. I knew that spring was coming, but I found mid-February to be mildly depressing.

When we arrived, I was reminded that, even in the winter, the tunnels in Grand Central Terminal are sauna bath-hot and steamy. When the train came to a stop, it seemed like the whole herd of humanity needed to get off that train at the same time and rush to its destination as if life itself depended on it. You don't walk up that tunnel, you speed walk, whether you want to or not.

It's easy to get caught up in that adrenaline high of moving briskly through the tunnel and then out into the massive, brightly lit main concourse of Grand Central Terminal. I'm a small-town girl at heart, and every time I see it, my pulse quickens. It's almost as if arriving at the center of a glamorous universe.

The New York offices of Continental Petroleum & Gas occupied the top three floors of a Park Avenue office building only a few blocks away. I hoofed it and silently gave thanks that it hadn't started raining yet. Glancing up between the skyscrapers, I saw the dark clouds promised precipitation. I wouldn't know if it was snow or rain until it actually happened.

Getting to my destination, I was mildly surprised to see a loud protest taking place on the street just outside the building where the CP&G offices were located. A raucous crowd of about eighty people held placards that read, "CP&G Kills Coral Reefs" and "Thank You Big Oil for the Global Warming" and "Keep the Earth Clean. It's Not Uranus."

Uniformed New York cops stood close by. A cluster of camera crews were shooting video. American broadcasters were joined by reporting teams from Japan, Sweden, and France.

As I got closer, I heard protesters chanting in unison, fists in the air, "Stop denying the Earth is dying. Stop denying the Earth is dying."

A racially diverse, but mostly young, crowd, the demonstrators were in their twenties and thirties. Worrying about the looming climate crisis and the future was a primary concern for millennials. After all, they were the ones inheriting the shitstorm we were leaving behind.

I glanced up at the office building and wondered if any of the oil executives in their ivory tower were even aware of what was going on in the street.

Ever the reporter, I took some photos, thinking I might use them should I write a freelance piece on the climate crisis movement. Then I crossed the street, where I was escorted into the building by two security men wearing tan slacks, white shirts, ties, and black sport coats. I briefly wondered if they'd been hired by the owners of the building, or if they worked for CP&G.

Taking the elevator up, I exited onto the forty-third floor where the reception room for CP&G was located. I had to identify myself and show ID before being buzzed through huge glass doors by yet another security guard dressed just like the two men on the ground floor.

The reception area was spacious and airy. Well-dressed men and women, most likely salespeople and vendors, sat on leather couches and chairs waiting to see their appointments. The walls were covered with massive flat-screen monitors running video of various scenes around the world—men working on offshore oil rigs, trucks rolling out of refineries, oil tanker ships moving through canals, workers building pipelines. The videos were bigger than life and showed the global power of the massive international energy company.

The front desk, a large glass and stainless-steel affair, was splashed with color by cut flowers in a silver vase. The receptionist could have been a fashion model. Perfectly coiffed hair, makeup, and smile, and wearing a chic, gray sheath dress.

I, on the other hand, no longer worried about impressing clients, was in my traditional jeans, sweater, and Doc Martens boots that kept my feet warm and dry in the winter. "I'm Geneva Chase. I have an appointment with Parker Lewis." I handed her a Lodestar Analytics business card that listed me as a "research analyst."

She consulted the electronic tablet on her desk, scrolling with her finger until she came to my name. "Yes, of course, I'll tell him you're here."

In the good old days, she would have called him on the phone or buzzed him on the intercom. But it's the twenty-first century, so she hit a virtual button on her computer screen. A second later, I heard a man's voice say, "Good morning, Elaine."

The woman smiled into the tiny camera on her computer. "Good morning, Mr. Lewis. Geneva Chase is here to see you."

"I'll be right there."

I had tried to book an appointment with Darren Reed, the

new CEO of the company, but I'd been told he was at a conference in Dubai. However, Parker Lewis, the longtime senior vice president, would be happy to meet me in his stead.

I'd researched as much about Mr. Lewis as I could find online. Most of it was in his biography on the company website. It told me that his parents had died in a car accident when he was a toddler, and he'd grown up as a foster child on a hardscrabble farm in Oklahoma. He'd joined CP&G in his teens and worked his way up from roughneck in the oil fields until he became second in command of one of the largest energy companies in the world.

Simple beginnings, small-town boy makes good.

Before he came out to fetch me, the receptionist offered to hang up my coat. When she came around the desk, I saw that she was tall, about my height, and leggy. Her dress looked expensive and was fashionably short. It showed a considerable length of leg and lower thigh. It reminded me of my short stint at Fox News.

A man in his sixties, with a full head of white hair, tanned skin, a bushy silver mustache, and a disarming smile, came out of a hallway in a rush, as if anxious to meet me. "Geneva Chase." He held out his hand, peering at me through steel-framed glasses. "It's so nice to meet you."

He had on gray slacks, white shirt, cuffs rolled at his wrists, yellow tie, and black shoes polished to a high gleam. When I shook his hand, it was warm and dry. His grin was genuine, and I swear his green eyes twinkled. As I evaluated him, the word *avuncular* popped into my head.

"Come on back to my office. Can I get you a cup of coffee?"

"No, thanks."

When he walked, it was in quickstep, albeit with a small limp, back up the hallway. He waved me into the entrance of his office where another receptionist sat behind a desk, typing at her computer. About my age and as beautiful as the woman in the foyer, she gave me the briefest of glances as we blew past her into Parker Lewis's inner office. To her, it was if I barely existed.

We entered a large space illuminated by track lighting and muted sunlight streaming through tall windows overlooking Park Avenue. On Parker's desktop were three massive computer screens. No files, no papers, and no books.

The office contained two brown leather couches, a small conference table with six upholstered chairs, bookshelves, potted plants, and a wet bar. Framed photos on the walls depicted scenes from oil derricks and refineries. Some of them appeared very old.

Parker slid around behind his desk and stood for a moment, head down as if thinking. Then he heaved a heavy sigh and turned his back to me, gazing out of his window at the scene on the street below. He didn't say a word. He just stared.

Still standing, I asked, "Does that happen a lot? The protesting?"

He turned back around to face me. The expression on his face told me that he was bothered by what he'd seen. "It depends on the news cycle. A report from NOAA came out yesterday saying that last year was the warmest year on record. When something like that hits the airwaves or the internet, all the eco-nuts fall out of the tree."

Eco-nuts?

He shook his head in disgust. "Plus, someone from our own company leaked the news that we'll be releasing a report of our own in a few days."

"Oh? What kind of report?"

He ignored my question and waved at one of the chairs on my side of the desk. "Please, sit down, Miss Chase."

The journalist in me kicked in and I insisted. "Tell me about the report."

He thought for a moment but then said, "Well, it's not like

you're working for the press, now is it? You're a research analyst, so you'll appreciate this."

He gave me that toothy smile again. "We've had a team of our own climate scientists working for over a year now. They've written the definitive study on the causes and effects of climate change, and I can assure you, Miss Chase, it's a natural occurrence, a recurring cycle that's happened over and over in the history of our planet. We don't argue that the earth is going through a change. But it's natural. It has nothing to do with burning fossil fuels."

Suddenly, the warm feeling I'd had when I shook his hand began to slide into impatience. I recalled what I'd read last night from the book *Uninhabitable Earth*. Only thirty pages into it, I was horrified. I wanted to take Parker Lewis by his shirt collar, shake him, and say, "You'd better hope that it's man-made and we have the spine to stop it. Because if things continue the way they are going and we can't stop it, humanity and this entire planet is in for an apocalyptic shitstorm." But I didn't.

Parker continued, adopting a sad expression. "As a matter of fact, as CEO emeritus, Morris was supposed to present that report to Congress in January when they came back into session."

I was confused. "That was a month and half ago. Why hasn't someone else made the report public?"

"It was our board's call, Miss Chase. They've waited, out of respect for Morris's memory."

I wondered if they really just wanted to wait until the bad publicity died down. I attempted a smile. "Call me Genie."

His grin broadened. "Then you have to call me Parker."

I had to admit, for a man his age, he had a nice smile and a handsome face. I guessed that he must get regular exercise because he appeared slim and fit. I'd bet that in his day, Parker was a lady killer.

Maybe he still is.

I glanced at his hands. He wasn't wearing a wedding ring. "Parker, it is. Did Mr. Rubin's office tell you why I'm here?"

His face faltered and his expression grew serious. "Yes, the Cutter estate has asked you to look into Morris and Julia's untimely deaths."

I took out my tiny recorder and set it on his desk between us. "How well did you know Mr. Cutter?"

The computer monitors were on metal tracks, allowing him to slide them to the side of his desk so he could see me with an unfettered view. "Probably better than any man alive. We were like brothers. Julia and Morris were my family. I never had any of my own. Their kids, Lisa and Eric, call me Uncle Parker. Hell, I was at their house for Christmas."

He sighed and shook his head. "When I'd heard what he'd done, I cried like a baby for days. I've known him for most of my life. Back when his family owned the company outright, before it went public, Morris, his brother, David, and I started working for CP&G at the same time back in the seventies. We were young bucks back then. Full of piss and vinegar. Morris's daddy had us working as roughnecks on oil rigs in Oklahoma. Same location where the company was started over eighty years ago by Morris's grandfather. That crusty old man was a wildcatter's wildcatter."

"Wildcatter?"

Parker stood up and pointed to a black-and-white photo that had been mounted, framed, and hung on the wall. It reminded me of the one I saw on Morris Cutter's desk at his house, only this one was obviously much older.

Parker took it down and handed it to me. It was a picture of a group of about twenty men posing together in front of an oil rig. Dressed in overalls and work boots, all of them were soaked with a black liquid that was obviously crude oil.

"A wildcatter was someone who would drill an exploratory well in a place that wasn't already known to contain oil. Some of these wells were out in remote, dangerous areas, and the men who drilled them were pretty wild. They called themselves wildcatters. The man in the center with the long black beard was George Cutter, Morris's grandpappy. That's an old photo of his first successful rig, back in 1935."

I handed the framed photograph back to Parker.

He carefully hung it up and sat down on a corner of his desk. "The Cutter boys and I started work on the CP&G rigs in Osage County, Oklahoma, back around seventy-two. Oil rigs didn't have the safety features that they have now. Back then it was hard, dangerous work."

"I'll bet it was."

"The Cutter boys' father, Henry, made his sons start at the bottom like he did. He wanted those boys to know the business inside and out, top to bottom. Of course, I knew that they weren't going to be roughnecks for very long, and sure enough, after a little more than a year, they both got jobs in the Oklahoma City office."

"How about you, Parker?" I was growing to like the man again, in spite of his backward view on climate change.

He gave me that toothy grin again. "They brought me along with them. The boys let me ride their coattails. They called us the Three Musketeers. Where they went, I went. Back then, we had each other's backs."

He stood up again and took down another photo from the wall. Three men in reflective vests, and camouflage coats and pants stood cradling hunting rifles with scopes in their arms. The photo had obviously been taken in a forest somewhere.

I was mildly startled to see that behind the three hunters posing in the picture, three deer carcasses hung limp from ropes thrown over a large tree limb.

"We used to do everything together. That's Morris on the right, David is next to him, and I'm right there." Parker pointed.

I guessed the picture must have been taken years earlier because Parker's mustache was a dark brown in the photo. "CP&G used to have a hunting lodge where we entertained clients and held corporate retreats. It was one of Morris's favorite places."

"Used to have?"

He nodded. "The company sold it years ago. Now if we want to entertain clients, the company has a beach house on the coast of North Carolina. And a sixty-five-foot fishing boat. Pretty slick, too."

I handed the photo back to him.

Parker hung the photo back up on the wall. "So, we all climbed the corporate ladder of CP&G together. I knew that one of them would eventually run the company. It turned out to be Morris." He spread his arms. "And now I'm second in command, senior vice president. Not bad for a kid who grew up in a foster home on the wrong side of the tracks."

I love a good Cinderella story, but I needed to get the thread back to Morris Cutter. "Did Morris have any enemies?"

He scrutinized me for a moment. "Does the Cutter estate think that it was something other than what the police investigation concluded? A murder-suicide?"

"Just covering all the bases."

"It's Eric, isn't it? That boy thought the sun rose and set on his daddy. He can't wrap his mind around the fact that his old man was human and capable of making such a horrible mistake. Sometimes when I think on it, I can't hardly believe it."

I gently repeated myself. "Did Morris Cutter have any enemies?"

"They say you can judge a man by his enemies. Morris was

highly respected, but he was also widely feared and despised. He was a top-notch businessman, and he played to win. For his family, for his company, and for his stockholders."

I leaned forward. "Anybody hate him enough to want to kill him?"

As he answered, he counted off the suspects with his fingers raised in the air. "Environmentalists, the global warmers, his competitors, the Saudis, the Russians, Venezuelans. Hell, there are some politicians who would have shot him if they'd had the chance. He could be a hard man to work for, so there're probably a hundred or so ex-employees he's fired or laid off over the years who would have loved to have cut his heart out."

That doesn't narrow it down much.

Parker added, "Even some of his own family hated his guts."

Now we're talking.

"Family?"

Parker leaned back in his chair with a pensive expression, stroking his mustache, as if considering whether or not to tell me a family secret. "It was in the newspapers, as recently as last year, so it's public knowledge. When old Henry, Morris's daddy, finally decided to retire, the company was still privately held by the Cutter family. Morris was named CEO by his dad, and David became the senior VP. At that time, I was VP of acquisitions. The troubles began right away. David was the older brother and resented being second banana. It wasn't unusual that when Morris made a decision, his brother would drag his feet and bitch about it. Morris didn't like being undercut by his brother, so he bought David out. Made him a very generous offer, which David jumped at."

I shrugged. "Sounds like a happy ending."

Parker leaned forward again. "Except that Morris had been secretly planning to take CP&G public. When that happened, the value of the company went through the roof. Instead of just being rich, David could have been filthy rich."

Rich, filthy rich, I didn't ask him what he thought the distinction was.

Parker continued. "David was livid. Took Morris to court. Took CP&G to court. Took me to court when he found out I'd taken his place as senior VP." He laughed. "Didn't do him a bit of good. About five years ago, he died of a heart attack, a bitter old man."

I mentally crossed David Cutter off my list of suspects. "You said something was in the newspapers just last year?"

"The hatred didn't die with David. His wife, Delia, is still alive and, along with their son, Stephen, is carrying on the litigious tradition of suing everyone they can think of."

Litigious, but not necessarily homicidal. But I recalled that Mike Dillon had told me to watch out for the nephew.

I put the recorder back in my oversized bag. "Morris's son told me that he kept an office here, even though he was retired."

Parker laughed and slapped at his knee. "Yeah, he actually kept his old office. Biggest one in the whole company. Never moved out of it. Came in here nearly every day. Darren Reed, the new CEO, had to use a smaller workspace, and it just about drove him batshit crazy. It was a big old burr under his saddle."

I smiled, thinking that Morris Cutter must have been one crusty old bastard. He had to have known that keeping the new CEO out of the "big" office would be a distraction. "Did Morris and Mr. Reed have a good working relationship?"

"They did not. Morris was from the old guard, and Darren is new blood. He was hired away from Exxon by our board of directors. They want to move harder to get permitting to drill off the Atlantic coast. They want us to invest more in fracking."

"Morris didn't want to do that?"

"The infrastructure's not in place on the coast. He thought it wasn't needed and that it would be too expensive."

"How about fracking?"

He waved a hand. "Morris didn't think the profit margins were high enough."

"After Morris died, did Mr. Reed ever move into the larger office?"

"I'll give Darren credit. He didn't do anything for about a week after we heard, for the sake of propriety. Then he had Morris's old office cleaned out and he moved in."

"I'm guessing Morris's things were sent to his son's address?"

Parker nodded. "We had everything shipped to Eric."

"You didn't happen to see Morris Cutter's laptop anywhere?"

He thought for a moment. "Nope, can't say that I did. Just a few notebooks he kept for the company history he was writing, and some photos that had been on his desk."

I asked a question that I already knew the answer to. "Did Morris Cutter keep track of his appointments on his phone, or his laptop, or is it possible he kept an appointment book?"

Parker chuckled. "Oh, Morris was old school. He kept an appointment book."

"Did you find one in his office?"

He thought again. "Afraid not. He carried it everywhere he went. Just like that damned beat-up laptop."

So, where the hell are they?

Chapter Six

"Ready for lunch?" I held the cell phone close to my ear, vainly trying to keep out the ubiquitous wailing sirens and traffic noises of the New York City streetscape.

"Nearly. Where are you?" Shana Neese's usually well-modulated voice sounded slightly out of breath.

"Just coming around the corner. Where do you want to go?"

Shana chuckled. "We're dining in. Gerald is in the kitchen whipping up something interesting for us." She'd lingered on the word "whipping."

I felt a little shiver. Gerald was a handsome young man in his early thirties who served as Shana's manservant. Shana was a professional dominatrix who owned a four-story brownstone on Sixth Avenue. The first floor was retail. The second and third floor housed the Tower, another name for Shana's dungeons and playrooms designed for expensive BDSM scenarios. She staffed the Tower with nine dominants, all women. The fourth floor was her gorgeous penthouse living quarters.

Gerald was her unpaid servant. Shana did give him an allowance and time off for good behavior, and in return, he willingly gave her his slavish devotion, affection, and total attention.

So, when Shana said that he was whipping something up for us, I felt a tiny vibration of sexual tension.

Shana is nearly as tall as I am, five-ten, possesses flawless chocolate brown skin, sculpted cheekbones, and fierce brown eyes. She's drop-dead gorgeous. With the exception of one experimental roll in the hay while in college, I'm totally heterosexual, but every time I was near Shana Neese, I felt a strange attraction.

Maybe it's because she exudes tiger-like power and a slinky sexuality, and somehow, I was attracted to that.

Still on the phone, I picked my way through the moving knots of pedestrians on the sidewalk. "I'm almost there."

"Come up to the third floor to the workout room. We're just finishing up now."

On the ground floor of her building are two storefronts, the Golden Dragon Chinese Restaurant and Arthur's Fine Liquors. Discreetly nestled between them is a nondescript door that opens into a short, carpeted hallway. At the end of that hall is an elevator. To use it, you punch a code into a keypad.

I did so, the door slid open, and I hit the button for the second floor where I was greeted by a muscular young man in a tight black T-shirt and black jeans, seated behind a gunmetal gray desk. Shana's only male employee, he served as receptionist and security. I nodded as I walked by. "Morning, Bill."

He nodded back. Bill had a remarkable memory. I'd only met him once, the last time I came to visit back in January, but he remembered my name. "Good morning, Miss Chase. Miss Neese is in the workout room."

"I know, she asked me to meet her there."

To get to the third floor, I climbed a metal, circular staircase that brought me to another short hallway. I tried to remember what rooms were on the third floor. The schoolroom? The doctor's office? I knew there were faux dungeons, for sure. All the doors were closed except for one that had just opened, allowing a tall brunette, clad in black leather bustier, chaps, and boots into the hallway. She held a leash that was attached to a pasty middle-aged man with a paunch who was wearing only a red thong and a dog collar around his neck.

The man looked slightly embarrassed and flushed crimson as the two of them approached me.

The woman gave me a knowing smile. "Fido here has been a bad dog and needs more training." She emphasized the words "bad dog."

Oh, yeah, now I remember. One of the rooms on this floor is called the Kennel.

I did everything I could not to snicker and, instead, nodded and gave her a feigned serious expression.

Shana's workout room was the last door on the right. I let myself in.

I'd been there about three weeks earlier. The walls and the floor were padded, the overhead lighting was bright. Two punching bags and a single-speed bag hung from the rafters. The scent of sweat hung heavy in the air.

Shana and a man I didn't recognize stood in the middle of the room. They were both slick with perspiration and were breathing hard. She smiled when I walked into the room. "Geneva, I'm so happy you're here. We're almost finished. This is Uri Tal, retired Israeli Special Forces."

They were both dressed in black, sleeveless, perspiration-soaked shirts and camo combat pants. Both were barefoot. Their faces and arms glistened with sweat under the bright lights in the workout room.

I'm always in awe of how Shana kept herself in fighting condition. Her arms were toned, her biceps buff, her shoulders were muscular, and her stomach was rock hard.

Uri Tal, with dark hair shaved close to his scalp, was built like a bull. Broad shoulders, bulging biceps, and pectoral muscles stretched the fabric of his shirt.

Lordy, I'd love to bury my face in that chest.

"Uri, this is Geneva Chase. I've shown her some basic moves, but perhaps you can give her a lesson or two sometime."

He smiled and had a slight accent when he spoke. "Anytime. So nice to meet you, Geneva Chase."

Shana ran a hand through her ebony hair and motioned toward a plastic chair against the wall. "Grab a seat. This won't take but a minute. We're just finishing. I want to see if I have this move down."

As I sat, the big man lunged forward, smashing Shana hard against the padded wall with his beefy forearm against her throat. Without missing a beat, she shot the palm of her left hand hard against his face and slammed his elbow with her right. His head flew back, and his thick arm slid sideways, like a deadbolt, from her throat.

That put him slightly off balance.

In short, swift, spiky moves, she lunged, punching his throat, and landed her elbow across his ear. Her foot swept his leg out from under him, and she hooked her arm around his neck and thrust him down. He landed with a heavy thud.

It had lasted less than two heartbeats.

He looked up at her and grinned, rubbing his ear with one hand where he'd been struck and his neck with the other. "I think you have it, Shana. I know you pulled your punches, but damn, lady, it still hurt."

She reached down and helped him up. "You're a hell of a teacher." Then she glanced over at me. "Do you want me to show you that?"

I held up my hand. "It happened so fast, I'm not sure what

that was. I'm still practicing what you taught me the last time I was here."

Krav Maga is a military fighting and self-defense method developed for the Israeli Defense Forces and was derived from a combination of techniques including boxing, wrestling, aikido, judo, and karate. Basically, it's the art of fighting dirty.

Mid-January, I had to be in New York to see Nathaniel in his office and stopped by to see Shana. She took the opportunity to teach me a few self-defense moves—elbow to the face, palm strike to the nose, punches to the ears, fingers strike to the throat.

Shana had told me that if I was ever attacked, I wouldn't have time to consider what to do. It would have to be instinctive, automatic. "Don't think, Genie. Do. And make it hurt."

So, practicing what she'd taught me, over and over again, was imperative if I needed to defend myself if in trouble. Or so Shana had said.

But her most helpful contribution was showing me how to meditate. Martial arts and Zen are both closely intertwined.

Shana was becoming my mentor, my confidante, my Yoda. I'd told her that I was trying to quit drinking. With no alcohol, I was having difficulties concentrating and sleeping, so she taught me how to turn in on myself, be in the moment, and find my inner strength through meditation. She said that it was all about control, being in command over your own body and mind.

Then, she'd told me something that surprised me. That once I'd learned complete control, I would be able to drink again but would be able to moderate my intake. Alcohol wouldn't control me. I would control it.

I found that hard to believe.

Over the years, I'd learned that once I start drinking, I can't stop. It had cost me three marriages and, up until then, every decent job I'd ever had.

And God knows, I've tried to quit cold turkey. I've tried hypnosis and twelve-step programs. Nothing worked.

Shana had said that John Stillwater had once had a drinking problem, but she'd taught him control and now he can drink socially and stop when he knows he's had enough.

Maybe someday I could achieve that. But I had my doubts.

Since the New Year, I'd started going for morning runs again, and I'd dropped five pounds. Some mornings, before waking up Caroline to get ready for school, I'd practice my punches and blocks. Then, before my shower, I'd spend ten minutes in the half-lotus position on my yoga mat, controlling my breathing and my mind.

Control.

Shana knew what it was. She came by it naturally.

I had to learn it.

———

While Shana showered, I sat in her uber-modern kitchen with a cup of coffee and watched Gerald put together our lunches. He was tall and easy to look at with rugged features, pretty blue eyes with long lashes, and a broad, shy smile. He was clean-shaven, wore his hair neatly trimmed, and had slim hips and broad shoulders. That day, Gerald wore a white long-sleeved collared shirt, tan slacks, and deck shoes.

I tried to picture him wearing a dog collar but couldn't quite conjure up that vision. "What are you fixing?"

He was slicing tomatoes. "A steak Cobb salad with creamy avocado cilantro lime dressing."

"Oh, yum." I admired the way he moved economically around the kitchen. "Are you sure I can't help?"

Honestly, I can cook if I really have to, but I don't enjoy it.

I'm not sure if I've ever even turned the oven on at our house. I asked him the question only out of politeness.

He smiled at me over his shoulder and moved on to peeling hard-boiled eggs. "I have this, Miss Chase. You just relax. Can I get you a glass of wine?"

I sighed. "No thank you. The coffee is fine."

"Anything you want."

I want to own a man just like you, Gerald. Oh, and that glass of wine.

"Anything new going on in your life?"

He shot me a puzzled look. "Just taking care of the house and Miss Neese."

I guess it was stupid question.

Gerald was totally devoted to his mistress. He'd once been a client of Shana's, then he chucked his successful career as an investment banker to spend his days and nights doing whatever Shana wanted him to. It seemed to be a mutually beneficial arrangement.

Better than most marriages.

Shana breezed into the kitchen dressed in jeans and a New York Giants sweatshirt. "How are we doing, Gerald?"

"Nearly finished, Miss Neese. If you two would like to sit down in the dining area, I'll bring Miss Chase another cup of coffee and you a glass of wine while I finish the salads."

She glanced at me. "No wine today, Gerald. Sparkling water will do."

We adjourned into her living room that also served as her dining area. The floor was polished hardwood, the walls were red brick. Dark brown timbers served as ceiling beams. A black leather sofa and two tan fabric chairs faced a cast-iron fireplace embedded in the wall. Off to one side of the large room, a bank of tall windows overlooked the busy street below.

The first time I'd been in Shana's apartment, it had been just before Christmas. The holiday tree had sat in the corner, off to one side of those windows. Now the dining table had been placed there along with two chairs facing each other. As we sat down, I admired the view she had of Sixth Avenue.

Then I glanced briefly at the framed photo of two little girls that hung above the fireplace. Shana and her sister, Lydia, from when they were children. Lydia had been sold into prostitution and beaten to death by a pimp when she was only fifteen. Her death had been the prompt for Shana to create a loose confederation of like-minded individuals who were dedicated to saving girls and women from sex trafficking and violence. The group, known as the Friends of Lydia, flew below the radar, was well-funded, and sometimes acted in a legal gray area.

Nathaniel Rubin was a close friend of Shana's, and Lodestar Analytics often did pro bono work for the Friends of Lydia. I sometimes wondered if Nathaniel might not be a client of the Tower. I wouldn't ask. I knew she'd never tell me.

Shana reached out and put her hand on mine. "We'll play catch up in a moment. Still sober?"

I liked, admired, and respected her. "It's hard. I'm still sober, but it's hard."

She squeezed my hand. "You're strong, Genie. I know you can make this work. You're in control. How's the new job going?"

"I'm so excited." I clapped my hands. "I got my first street assignment."

"Will Nathaniel let you tell me what it is?"

"It's not a secret. Do you remember reading about the murder-suicide of the retired oil executive and his wife on New Year's Day? We've been hired by the estate to reopen the investigation."

Her eyes narrowed as she smiled. "Oh, my, Nathaniel gave you a juicy one. He must have a lot of confidence in you." She had a very distinctive way of talking, savoring each word as if she were tasting it. Added to that was her sophisticated Southern accent that made almost everything she said sound subtly seductive.

"I'd like to hope so. I'm a little surprised he didn't give it to John."

After he'd left the NYPD, John Stillwater had gone to work for Nathaniel. I had a chance to spend some quality time with him just before Christmas, after I was threatened by a violent thug, and John had volunteered to be my bodyguard, sleeping on my living room couch.

John was in his forties, tall, about six feet, and I guessed he weighed in at about two-ten. He was clean-shaven, had a strong jawline, a pleasant smile, and blue eyes that seemed fatigued, like he'd seen much more than he could ever possibly forget. The lines around his eyes and the sides of his mouth gave him character. The way his full head of brown hair fell over his ears and the back of his collar made John always look like he was two weeks overdue for a trim.

The square, black-rimmed glasses he wore gave me the impression that he was both intelligent and vulnerable.

One night, back at my house, while he was keeping me safe, I'd walked in on him while he was sacked out on my couch. Only he wasn't where he was supposed to be. He'd heard me start down the stairs and, always on guard, he was hidden in the shadows by the time I got to the ground floor. When I finally saw him, he was wearing nothing but his boxers. The man has a smokin' hot body.

When's the last time you had sex, Genie?

I thought for a moment. It had been last October. There was a shame-filled romp in a hotel room with a sleazy actor after too many cocktails over dinner.

Just another reason to give up drinking.

Shana smiled at me when I mentioned John's name. "He's doing some pro bono work for the Friends of Lydia."

When she didn't say anything more, I asked, "I'm guessing that you can't tell me about it?"

She shook her head. "I'm sorry. I don't want to do anything that might put John in danger. Did the two of you ever connect after the holidays?"

"No, but I wouldn't mind if we did," I said, blushing.

She hesitated before she said anything more. Then, "You know I adore John."

"But?" I sighed.

She shrugged. "When he's on the job, that man is focused, laser sharp."

Now there was an alarm bell going off in my head. "Oh?"

She put her hand on mine again. "Just that sometimes he loses sight of the other things around him, no matter how important they might be."

I sat back in my chair and considered what Shana had just told me. I'd been in a lot of unhappy relationships. The last thing I wanted was to be second best to a man's job. Been there, done that.

Just then, my phone warbled. "I'm sorry." I took the phone out of my bag and looked at the number on the screen. I didn't recognize it but answered anyway. "Yes?"

It was a man's voice. "Geneva Chase?"

"Yes?"

"My name is Leonard Ryan, with Fisher, Evans, and Sinclair. We're consultants for Continental Petroleum & Gas. I wonder, if you're still in town, if we might meet for a cup of coffee."

How did you get my number?

I took a guess that right after my meeting at CP&G, Parker Lewis must have gotten on the phone with Fisher, Evans, and Sinclair.

"Might I ask what this is about? I'm right in the middle of

lunch." I eyed Shana who smiled back at me. I saw Gerald from the corner of my eye emerge from the kitchen with a tray containing our salads and Shana's sparkling water.

"We might be able to help you with the inquiries you're making at the request of the Cutter estate. Please, finish your lunch. Perhaps we can meet at the Starbucks on Forty-Second Street, near the corner of Fourth, up the block from the Grand Hyatt Hotel. Say around two?"

I glanced at my watch. It was twelve thirty. That would still give me plenty of time to catch up with Shana.

"What kind of consulting do you do?"

"Oh, we're a full-service agency." He stopped for a melodramatic moment. "We have a wide range of services."

I'll just bet you do.

Chapter Seven

A chilly drizzle was falling when I left the front door of Shana's brownstone. I reached into my oversized bag and pulled out a retractable umbrella. I'd bought it from a street vendor last summer when I was in the city and had gotten caught in a downpour. It'd cost me ten dollars, and I was surprised that it had survived this far into winter.

Even in the adverse weather, the sidewalks were crowded with pedestrians. Men and women in expensive coats and shoes walked past blue-collar workmen in sneakers or work boots who walked past homeless panhandlers sitting on flattened cardboard boxes placed on the cold cement. Most of those held out plastic cups for change next to hand-scrawled signs pleading for help.

I stopped when I read a sign begging for money…for a cell phone.

At first, I thought it was pretty dumb request. Shouldn't he be asking for money for food? But in thinking it through, though, it made sense. You can't get a job without a phone. You can't get a place to live without a phone. You can't do much of anything without a phone.

I went back and dropped a couple of bucks in the guy's cup.

Feeling both good about myself for doing a good deed, and bad for being a potential sucker, I continued my trek, bag slung on my shoulder, umbrella over my head, ears soaking in the cacophony of the traffic.

Walking into the warm, quiet, coffee-scented interior of the Starbucks was a nice transition from outside. The shop was much like all the others. The walls were a deep green imprinted with the company's bizarre mermaid logo. The counters were plastic magically made to look like wood. The gleaming glass showcases were filled with inviting pastries and sandwiches. One barista behind the counter took orders and two others put them together like modern-day alchemists.

I got in line and glanced around the shop to see if I could spot Leonard Ryan. My eyes danced from face to face until they landed on a man who was in his fifties with curly brown hair receding from his forehead. He had a thin face and gray eyes. He wore a conservative charcoal gray suit, white shirt, and red tie.

The way he stared at me, smiling, was unnerving. He gave me a brief nod.

Parker Lewis must have told him what I looked like and what I was wearing because it was obvious that he'd spotted me the moment I came through the front door.

I nodded back at him and focused on the barista, ordering a grande latte, which sounds bigger than it is. Tall means small, grande means medium.

Who the hell thinks this up?

When my order came, I turned and picked my way across the crowded shop to the table. There were four chairs, and the man sat in one and his black overcoat was draped over a second. I did the same with my own coat, and he stood up, reaching across the table. "Geneva Chase? I'm Leonard Ryan." He had a faint Long Island accent.

I shook his hand, sat down, and lifted the plastic cap off my paper cup to let my coffee cool. "So, Mr. Ryan, why are we here?"

He broke into a grin that exposed impossibly white teeth gleaming through thin open lips. His eyes, framed by heavy eyelids and bushy eyebrows, reminded me vaguely of an iguana's.

He handed me an embossed business card with the name Fisher, Evans, and Sinclair. I noticed that he seemed to have exceptionally long, claw-like fingers.

The card told me that Leonard Ryan was an account director. "We want to know how we can help you in your investigation into the deaths of Morris and Julia Cutter."

I cocked my head. "Help me how?"

He folded his hands on the tabletop. "By offering whatever resources you think you'll need to expedite your research."

I blew at the surface of my latte and took a cautious sip. "What interest does"—I glanced at the card again—"Fisher, Evans, and Sinclair have in my research?"

Never taking his eyes off my face, he answered, "As I said on the phone, we're consultants for CP&G. It's in everyone's best interest if your investigation comes to a speedy and successful conclusion. We'd like to keep this all from being fodder for the news media again. It was tragic enough the first time. We'd like to maintain the loyalty and respect that the public still holds for the Cutters, both for his business acumen and for their philanthropy. No need to drag their names through the press one more time."

I tapped the corner of his card on the table. "How speedy is speedy, and what does your company consider to be a successful conclusion?"

He leaned forward to keep his voice low. "Oh, we'd love to see this concluded by Thursday, end of day, latest. And we're certain that your findings will parallel law enforcement's." He glanced around him to see if anyone was listening to our conversation. "That it was murder-suicide."

I blinked when I heard what he'd just said. He thought I could legitimately close this case by Thursday? "Today's Monday. That doesn't give me a lot of time, Mr. Ryan."

"I believe you already have the police case file. I suggest that they've done most of the legwork already."

I sat back in my chair, interested in seeing how far his consulting firm would go. "So, Mr. Ryan, what resources are you offering?"

"Financial," he said, as if it should have been obvious.

"Are you offering me a bribe?"

His brows furrowed and, for the first time, his lips compressed into a frown. Ryan shook his head slightly from side to side. "We're offering financial assistance to help with your expenses."

I cocked my head. "My company is pretty good about covering my expenses."

"This is above and beyond what your company is offering."

Sounds like a bribe.

"I see. So, is there a cap to the resources your firm is offering?"

His smiled again, thinking that he had drawn me into his web. "We have two hundred fifty thousand dollars available to bring this investigation to a swift and successful conclusion."

What? A quarter of a million dollars?

For a moment, that took my breath away. I gave myself a couple of seconds to regain my composure. I cleared my throat. "What if we feel that your resources won't be necessary?"

His eyes narrowed and his voice turned into a growl. "As I said, it's in everyone's best interest if we can tie this up quickly and quietly."

My nerves jangled and the hair on my arms stood up. "That sounds like a threat, Mr. Ryan."

He held out his hand for me to shake. "Not at all. I hope we're all on the same team here."

I stood up without touching his outstretched hand and slid into my coat. Then I picked up his card from the table, put it in my pocket, and snapped the plastic top back on my latte. "I'm not much for joining teams. I like working alone. If I need your help, I'll call you."

As I found my way across the café to the door, I could feel his gray eyes boring into my back, like the laser sight of a rifle. I had a nasty feeling it wouldn't be the last time I'd hear from Leonard Ryan of Fisher, Evans, and Sinclair.

———

Back on the busy sidewalk, I held the umbrella over my head with one hand. With the other, I rummaged in my bag until I found my phone. I wasn't in a particular rush to make my next phone call, but I knew I'd have to do it sooner or later. I huddled, face-first, against the brick facade of a building to try to reduce the din of the city.

Frank Mancini answered after the third ring, recognizing the caller ID. "Genie? What a nice surprise."

"Yeah, look, you already know that I've been hired to look into the deaths of Morris and Julia Cutter. Getting a phone call from me can't be too much of a surprise."

His voice was like warm honey. "When I talked to Mr. Rubin, he told me he'd be assigning his best researcher to this case. I was a little taken aback when he told me it was you. I didn't even know you weren't working for the newspaper anymore."

Nathaniel said I was his best researcher?

"I quit to go freelance about a month ago. Are you going to be okay with me working on this?"

He chuckled. "Of course. I know that once you have your arms around something, you don't let go." His words sounded mildly seductive.

I started walking slowly toward Grand Central Terminal, careful to not get in the way of fast-moving pedestrian traffic. "What are you hoping the outcome will be?" After I asked the question, even I wondered what I'd meant. Was I asking what he hoped the end of the investigation would look like? Or was I asking what he hoped the outcome of our newly formed business relationship would be?

Jesus, Genie, get a grip.

He was silent for a moment. "Look, how about we have dinner tonight to talk about it?"

I closed my eyes for a moment. "How about I just meet you in your office?"

"Dinner. I have a lot to tell you. Genie, it's just two friends having dinner."

When I'd last seen him back in October, he'd been good about not trying to get me into the sack. Back then, emotionally, I was in a bad place, and I needed a friend to talk to. If nothing else, Frank was always a good listener.

"Okay, how about Harbor Lights at seven?"

"See you there." Then I recalled the real reason I'd called. "Hey, I need to get into the Cutter house. Does the Realtor have a key?"

"Yeah, unofficially, they're still trying to sell it. Although, while murder scenes have a certain novelty, they're seldom a selling point. I have a feeling it's going to be on the market for a while."

"Can you call the Realtor and see if I can either get a key or have one of their people let me in?"

"Not a problem. See you tonight."

The connection broke off, and I called Nathaniel.

"Genie?"

I summoned up a picture of him, sitting at his desk in his apartment that doubled as his office, the window giving him a beautiful view of the East River. He'd have his cell phone to his ear with one hand and he'd be adjusting his bow tie with the other. "Hi, Nathaniel. I had my meeting with Parker Lewis at CP&G. Is there anything else you need me to do while I'm in town?"

"Did CP&G have Morris Cutter's laptop?"

"They said they didn't. They also said they didn't know where Cutter's appointment book is. I stopped by the Sheffield PD early this morning, and they didn't recall either a laptop or an appointment book being tagged for evidence. I'm going back to the Cutter house to take another look for myself."

There was a momentary silence, as if giving himself time to think. "Overall, was Parker Lewis helpful?"

"I think he gave me as much as he had. I don't think Mr. Lewis was hiding anything. He told me that Morris Cutter had a boatload of people who wanted him dead. He also said that Morris Cutter was only days away from giving some study to Congress about the role of fossil fuels and climate change."

"What?"

"According to Mr. Lewis, CP&G had hired their own team of scientists to write a report claiming that burning oil and coal doesn't cause global warming."

Nathaniel sounded disgusted. "Ugh, just what we need. More reasons for the science deniers to hide their heads in the sand."

As I walked, the light drizzle matured into a steady rain. "Have you ever heard of the consulting firm Fisher, Evans, and Sinclair?"

Nathaniel's voice went low. "Yes, why do you ask?"

"I just had coffee with one of their people. A creepy corporate troll by the name of Leonard Ryan offered me a quarter of a million dollars to close the Cutter case. He said he'd like the case shut down by Thursday."

"Fisher, Evans, and Sinclair does a lot more than just consulting, Genie. Did he threaten you?"

I smiled. "Not directly, just offered me money. He called it 'available resources to help expedite the investigation.'"

"Watch your back when it comes to those people."

I felt a chill. I thought back to Leonard Ryan's creepy smile and lizard eyes. "Are they dangerous?"

He didn't answer directly. "Black hats doing black ops."

"What?"

"A company that primarily recruits mercenaries. They've been known to post false stories with the press and create smear campaigns against their enemies. If that doesn't work, they use intimidation…or worse."

"Yikes."

"If they contact you again, let me know."

"I'm guessing that after I left his office, Parker Lewis must have called them to run interference."

Nathaniel cleared his throat. "Maybe, maybe not. I might have leaked something to the press."

"Excuse me?"

"I might have let a reporter friend of mine know that you've been retained by the estate to look into the Cutters' deaths."

Why in hell did you do that?

He didn't wait for me to ask. "Look, going public with this might shake the branches enough that a new witness falls out or someone comes up with useful information."

I felt a headache coming on.

He had one more thing to add, his voice tinged with a touch of good humor. "Plus, it tweaks Darren Reed."

"The new head guy over at CP&G?"

"While I was with the *Times,* I did a piece on him when he was with Exxon. He didn't like what I wrote and sued the paper, then tried to get me fired. The lawsuit got thrown out. I got promoted."

The last thing I needed was to get in the middle of a pissing match between Nathaniel and the CEO of a major oil company.

I walked past the busy doorway of the Grand Hyatt Hotel. I could see Grand Central Terminal just up the block. "Unless I'm needed here in the city, I'm heading back to Connecticut."

"Travel safely. And, I can't stress this enough, watch your back."

We said our goodbyes and I moved close to the building to check if I had any texts. Not seeing anything, I dropped the phone into my bag and glanced behind me so I could get back into the flow of pedestrians without getting bowled over by someone hurrying to the train station.

My heart did a slow roll when I spotted a man wearing a full-length black leather coat, holding an umbrella, and standing in front of the entrance to the Grand Hyatt, about thirty feet behind me.

He was staring straight at me.

When he saw that he'd caught my attention, he casually turned and walked slowly into the hotel.

Was I being watched?

Paranoia—welcome back, old friend.

Chapter Eight

I enjoy getting into Manhattan when I can for, if nothing else, the shopping. But for quick trips like on that day, it's a pain in my tush. Especially since I had to take an hour-long Metro-North back to Sheffield, then pick up my car at the station and backtrack to the Realtor's office in New Canaan. It was close to four by the time I parked in front of the Pullman Realty Group's storefront office.

Before I got out of the car, I called Caroline's cell phone. She answered on the second ring. "Hey, Genie."

"It looks like I'm going to be late tonight. I'll grab dinner while I'm out."

I obviously didn't tell her that I was having dinner with an old lover. I'd never told her about my shameful affair with Frank, and it would be a cold day in hell before I ever would. Another mistake in my life I didn't want her to repeat.

"No worries. I'm home and I've already let Tucker out back for a run." She sounded pretty chipper. Not like the snappish, surly teenager from last night.

"Awesome. There's still that pasta you can nuke from last night."

"I'm good. What time do you think you'll be home?"

I had that momentary inward cringe again that she and Tyler Greenwood would be up in her room canoodling and she wanted to know what time to get him out of there before I got to the front door.

You've got to trust her, Genie.

"No later than nine."

"I've got plenty of homework to keep me busy."

"That's my girl. If you need anything, I'll have my phone with me."

Dropping the phone into my bag, I got out of the car and went into the real estate office. The reception area was tastefully appointed with a couch and two upholstered armchairs, a coffee table replete with magazines like *Martha Stewart Living, Architectural Digest,* and *Elle Décor,* an espresso machine on a counter, and four wide-screen monitors on the walls simultaneously showing video of the interiors and exteriors of the ultra-expensive homes their company listed.

The receptionist sat at a tidy desk, her face hidden behind a laptop. When she saw me come in, she took off her glasses, placed them on the top of her expertly colored auburn hair, and sized me up. Because I was wearing my jeans, sweater, Doc Martens, and heavy coat, she quickly concluded that I wasn't there to buy a multimillion-dollar mansion.

She warily asked, "Can I help you?" Her voice made the question sound like I'd wandered in by accident looking for a bathroom.

I smiled. "Yes, I'm Geneva Chase, representing the Cutter estate. I need to get into the Cutter house. Their attorney, Frank Mancini, should have called you."

Without saying a word, she stood up, turned, and disappeared down a hallway.

While I waited, I took my phone back out and checked the *New York Times* website. One of the headlines screamed that an ice sheet the size of Rhode Island had broken off from Antarctica.

Climate change, the gift that keeps on giving.

When the receptionist came back through the doorway, she was followed by a man who was about forty pounds overweight for his five-foot-eight frame. He wore tailored slacks, a white shirt, and a pink-and-blue-striped tie loosened at his open collar. Attached to his pocket was a metallic nameplate with the Pullman Realty Group logo and the man's name, Arnold Allen. He reached for my hand. "Frank Mancini called and told me you'd be by. He said you wanted to get into the Cutter house. May I ask why?"

The soft illumination from the track lighting in the ceiling glistened on the man's bald head. His brown eyes didn't appear to be defensive. Only curious.

So instead of giving him a wiseass answer, I stuck with the truth. "I've been hired to investigate the deaths of Morris and Julia Cutter."

The receptionist's eyebrows shot up, and the man's mouth formed a surprised *O* at exactly the same time.

The man spoke first. "You're a private investigator?"

"I prefer research analyst."

It makes me sound like a sexy scientist.

"Let me get my coat." He turned for a moment to head back down the hallway but stopped in midstride and looked back to me. "I'm Arnold Allen. You can call me Arnie."

"Genie Chase."

"Nice to meet you. I hope this will all be kept quiet. The last thing we need is any more press. It's going to be hard enough to sell that house as it is."

———

While we took his Lexus SUV back to Sheffield, Arnie told me how he and his wife had moved from Minneapolis to Stamford a dozen years ago, how he got into real estate, how he landed a sales position with the exclusive Pullman Group, and how fucking hard it was going to be to unload the house in front of which we had just parked. "Dead bodies and real estate sales don't mix, Genie. It's just bad juju."

He stopped talking long enough for us to walk up the sidewalk, climb the steps, and unlock the door. "I'll be just a second." He entered the house, and I watched him push the code into the alarm box. "Okay, come in."

So, now I was certain that someone from the realty company could have had access to the house on the day of the murders. But would one of them have gotten close enough to kill two people and make it look like murder-suicide? And what the hell would the motive be?

Sizing up Arnie Allen, I decided he didn't look much like a killer.

The atmosphere inside had the quiet, empty feeling that houses take on when they haven't been lived in for a while. Knowing that two people had died so violently, meant the stillness took on a haunted quality for me.

At least when I'd been there yesterday, it had been in the comforting company of Nathaniel.

Arnie flipped on some lights, and I gazed around the spacious living area. Like a spooky magnet, my eyes were drawn to the kitchen doorway.

If there are ghosts in this house, that's where they'll be.

Even though the heat was still off and there was a distinct chill in the air, Arnie slid out of his overcoat and tossed it onto one of the plastic-covered couches. "Okay, here we are. What do you want to see?"

Keeping a neutral expression on my face, I answered, "I want to start with the library."

"Okay, let me show you where it is."

I held up my hand. "I know where it is. I'd like to do this alone, Arnie."

He grimaced. "I'm not supposed to let folks wander around the house on their own."

"Why not?"

He gestured vaguely with his hands. "Lots of valuable knickknacks sitting around. I'm responsible if something comes up missing."

I frowned. "Really? People who come out to look at multimillion-dollar homes are likely to walk out with a paperweight?"

He nodded and appeared earnest. "You'd be surprised, Genie."

I made a cross on the front of my chest. "I promise. I won't steal anything."

He considered for a moment. "Okay, I've got a closing coming up tomorrow in Redding and there're a few details that need to be ironed out. I'll be here on my phone if you need me."

I gave him the thumbs-up and then went down the darkened hallway until I got to Morris Cutter's library. Opening the door, I turned on the light switch and two table lamps blinked to life. Gazing around the room again, I marveled at the number of books Morris Cutter had accumulated.

Had he read all of them?

The two empty armchairs silently stared into the cold, dark maw of the stone fireplace, swept clean of ashes by the estate's cleaning crew. I went to the tall window, pulled away the curtain, and studied Long Island Sound through the glass, the surface of the water reflecting the cold gray winter sky.

Then I sighed and turned. Shadows fell across the deer heads and dead fish that hung on the wall, their cold, lifeless eyes staring blankly into space. I felt slightly queasy.

I sat down at the desk in a comfortable leather swivel chair. The same books I'd seen yesterday were still stacked on the desktop. One at a time, I opened the drawers as Eric had done. I found containers of paper clips, a stapler, pens, pencils, and unused notebooks. In one drawer I found hundreds of business cards, held together with rubber bands. In another was a stack of household bills that had been opened and then, I surmised, paid and stored until needed for tax purposes.

Nosy, I opened the envelope on top from American Express. I scanned the line items, noticing that back in December, on two separate occasions, Morris had purchased a pair of round-trip Acela tickets from Stamford to Washington, DC.

I was willing to bet that if he'd still been the CEO of his company, he would have taken the company jet.

But I wondered why he was going to DC.

To see his daughter?

Eric had said that Morris and his daughter weren't close. I made a mental note that I'd have to see how much money she'd inherited and if she had an alibi for New Year's Day. I recalled Nathaniel telling me that the gun that killed Morris and Julia was just the right size to fit in a woman's hand.

Not finding Morris's appointment book or anything else of interest, I sat and wondered how well the police had searched the rest of the house. If they believed that it was murder-suicide, might they have given certain rooms only a cursory look?

I turned off the lights in the library and went back into the living area, where Arnie had peeled back the plastic covering and was seated on a couch, phone to his ear, softly asking and answering questions. Without catching his attention, I silently climbed the carpeted steps to the second floor.

I slowly went down a long hallway, opening and closing doors. I knew the house had nine bedrooms, and I peeked into eight of them before I got to where the Cutters must have slept. Much larger than the others, a king-size four-poster bed dominated the room that boasted bureaus, large mirrors, another fireplace, and a window overlooking the wooded area beyond the tennis court. This room also had a desk, much smaller than the one in the study, and painted white.

Morris and Julia each had their own bathroom and walk-in closet. From the clutter of high-end cosmetics, I could easily tell which of the bathrooms Julia used. I glanced back at the desk where photos in heart-shaped frames sat. One of them was of Eric, Olivia, and their baby. Another was the graduation photo of a young lady I hadn't met yet. Most likely their daughter, Lisa.

This desk was obviously Julia's.

Sitting down, I opened the desk drawers. The first one gave me what I was looking for. Julia kept an old-school appointment book much like her husband had. I opened the flower-patterned cover, scanned through a few pages, and saw that she had two dates with her daughter's name on it. The same two dates on the American Express bill for the train tickets.

Interestingly, there was a date marked for January 4, three days after the Cutters had died. It was marked "Morris—Shadow Hill."

What's Shadow Hill?

I rooted around in my bag, which was still hanging from my shoulder, until I found my phone. I called Eric Cutter's number. Evidently, the number he'd given me must have been their landline because Olivia picked up. "Hello?"

"Olivia? This is Genie Chase. We met yesterday?"

"Of course, I remember."

I heard a baby crying in the background. "Do you need to go to see what's going on with your daughter?"

"No, Maria is here. Someone just has a poopy diaper. Maria's got it. What can I do for you?"

It must be nice to have someone to change those poopy diapers.

"Is Eric available? I have a couple of questions I need to ask him."

"I'm sorry, he's out right now inspecting a jobsite. I can give you his cell phone if you like."

I wanted to know who else came and went in the Cutter household, who else might have had a key and knew the alarm code. "Do you know if Morris and Julia had a live-in housekeeper or maybe a cook?"

"Live-in? No. They had a housekeeper who came in three times a week, and a cook who came in on weekends and on special occasions. Every so often, the help might stay overnight if Morris and Julia were entertaining."

I inwardly chuckled. Regular folks throw parties. Rich people entertain.

I asked, "How about security? Did they stay overnight at Eric's parents' house?"

The crying in the background stopped. "When Morris was still working, he had around-the-clock armed security. I know they used one of the bedrooms for one of them to catch naps while a second man was on duty. After Morris retired, the company stopped paying for security." Her voice sounded bitter.

"Do you know if any of the security people had a key and access to the alarm?"

"I honestly don't know."

"How often did Morris and Julia go to DC to visit their daughter?"

"Morris would go to Washington fairly often, but not to visit with Lisa. They weren't close at all. But when he *did* fly to DC, Julia would go with him, and she'd have lunch with her daughter while Morris did whatever Morris did. Usually it was to put the arm on some politician."

I looked down at the appointment book again. "Do you know where Shadow Hill is?"

She offered a clipped laugh. "That's what Morris called Congress…Shadow Hill. You know, Capitol Hill? He said that everyone on the Hill has an agenda, deep secrets, doing things they didn't want you to see. He said they were all like cockroaches scurrying around in the shadows. Shadow Hill."

"Do you know if Morris was in Washington a lot?"

"It was part of his job. Influencing the influencers. That's what he called it. That was back when he'd been taking the company jet, of course. Julia had mentioned that when they went down after his retirement, they'd take the train."

"Thanks, Olivia."

Saying goodbye and disconnecting, I looked back down at Julia's appointment book and flipped through the pages. She mentioned going to DC multiple times. The only time the words Shadow Hill were mentioned was three days after she and her husband died.

I recalled my interview with Parker Lewis. That must have been the date Morris Cutter was going to make the presentation of the CP&G study to Congress.

Chapter Nine

I dropped Julia's appointment book into my bag and went back downstairs. Arnie spotted me coming down the steps and frowned. "I didn't know you were upstairs. You didn't tell me you wanted to look around upstairs."

Is that fear in his voice? Or anger?

I smiled at him. "I hope that wasn't a problem."

He glanced down at my bag, and for a second, I thought he was going to ask me to empty it out so that he could see if I'd pocketed any expensive baubles that I might have found.

Nope, no baubles, just an appointment book, Arnie.

After an awkward silence, he said, "Okay, do you need to look at anything else?"

I glanced toward the kitchen and shivered. "Nope, good to go."

He clapped his hands together. "Let's saddle up."

He drove me back to the realty office, and I got into my car. Before I backed my Sebring out of the parking space, I saw that Arnie was still sitting in the driver's seat of the SUV and was having a heated conversation with someone on his cell phone.

Telling someone that I had taken an unauthorized tour of the bedrooms?

As I pulled onto the Merritt Parkway, I got an incoming phone call from my old boss, Ben Sumner, publisher of the *Sheffield Post*. "Ben? So nice of you to call. Do you have an assignment for me?"

"Genie. I think you have your hands full with the one you're already working on. I just fielded a call from a reporter from the *New York Daily News*."

"Did you get a name?"

"Brenda Zafiro. Do you know her?"

I checked my rearview mirror and changed lanes, anticipating the next exit off the highway. "Nope. What did she want?"

"She looked you up online and discovered that you used to work here. She's digging for some background information about you for a piece she's working on."

"Did she tell you what it's about?" I was pretty sure I already knew. Nathaniel said he'd leaked to the press that morning that we were reopening the investigation into the deaths of Morris and Julia Cutter. When this hit the papers, the executives at CP&G were going to have a whole herd of unhappy cows, and it would be a long time before poor Arnie Allen saw a dime of commission from the sale of the Cutter house.

"She told me you're investigating a murder-suicide. She said the cops have already closed the case. I got her phone number from caller ID. You want it?"

"Sure, but text it to me, I'm driving. By the way, what did you tell her about me?" I flipped my turn signal on.

I could almost hear him smile over the phone. "That you're the best damned crime reporter I've ever worked with."

I put a hand on my heart. "So sweet, Ben. How are *you* doing?"

"Oh, you know. I'm suing Galley Media, they're suing me. This thing will be in the courts for years."

I asked him, "How's Darcie doing?" She was the young journalist who had originally taken my place on the crime beat.

"I put her back on features. She's five months pregnant now, and between her swollen ankles and her difficulty getting in and out of her tiny little car, it's just easier to let her work from here."

I pulled onto the exit ramp. "I hear you hired Colby Jones to cover the cop shop."

"Yeah, you know him? His resume says he used to work for the *Boston Globe.*"

I waited at the stop sign until I could see a break in the traffic onto Main Avenue. "I remember him."

"He told me that the two of you had worked together."

"Yeah? What else did he say?"

Ben was silent for a moment. I'm sure he was wondering if there was more to the story that he hadn't heard. Ben had seen me at my best, and he'd seen me at my worst. "Nothing. Just that you'd worked together."

I recalled that Jones was a very good reporter but had an ego the size of Faneuil Hall. "Tell him that I wish him luck on his new job."

What's a hotshot like Colby Jones doing at a Podunk newspaper like the Post?

Of course, I'd also been a hotshot journalist who ended up at the *Post.* But for me, it was the last paper in the world that would hire me after drinking myself out every other good job I ever had.

Yet another good reason to stay strapped onto the sobriety wagon.

"I've got to go, Ben. Fight the good fight, my friend."

"Keep checking in. I'll send a freelance assignment your way."

"Bye, Ben."

I pulled into the parking lot of a Dunkin' Donuts and looked for the text where Ben sent me the phone number for Brenda Zafiro from the *Daily News.* I punched it in.

On the third ring, she answered. "This is Zafiro." Her words were clipped. Her voice low and smoky like she'd just had a cigarette and a shot of bourbon.

"This is Geneva Chase. I understand you called my old boss today. Ben Sumner at the *Sheffield Post*?"

She was quiet for a moment, as if I'd caught her by surprise. "Yeah. He told me you're working freelance now. Gutsy move. I've thought about it for years. Look, thank you for calling me, Miss Chase. I understand that Lodestar Analytics has been hired by the Cutter estate to reopen the investigation into the deaths of Morris and Julia Cutter."

"That's correct." I mentally questioned, again, Nathaniel's wisdom of sharing that with the press.

"The police concluded that it was a murder-suicide. Is there new evidence? Is that why you're taking another look?"

Since I knew what it was like to be in Brenda Zafiro's sneakers, I was professional but polite. "I'm afraid I can't speak about that."

"Can you tell me what prompted the estate to reopen the investigation?"

Same question asked just a little differently.

"I'm afraid I can't speak about that either."

"There's a rumor that Morris Cutter's company will be presenting something called the Ekmann Study to Congress later this week that purports climate change has nothing to do with burning fossil fuels. Does that have something to do with your investigation?"

Well, now I know that it's called the Ekmann Study.

The protestors in front of the CP&G offices already knew about the study, and now the press was wise to it. It didn't seem to be much of a secret.

I answered honestly. "I'm afraid I can't comment."

"I don't have a rat's ass chance of getting you to say anything, do I?"

"I'm sorry. If it makes you feel any better, I can sympathize."

"Who knows, maybe we can compare notes about our glamorous lives in journalism sometime." Her voice hummed with sarcasm.

"Maybe."

"Can you at least point me in the direction of someone who might be able to shed some light on this?"

"Sorry."

"Just so you know, I'm going to reach out to the executor of the estate, Eric Cutter."

"I'd do the same thing, Miss Zafiro. But I doubt he'll talk to you. You might have better luck talking to the estate's attorney. His name is Frank Mancini. You can Google his contact information."

"Call me Brenda. Good luck with your investigation. If you come up with anything you'd like to share, I'd appreciate it if you'd call. I know you have my number."

After we disconnected, I felt a pang of regret that I couldn't tell her anything. I liked how she sounded on the phone.

I couldn't tell her anything because at that point, I didn't have anything more than what was in the police report.

It wouldn't take long for that to change.

Chapter Ten

I glanced at my watch and saw that I had a little over an hour before my dinner appointment with Frank. I felt the urge to shower, fix my face, and change into something a little nicer than jeans and hiking boots.

When I walked through the front door of the house, Tucker dashed up to me as usual and begged me to pick him up. I swept him into my arms as Caroline came downstairs. "Hey, Genie. I didn't think you were coming home until late."

I involuntarily glanced up the stairs and silently wondered if we were alone in the house.

Seeing where my eyes had gone, she folded her arms and stated, "Nobody's up there. Want to check under the bed?" She sounded testy again.

Yes.

Hearing the angry sarcasm, I kept my voice calm. "Why would I want to do that? How was your day?"

"You know, after yesterday, I'm not sure if Jessica or Tyler will ever want to come back here."

Really? The kid's trying to guilt me?

It was working. "I'm sorry." I asked again, "How was your day?"

"Nothing special. Had about a dozen kids out with the flu. Oh, and I was asked if I wanted to be on the school paper."

My jaw dropped. "Really? What did you say?"

"I said sure."

"Do you know what you're going to be working on?"

She nodded. "I'm doing a piece on how the city is working to keep the schools safe from gun violence."

"That has awesome written all over it." I put Tucker down and rushed up to hug her.

To my surprise, she hugged me back. Even through our differences, I knew we loved each other, although it wasn't always easy. "What made you think about writing that?"

"We had another active shooter lockdown drill today. Every time we do that, my stomach hurts." She absently rubbed her tummy.

That broke my heart. It's not how kids are supposed to feel while they're in school. They're there to learn and be safe, not to practice hiding from a maniac with a gun.

I understood the school's concern. Sheffield was only thirty minutes from Newtown, Connecticut, where twenty children and six adult school staff members were gunned down by a nutjob with an AR-15 semiautomatic rifle. "I'm so sorry you kids have to go through that."

She shrugged. "Hey, I meant to tell you, it looks like someone stuck something weird in with our mail today."

"What do you mean something weird? Where is it?"

"Kitchen table. I don't want to be rude, but I've got to get back upstairs and tell Tyler to put his clothes back on."

I felt my face flush. "What?"

She laughed. "I'm kidding. I have an essay to write for my science class about single-use plastics. What time do you think you'll be home?"

I took a breath and tried to regulate my blood pressure. Her joke had been jarring. "Don't know. I'm having dinner with a business colleague. I won't be late."

I watched her trudge back up the steps, and then I went into the kitchen wondering where that kid got her snarky sense of humor.

On the table, a small stack of mail sat on top of a single trifolded sheet of paper. I moved the envelopes aside and unfolded the sheet of paper. It was a black-and-white photocopied Associated Press story picked up from the *Sheffield Post* about how last year had been the warmest on record. Handwritten in Sharpie across the top of the page were the words **Morris Cutter is burning in hell.**

Great, now all the crazies knew I'm working this case.

And where I live.

I fought the urge to pull the *Daily News* website up on my laptop in my bedroom to see what Brenda Zafiro had posted. But I didn't; the clock was ticking, and I still wanted that shower.

———

Harbor Lights was a restaurant in Norwalk that was, appropriately, right on the edge of the water. Overlooking the harbor, diners had a beautiful view of the marina, a city park, and the entrance to Long Island Sound. During the summer months, the line of people waiting to dine in the restaurant would be out the door. That time of year, however, the place was half-empty. We even got a table by the window. I glanced out at the lights on the black surface of the water as I walked through the dining room.

"You look great." Frank had already been seated at the table when I walked in. Grinning, he stood up, we hugged, and he held my chair out for me. Ever the handsome gentleman, he had on charcoal gray slacks and a collared white shirt under a tan cashmere sweater. His chocolate eyes glittered in the candlelight, and he looked absolutely delicious.

I blushed at his compliment and returned, "You always look great, Frank."

I'd decided on black slacks and a conservative white long-sleeved, off-the-shoulder top, with the top three buttons undone, offering the hint of cleavage without giving away the mystery.

Not that it was much of a mystery to Frank Mancini.

When the waiter came to take our drink order, and I asked for a club soda with lemon, Frank's eyebrows shot up. "No vodka?"

I slowly shook my head. "A new leaf, Frank."

Glancing up at the expectant young man, Frank shrugged and ordered the same.

He gazed over the flickering candle at me. "You weren't arrested again, were you?"

He was referring to the infamous incident about two years ago when I got into a fistfight with his wife in a bar and accidentally clocked an off-duty cop. Part of my punishment, in addition to a night in jail, was court-forced sobriety.

That had been an utter failure.

"No arrests. I just felt it was time."

"That's cool. It's healthy to evolve."

I could tell from his voice he wasn't sold on what I'd told him.

The glasses of club soda arrived, and the waiter asked if we knew what we wanted to order. I ordered the Filet Lavraki, which is Greek sea bass over jasmine rice and spinach with a lemon and olive oil sauce.

Frank asked for the seared yellowfin tuna, done very rare.

We clinked glasses and I asked, "So, what about you, Frank? Have you evolved?"

He sipped his club soda and smiled. "How can you improve on perfection?"

"Cute. How's Evelyn?"

He grimaced, not expecting me to inquire about his long-suffering wife. "She's good. Planning her next vacation with one of her girlfriends."

"Where to?"

"India. Something about going to where yoga originated."

Not actually caring where his wife was going to vacation, I moved on. "Mind if we talk business?"

"Good, right to it. I don't mind at all. I can write this dinner off as a business expense. But before we begin, you almost gave Mr. Arnie Allen a heart attack."

The Realtor from the Pullman Group. "Are you the one he called after we got back to his office?"

Frank smiled. "He told me how he caught you wandering around the house unescorted."

"I wasn't wandering, I was snooping. There's a huge difference."

"Poor guy thought I'd pull the listing."

"Eric told me the house isn't officially on the market."

"It's not, but if we can sell it, nobody's going to bitch."

I changed the subject. "How did Eric and Lisa Cutter make out when the wills were read?"

He studied my face. "Looking to see if the children had motive? Well, they both made out very well. They each inherited a third of everything."

I frowned. "Where did the last third go?"

"Into a trust fund for the granddaughter."

"How much are we talking about?"

He glanced up at the ceiling, as if doing a fast tally in his head. "Well, part of that depends on how much the house sells for, if it sells at all. But we're looking at about twenty-one million dollars total, split three ways. Not counting the house."

"That's a lot of money."

Frank raised an eyebrow. "You suspect the kids?"

"For right now, Eric's off my list of suspects. He's the one who reopened the investigation. I haven't met the daughter yet. What makes Eric think that it wasn't a murder-suicide?"

He cocked his head in surprise. "Well, you should probably ask Eric that, but I think it's got something to do with the baby. Amelia Cutter is Morris and Julia's first and only grandchild. According to Eric, his parents doted on that kid. They were looking forward to seeing the baby on New Year's Day." Frank shook his head. "Honestly, I have some doubts myself. I knew Morris. He wasn't the kind of guy who'd go out that way."

"Do you think this has anything to do with something called the Ekmann Study?" I watched his face to see if that would cause any reaction.

He tapped the top of the table with his fingertips. "Morris had mentioned that study to me in passing. It's another reason I have doubts about Morris Cutter killing himself. He was just days away from presenting it up on the Hill."

I smiled. "Shadow Hill?"

He laughed and nodded. "Did Eric tell you that's what Morris called Congress?"

"Olivia."

Out of the corner of my eye, I saw our young waiter emerge from the kitchen with a basket of warm bread. He placed it on our table and let us know that our dinners would be out shortly, then discreetly melted away.

I opened the cloth covering the warm bread and took a slice, placing it on my plate. "How well did you know Morris Cutter?"

Frank shrugged. "He's done business with my firm for years. I handled his will and a few other legal items for him. We never socialized."

I fixed him with my eyes. "What other legal items?"

Frank held up his hand. "Attorney-client confidentiality. I'm sure you understand."

Watching him take a roll and then pour olive oil onto his bread plate, I said, "You're writing the checks to Lodestar for this investigation. How thorough does the estate want me to be?" I looked him in the eye. "We're on the same team here, Frank."

He dipped a piece of his roll into the oil and took a bite, chewing slowly and considering my question. Then Frank swallowed and nodded. "Okay, what do you want to know?"

"I need to know his state of mind. Was there something that could have driven him to suicide? Maybe something even his son doesn't know?"

He took a sip of his club soda and appeared to struggle with how he should frame his answer. "There's no diplomatic way to talk about this. I can't emphasize how important this is that it never gets into the press. Even the Cutter kids don't know about it."

I crossed my heart. "I won't say anything."

"Look at me, talking to a reporter."

"Research analyst," I corrected.

He leaned forward and his voice dropped. "Two months before he died, Morris Cutter came to me. He needed to form a shell corporation to put some money into and then write some checks." He took another drink of his club soda.

"Why?"

Frank put the glass back down. "He'd been having an affair. He wanted to give the woman some money."

I watched Frank twist in his chair, clearly uncomfortable.

"The woman he had an affair with?"

Frank bobbed his head.

I continued, "Hush money? Blackmail?"

He glanced around his again. "He never said. I never asked.

He just told me how he wanted me to set up the shell corporation and what amount the checks were to be and to whom to write them."

I folded my hands on the table. "To whom did you write them?"

Frank rubbed his face. "A woman by the name of Nikki Hudson."

"Who is she?"

"She's a second-rate model trying to break into the big time. When Morris met her, she was working a golf tournament as hired eye candy."

"He didn't knock her up, did he?"

Frank shook his head. "Not that I'm aware of. Look, if she was threatening to tell his wife, maybe that's what pushed him to…you know."

"How much money changed hands?"

He took a deep breath before answering. "Three separate checks totaling two hundred and eighty thousand dollars."

I could tell Frank wished that this had never come up. I reached across the table and put my hand on his. "Okay, end of business discussion. You're clearly uncomfortable. How are your kids?"

"Paul's already talking about what colleges he wants to look at. Stacey is going to be taking equestrian classes this summer." He tore another corner of his bread apart and popped it into his mouth.

I let his hand go. "And your wife is going to India."

He shrugged.

I grinned at him. "How are *you* doing?"

He gave me a shy smile. "I miss us being together."

I looked at him from across the table. The flickering candlelight made the shadows dance on his handsome face. "Sometimes I miss it, too."

"We could be together again."

I frowned. "We were never *really* together, Frank. You're married, and I was a piece of ass on the side."

He frowned. Frank never liked it when I gutter-talked. "We were together, Genie. I admit we were a nontraditional couple. But, we were good together. I miss our desserts." He was referring to sex, being at his most charming.

Noticing that his voice had gone low and seductive, I narrowed my eyes. "No desserts, Frank." I offered an evil grin. "Your dessert is at home. No sugar here for you, sweetie."

Chapter Eleven

The next morning, while I was still in my ratty bathrobe, peeling a hard-boiled egg over the trash can, Caroline sat at the kitchen table spooning Cheerios into her mouth. I couldn't help but notice that she kept eyeballing me. Finally, I shot her a glance. "What?"

She dabbed at her lips with a paper napkin. "Trying to figure out the best way to bring this up."

Dear God, please don't let her be pregnant.

"Just say it."

"The school's got a Valentine's Day dance planned for this Saturday. Tyler asked if I wanted to go to the dance with him."

"You mean, like a date?"

She puffed out her lower lip and nodded. "Yeah, kind of like a date, I guess."

And so it begins.

This would be her first official date. Oh sure, she'd gone out with groups of her friends for pizza or to the movies, but this would be her first time going out one-on-one with a boy. I could feel the anxiety growing in the pit of my stomach, souring the coffee I'd already consumed.

"What time is the dance over?"

She shrugged. "I can check. Around ten, I think."

"Who's driving you there and picking you up?"

She scrunched up her face. "I'm guessing that you are."

"Damned right I am," I said, smiling.

Caroline's eyebrows shot up. "So, it's okay if I go?"

You've got to give the girl some room, Genie.

I finished peeling my egg. "Sure. Do you need something special to wear?" I lowered my voice for effect. "Do I need to take you shopping?"

That would be fun. The two of us hadn't been out shopping since the beginning of the school year.

"It's not going to be a fancy kind of dance. I think I can find something in my closet. I may need some help with my makeup and hair, though." She cocked her head, puckered her lips, and gave me her "I'm cute" expression.

I gave her a head nod. "I'm your girl. You'll be the prettiest one there."

———

I wanted to ask her more about this boy Tyler, but we were out of time. After one of Jessica's moms picked up Caroline to take the girls to school, I sat down at the kitchen table, still wearing my bathrobe, and searched the internet for Nikki Hudson, Morris Cutter's alleged lover. Aged twenty-three, she worked for the Triton Modeling Agency based in New York. According to her biography, she was five-seven, had lustrous black hair and emerald-green eyes, and had been in the business for a little over two years.

She'd worked at some of the top automotive shows, boat shows, and golf tournaments on the East Coast.

I didn't see any mention of magazine shoots, though.

There were half a dozen professional photographs that accompanied her bio. Two headshots, four glamor shots in gowns, and two "make love to the camera" bikini pictures. The girl had a rock-hard body.

Morris Cutter must have thought he'd died and gone to heaven.

Until the girl asked for money. Frank didn't know if she'd been blackmailing him or Cutter just wanted an insurance policy that kept her quiet.

I called the modeling agency. When the receptionist picked up, I said, "Hello, I'm looking for a way to contact one of your models."

The woman's voice on the other end of the phone sounded bored. "Which one?"

"Nikki Hudson."

"Let me look up her information, and I'll put you in touch with the appropriate agent here."

After a few moments of silence, giving me time to check the weather on my laptop, the woman came back on the line. "I'm sorry, we can't help you. Miss Hudson is no longer a client of ours." She disconnected without any further courtesies.

She'd recently received over two hundred and eighty thousand dollars. Probably didn't need to work for a while.

No worries, it just means I'll have to dig a little deeper.

Before I focused on Nikki Hudson again, I Googled Morris Cutter. A wide range of news stories and photographs came up. In one, Morris was shaking hands with George W. Bush in the White House. In another, he was posing with Donald Trump onstage at one of his raucous rallies. Press releases posted by media flacks for CP&G described Morris Cutter as a champion of energy independence. In one, he talked about the importance of opening national park land to oil exploration. In yet another, he argued that the earth was going through a natural cycle and the climate was warming of its own accord.

But in various Associated Press stories, he was vilified by environmentalists and climate-change activists as being the worst of the worst in the energy industry for polluting the air and water and contributing to the carbon content in the atmosphere.

I pulled up Julia Cutter. She had fewer entries, and they were much more genteel. One piece talked about how the Cutter family gave Sheffield Hospital a million dollars toward expanding their birthing center.

That was about the same time that Julia's granddaughter was born.

I found a photograph of Julia handing a check for a half-million dollars to the Sheffield Library. In another, she was donating the same amount to the Fairfield County Suicide Prevention Center.

If that doesn't drip with irony, I don't know what does.

Then, of course, there had been a ton of press on their deaths. Some of the stories that appeared were my own, written while on staff at the *Post*.

I took another sip of coffee and was about to get back to doing a deep dive on Nikki Hudson, but before I could bring anything up on my browser, the doorbell chimed, Tucker started barking, and I panicked.

I'm in my freakin' bathrobe, with bed-head hair, and no makeup.

Hoping that it was a just visit by the Jehovah's Witnesses, I shushed the dog, went to the front window, pulled away the curtain, and peeked at who was standing on my front stoop. It was a woman in a hooded parka, jeans, and hiking boots. I couldn't view her face clearly enough to see if I knew her.

I took a deep breath and opened the door. "Can I help you?"

I must have been a hell of a sight. She blinked when she saw me.

The woman pulled her hood back so I could see her face. She was in her early thirties and had long chestnut hair, brown eyes, freckled nose, pink cheeks, and a nervous smile. "I'm looking for Geneva Chase."

"I'm Geneva Chase. I might not be at my best right at the moment, but I'm Geneva Chase. Who are you?"

"I'm Dr. Lisa Cutter."

———

I invited her in, took her coat, ushered her into the kitchen, and got her a cup of coffee. Then I excused myself, dashed upstairs, ran a brush through my hair, and slid into a pair of jeans and a long-sleeved top. Skipping the makeup, and still barefoot, I descended and reentered the kitchen where I found Lisa Cutter sitting at my table with Tucker on her lap.

The little guy is pretty good at entertaining people, even strangers. Tucker had his eyes closed and seemed very relaxed as she held him.

"I love your dog."

I reached down and gave him a scratch behind the ear. "That's Tucker."

I topped off my coffee cup and sat down with her. "Let's start by my asking you, how did you find me?"

She grinned, showing me a set of nearly perfect teeth. Lisa was girl-next-door pretty. Freckles, pert nose, wide eyes. "I get an alert any time my parents' names pop up on the internet. Last night, the *New York Daily News* posted a story that you were reopening the investigation of their deaths. I called Eric, who confirmed that he asked the estate to do just that. Looking up your address is child's play. I took the first train from DC to Stamford and got an Uber to bring me here from the station."

Is that how that flyer found its way into my mailbox? The one that said her father was burning in hell.

I fought the urge to reach out to my laptop and look up the piece in the *Daily News*, even though I was dying to read it.

I took a sip of my coffee. "You must have gotten up at the crack of dawn."

She gave me a shy smile. "Oh, well before dawn. But I do that almost every morning."

You silly girl.

"Eric told me that you work in DC. He didn't say what you do exactly. You're a doctor?"

"I'm a climatologist. I work for NASA."

"That must have made for some interesting dinner conversation when you visited your father."

She frowned. "Over the last few years, we'd pretty much stopped talking to each other."

I had a ton of questions, but I left them unasked for the time being. "What can I do for you?"

Lisa looked down at the floor. She answered hesitantly. "I guess I'd like to know what you've found so far. The police were pretty certain that it was..." Her voice trailed off, not wanting to say the words "murder" or "suicide."

"We're really just getting started. I've studied the police reports, I've talked with Parker Lewis at CP&G, I took another look through your parents' house, and I met with the attorney handling the estate."

I obviously wasn't going to mention Nikki Hudson.

"I haven't found anything definitive so far. Is there something *you* can tell me? Was there someone who wanted to harm your parents?"

She looked up at me. "My father's stance on the environment was abysmal. We argued about it every time we were together.

There are activist groups who would have jumped at the chance to do harm to my father."

I went to the kitchen counter and opened my junk drawer. It contained old keys, rubber bands, expired coupons, and receipts I no longer needed but was too lazy to toss in the trash. It was where I also kept a few extra reporters' notebooks. I sat back down and opened one, holding my pen in the air. "What're the names of these activist groups?"

"I'm not saying any of them did anything."

"I understand."

She hesitated. "Okay, Climate Army. Maybe Crisis Warriors. Gaea, for sure."

"Gaea, what's that stand for?"

"It's not an acronym. It's the actual name of the organization. In Greek mythology, Gaea is the primal Earth Goddess, the personification of Earth, the ancestral mother of all life."

"Got it, mother of all life. Do you think any of these organizations are capable of hurting someone?"

She held up her mug. "Can I get a warm-up on this coffee?"

"Oh, of course, I'll get it for you."

"No need, I see the pot."

She stood up and went to the counter. It gave me a chance to give her another look. She seemed too young to have a PhD in climatology. She looked more like she could be a weather girl on television.

Christ, Genie. When did you get so sexist? Or so old?

Lisa had on blue jeans and a gray sweater. Everything appeared like it was off the rack. Nothing about her gave away the fact that she was the daughter of a very wealthy man and had just inherited millions of dollars.

For some people, that was motive enough to kill.

She topped off her cup, came back to the table, and sat down.

I repeated my question. "Do you think any one of these organizations could have had anything to do with the deaths of your parents?"

She sighed. "Gaea was the group that hacked into Exxon's computers last month and shut down their refinery in Texas for three days."

It's not murder, but it's extreme.

"They also published photos of Senator Ted Wilkins last year in bed with a hooker. Wilkins was on the Senate Committee for Commerce, Science, and Transportation. He's repeatedly called the climate crisis a hoax. He's since resigned from the Senate."

"But no physical harm."

"Three months ago, they blew up a natural gas pipeline under construction in Virginia. It put three people in the hospital. The Department of Homeland Security has them listed as a terrorist group." She was quiet for a moment, but Lisa wasn't finished. "I don't agree with Eric, Genie."

"How's that?"

"I don't think it was a double homicide. I think the police are right. I think my father killed my mother and then turned the gun on himself."

"Why do you think that?"

"Because Mom was having an affair, and Dad found out."

My heart took an extra beat. "How do you know your mother was having an affair?"

Were the Cutters both unfaithful?

She ran her finger slowly around the lip of her coffee cup. "She told me when I was up here for Christmas. She'd been having an affair for over a year."

"When she told you, was the affair still going on?"

Lisa shook her head. "She said she'd called it off. But he didn't want to let her go."

I leaned in close. "What else did your mother tell you?"

She reached into the pocket of her coat and pulled out a tissue, dabbing it at the tears that had welled up in her reddening eyes. "Mom was religious about going to the gym nearly every day. She was very physically fit. She was fifty-two but had the body of someone who was twenty years younger. Mom called it her insurance policy against getting old."

I took a sip of my tepid coffee and considered putting it into the microwave to warm it up. I decided against it, not wanting to break the flow of conversation.

Lisa continued. "She met a man there. He worked out nearly every day as well. She told me he was a retired police detective. She said that now he sells real estate part time."

I interrupted. "Do you know if he was a municipal cop or, maybe, state?"

"She didn't say. I don't even know his name."

"Why do you think she told you about the affair?"

"She was afraid."

"Afraid of what?"

"She said that when she broke off the affair, the man was so distraught he threatened to tell Dad. He'd even threatened to kill himself."

I sat back in my chair. "Did you tell the police this when they were doing their investigation?"

She nodded. "Yes, but I don't know if they ever followed through."

If the ex-lover is a retired cop, would that have colored the investigation? Did this man actually confront Morris Cutter over his wife's infidelity?

"What gym did your mother go to?"

"The Solstice Club here in Sheffield."

"Tell me about your relationship with your father."

"It had started going south about ten years ago when I told my parents that I was gay. Mom handled it pretty well, but Dad went ballistic. Then, when I got my doctorate in climatology, our relationship was pretty much done. We'd gotten so we could barely stand being in the same room together."

"I'm sorry."

She shrugged. "Look, climate change is real. Dad was a major contributor to the problem. From what I understand, now his company is getting ready to release their own study on how other factors are at fault for the changes that are happening. They claim that burning fossil fuels does nothing to harm the environment."

"Did you know your father died a few days before he was supposed to present that study to Congress?"

She nodded.

"How did that make you feel?"

"Pissed off. How do you think I'd feel?"

I rapped my knuckles gently against the top of the table. "Do you think anyone will believe CP&G's study?"

She sighed. "Public opinion is shifting in our favor. But a lot of people are stupid, Genie. And a lot of people just want to hear what they want to hear. They live in their little silos, listening and reading news that reinforces their beliefs. They don't want to have to face something that could very well be the end of life as we know it on this planet."

"I believe your father was reading a book by the name of *The Uninhabitable Earth*. Do you know it?"

She openly laughed. "Really? He was actually reading it? I had it sent to his house as a Christmas present. Are you sure he was reading it?"

"Yeah, I think so. It was on his desk in his library and there was a bookmark toward the end that led me to believe he was almost finished with it."

"I'm shocked he didn't throw it into his fireplace. I sent it as kind of a fuck-you present."

"It was on his desk along with his books about dead presidents."

"Well, I'm sure he wasn't taking it seriously." She chuckled. Then she shifted the subject. "You know, I'm surprised that CP&G has waited this long to release their bogus report."

"What do you mean?"

"From what Mom told me back around Christmas, Dad was going to DC to present the study to the Senate Committee on Energy and Natural Resources sometime after January first."

I frowned. "Do you know the exact date when he was supposed to do that?"

She thought for a moment, searching her memory, then she took her phone out and checked the calendar. "January fourth. Mom was coming down with him, and she and I were going to have lunch while Dad did his sideshow in Congress."

That corresponded with the date marked *Shadow Hill* in Julia's appointment book.

I echoed one of her earlier thoughts. "Any idea at all why CP&G put the brakes on making the report public?"

Lisa took one more sip of her coffee. "No clue. Unless they wanted to wait for the dust to settle from the news about Mom and Dad. And I'd be willing to bet the new CEO himself, wanted a little time to go by. I'm sure he wants to take full credit for the study. I met him briefly when he was at Exxon. Darren Reed is an ass."

I took a deep breath, and then asked the question I really wanted an answer to. "Where were you on New Year's Day?"

She eyed me suspiciously. "You mean do I have an alibi?"

I didn't answer.

"My partner and I were out late with friends partying on New Year's Eve and slept in late that morning. I got up while she was still sleeping, went for a run, and when I got back to my apartment, I made lunch."

"You were both there all day?"

Her eyes narrowed. "Janice and I were there all day. She made us a nice pot roast for dinner."

"Have you and your partner been together long?"

"I've known her since I was six. When we'd decided to move in together, we both came out at the same time. The difference was that her father was supportive."

I was done asking her questions, so we finished our coffee, made some uncomfortable small talk, then Lisa told me that she was going to stop by her brother's house and see the baby before she headed back to DC.

After she left, I looked up the *New York Daily News* story online. I was greeted by the headline, "New Investigation into Millionaires' Deaths."

Brenda Zafiro's first paragraph read, "Sheffield, Conn., police have called the deaths of Morris and Julia Cutter a murder-suicide. A fresh investigation spurred on by the family is looking at it as a double homicide. Lodestar Analytics, a privately owned investigation firm, stated that crime journalist Geneva Chase is heading up the inquiry. Miss Chase refused comment on the investigation. A spokesman for the Sheffield Police Department said that they stand by their findings of murder-suicide."

It seemed odd to see my name as part of the story and not the byline.

The story continued, "Morris Cutter retired as CEO of Continental Petroleum & Gas late last year. Darren Reed, current CEO of CP&G, stated that his thoughts and prayers go out to the family, and he hoped that the inquiry would come to a swift conclusion."

The rest of the piece was a rehash of Morris Cutter's career and the charitable contributions made by Julia Cutter. Brenda Zafiro also reopened the wounds from when Morris's brother was bought out of CP&G just before the company went public. She outlined the bitter lawsuits brought about by David Cutter, then after his death, more litigation from David's wife, Delia, and son, Stephan.

Then in a sidebar, I read that someone, just that morning, had hacked into a CP&G computer network and shut down three of its refineries, one in Texas and two in Louisiana. Darren Reed was quoted in that piece as well. "I hope the authorities find the terrorists behind this and prosecute them to the fullest extent of the law. These extremists are putting lives, jobs, and the energy security of this country at risk."

My cell phone chattered and I saw Leonard Ryan's ID on my tiny screen. I reluctantly answered. "Yes?"

"Miss Chase, this is Leonard Ryan of…"

I cut him off. "I know who you're with."

"Have you seen this morning's *Daily News*?"

I glanced down at my laptop. "I was just looking at it online."

"Did you leak this to the press?"

I smiled at the thought that Nathaniel had been the one to let the press in on our investigation. "Wasn't me. Didn't you see the part about Geneva Chase refusing to comment?"

"That the press has already gotten wind of your investigation is deeply upsetting. It makes getting to the successful conclusion in a swift and timely manner all the more important. Our company is willing to raise the amount of resources we can offer you to half a million dollars."

Holy crap, they're serious.

"So, just so I'm clear. You want me to say that it was murder-suicide."

"We want you to concur with the results of the police investigation. Yes."

"By Thursday."

"Yes."

"Why?"

There was silence on the other end of the line.

Finally, I said, "I don't think a legitimate investigation can be done in that short amount of time."

The man's voice went low. "Then that, Miss Chase, would be unfortunate for you."

Chapter Twelve

"Fisher, Evans, and Sinclair just upped the ante. They've put a half million dollars on the table if we wind this up their way by Thursday."

Nathaniel was on the other end of the line. "Why?"

"That Ryan guy didn't say. He just told me that if it dragged out any longer than that, it would be unfortunate. I think that CP&G wants to present their bogus climate report to Congress sometime soon. Who knows, maybe as early as Friday. I talked with Lisa Cutter this morning, and she thinks they want this whole thing behind them."

"I'll take a look at the congressional schedule. Give me a minute to look it up online. While I'm searching, I have a question. Did you ask Lisa Cutter where she was on New Year's Day?"

"She says she was home with her partner."

"Partner. Is she gay?"

I smiled to myself. "Her partner's name is Janice. What do you think?"

"Okay, I found it. The Senate Committee on Energy and Natural Resources is meeting on Friday. Darren Reed is on the agenda."

"That's why they want this tied up by Thursday. They don't want us to muddy the waters."

"Genie, keep plugging but watch your back. Back when I was with the *New York Times*, I did a piece on Fisher, Evans, and Sinclair. They play dirty. Darren Reed, the CEO of CP&G, is no saint either."

"Lisa Cutter says he's an ass."

Nathaniel offered a dry chuckle. "King size."

After we disconnected, I grabbed a shower, fixed my face, and threw on some street clothes. Then I went back downstairs and looked up the contact information for Delia and Stephen Cutter. When I called, a woman answered. "Hello?"

"Am I speaking to Delia Cutter?"

She was slow to answer, wondering if this was a sales call or a phone scam. "Who's asking?"

"My name's Geneva Chase, Mrs. Cutter. I work for a company called Lodestar Analytics, and we've been hired by the Cutter estate to take another look at the deaths of Morris and Julia Cutter."

There was an icy silence on the other end, and for a moment, I thought we might have been cut off.

Finally, the woman came back on the line. "Why? The police concluded that that greedy son of a bitch shot his wife and himself. Why does the estate want to open this dirty affair back up again?"

What could I say? I didn't want to admit that there was really no evidential reason to reopen this investigation.

"It would be easier to discuss if I could meet with you face-to-face."

"I'll want my son, Stephen, here."

Even better.

"By all means."

She gave me her address, and we set the time for one o'clock that afternoon. While I sat in my kitchen killing time, I looked up her Easton location online. Knowing that the late David Cutter was Morris's brother and that he'd been cheated out of a fortune, I couldn't help but make comparisons between their homes.

David's was worth a little over a million dollars. His older brother's house was worth eleven million. Looking at the photos on my laptop, I noticed that the two homes had a lot in common. They were both Tudors, built with fieldstone, brick, and heavy timbers.

But David's was considerably smaller.

Morris's house had nine bedrooms. David's had four and sat on a little less than an acre of land, with no tennis court or pool or Long Island Sound to look at. Nonetheless, from the photos of the exterior and the interior, it was a beautiful home.

Just not nearly as grand as his brother's.

While he was alive, it must have been galling for David to know that his brother had cheated him out of so much money.

And like a slow acid drip for David's widow and son.

———

I parked my car next to a Tesla Model 3. The car was a beautiful deep blue. I thought the low-slung design of those cars was stunning. I loved the look, but still harbored doubts about driving an electric car.

I'd once asked Darcie, the newspaper's resident millennial, what the allure of the Tesla was. She'd told me, "It's not a car, Genie. A Tesla is a gorgeous, well-designed, smart device that takes you places."

Before I climbed the stone steps up to the front porch, I glanced back at the car one more time and quickly looked it up online. I saw that the price tag on that car was between fifty and seventy thousand dollars, depending on the bells and whistles. Sitting next to it, my ten-year-old Sebring was looking kind of punk.

Yeah, it's time to be looking for another car.

I was greeted at the door by a tall, good-looking man in his thirties. Eric Cutter's cousin bore a faint resemblance to him. Stephen had dark eyes, a carefully trimmed black beard, and hair that was brushed straight back from his forehead. He had on tan slacks, a dark green V-neck sweater, and loafers.

What he wasn't wearing was a smile.

"I'm guessing you're the detective?"

I extended my hand. "I'm Geneva Chase. Are you Stephen Cutter?"

He reached out his own, and we briefly shook. "I'll be very frank with you, Miss Chase. We're not happy that my cousin has reopened the investigation. My mother and I don't see the value in dragging the family name through the mud one more time."

Why? Do you have something to hide?

I attempted a weak smile and thought about the hypocrisy of his statement. It hadn't stopped him and his mother from filing lawsuits against CP&G or the Cutter estate itself. I answered, "We want to wrap this up as quickly and as quietly as possible."

"Please follow me." I walked inside, and he closed the door behind me. Then Stephen led me through the foyer and into the living area.

My eyes were drawn immediately to the woman sitting in a wheelchair wearing a hospital gown with a colorful quilt across her lap. A rubber tube ran from an oxygen tank, hung from a metal rack, to her nose. Her eyes were gray and rheumy. The pale parchment-like skin on her face was mottled with pink patches. She was seated in front of a large-screen television mounted on the wall. I noticed that it was tuned to *The View.*

Next to where she sat was an end table with a lamp and a landline telephone. That was how she was able to answer the phone when I called.

She watched us come into the room. When the woman spoke, her words were little more than a whisper, her breathing labored. It was obvious that she was struggling for air as she talked. "Pardon me if I don't get up to greet you. I'm having a particularly bad day."

I moved past Stephen and extended my hand. "Please don't worry about that, Mrs. Cutter."

I knew that if David Cutter was alive, he'd be sixty-five. I surmised that Delia Cutter had to be around that age as well, but she looked at least twenty years older.

The woman made no attempt to shake my hand but eyed me suspiciously, like a sparrow watching a cat. "What do you want?"

As a journalist, I knew that when approaching a hostile subject from whom you wanted information, it was best to be as sympathetic as possible. "From all the stories I've heard, Morris Cutter treated your husband poorly. I'm hoping you can tell me more about that."

Delia's eyes were little more that wet slits as she studied me. She waved her hand. "Sit on the couch over there. Can Stephen get you anything? Water? Coffee?"

"Nothing, thank you." I glanced around the room. As dark as the living space was in Morris Cutter's house, this room was open and bright with plenty of windows. The walls were a light peach; the two fabric-covered couches and love seat were off-white and pastel blue. The floors were a pale-stained hardwood, and there was a simple white throw rug in the center of the room. Against one wall was a brick fireplace framed by a wooden mantle. Off to one side sat a black baby-grand piano.

I took off my coat, and Stephen silently took it, hanging it in a closet in the foyer. I sat on the couch closest to Delia. "Thank you for allowing me this time."

Stephen came back into the room and sat on the loveseat, his hands folded in his lap.

Delia licked her lips and started. "Morris Cutter was the most evil motherfucker that ever walked this earth."

Okay, good. She wasn't going to sugarcoat this.

I nodded empathetically. "So I've heard."

She pointed a bony finger at me. "We wouldn't be living in such a tiny house if he hadn't cheated my husband out of what was rightfully his."

Seriously? You want to see a tiny house, come over to my place.

"Please, can you tell me about it?"

She closed her eyes for a moment. Then opened them back up, staring straight at me. "Thirty years ago, my husband's father retired and made David senior vice president of CP&G and named Morris the president. I don't know if anyone's told you this, but David was the older of the two. If anyone should have been running that company, it should have been my husband."

I leaned forward. "That must have been very upsetting to your husband. I can't imagine why their father would have done that."

Delia nodded and gripped the arms of her wheelchair hard enough that her knuckles went white. "David knew why. Just before his father retired, the *Exxon Valdez* ran aground, and eleven million gallons of crude oil spilled into Prince William Sound in Alaska. That oil slick covered thirteen hundred miles of coastline and killed hundreds of thousands of seabirds, otters, seals, and whales. Even now, after so many years, every so often they still find a pocket of oil that they haven't managed to mop up."

Stephen explained, "It was the country's biggest oil catastrophe right up until the Deepwater Horizon disaster took place in 2010."

I was confused. "What does the *Valdez* have to do with CP&G?"

Delia frowned. "David was concerned. Seeing what happened in Alaska appalled him. He never wanted something like that to happen with CP&G. He moved to institute safety measures for all of the company's ships." Delia cocked her head. "Expensive safety measures."

"I see. His father didn't agree?"

She slowly shook her head. "He put Morris in charge. And instead of increasing the safety measures for their ships, Morris went to Congress to weaken them."

Stephen spoke up again. "Uncle Morris was all about the money…lowering costs, maximizing profits, and damn the consequences."

Delia licked her lips again. "Stephen, can you get me a glass of water?"

"Sure." The young man sprang up from the love seat and disappeared through a doorway into what I assumed was the kitchen.

She glanced after him. Delia leaned forward and whispered, "Even though he has his own place, Stephen spends as much time here as he can. He's such a good son."

I wanted to get the conversation back on track. "Your husband must have been very frustrated."

She frowned. "David constantly questioned his brother's decisions, especially the ones to cut costs. He was certain that sooner or later, a *Valdez*-like accident would happen to CP&G."

"Did it?"

Delia leaned forward again. "Yes, one of the derricks off the coast of Texas sprang a leak in 1992. It wasn't nearly the size of the Deepwater Horizon spill, but it was the result of cutting back on safety equipment and inspections. It was only about a half million gallons, but it was enough that people in Texas and

Louisiana were finding tar balls on their beaches for months, and seagulls and pelicans were showing up covered in crude."

"I don't remember hearing about that."

Stephen walked back in with a glass of water. Handing it to his mother, he looked at me. "You didn't hear about it. Uncle Morris and his lapdogs at Fisher, Evans, and Sinclair kept a lid on it."

"How did they do that?"

"Bribes, intimidation, blackmail."

I frowned. "I thought Fisher, Evans, and Sinclair was a consulting firm."

"They're way more than that, Miss Chase."

I was just starting to understand the scope of the consulting company's reach. "So it never made the newspapers."

Stephen shook his head and sat back down. "Nope, and Dad raised holy hell. He threatened to tell the press unless Uncle Morris changed the way the company did business."

Delia took a dainty sip of water and set the glass on a coaster on the end table next to where she sat. Then she brushed a wisp of white hair away from her eyes. "Morris wanted him silenced and out of his hair. He made David what looked like a sweetheart deal to sell his share of the company."

I knew the story, but I feigned ignorance. "It wasn't such a good deal?"

The woman slowly shook her head. "He screwed David six ways to Sunday. Morris had quietly been getting ready to take the company public. Once he did, the value of CP&G skyrocketed. He'd cut his own brother out of the deal, costing us tens of millions of dollars."

I raised my eyebrows in faked astonishment. "Wow. David must have been furious."

Her eyes narrowed. "To put it mildly."

"Enough to want to kill his brother?"

Stephen, turning a bright crimson, interrupted in anger. "I think that's enough, lady. Time for you to go."

I held up a hand. "Did David continue to lobby for more safety measures?"

Stephen stood up. "My father was an outspoken, impassioned environmentalist."

"What did Morris think about that?"

Delia bobbed her head slightly. "It drove Morris crazy to see David standing in front of his building with a group of protesters, chanting and carrying a placard."

"Did he believe that CP&G was contributing to climate change?"

Stephen managed a twisted grin. "Wholeheartedly."

Looking back at Delia, I asked, "When did your husband pass away?"

"Two years ago. He died of a stroke."

I stood up, directing my next question directly to Stephen. "How about you? Do you believe that CP&G is damaging our climate?"

"Of course, it is. It's an oil company."

"Is that your Tesla out there?" I jerked my thumb in the direction of the front door.

He looked slightly embarrassed. "Yes, it is."

"It's a nice ride."

"We all have to do our part."

I glanced at him, curious. "Do you mind if I ask what you do for a living?"

He stood up a little straighter. "I do public relations work for a nonprofit organization called Gaea. Have you heard of them?"

Just that morning, Lisa Cutter had told me how Gaea had shut down refineries and blown up a pipeline. "Yes, I have. I heard that the Department of Homeland Security has labeled Gaea a terrorist organization."

Stephen's nostrils flared, and I watched his jaw muscles move as he ground his teeth. When he answered, it was in a low, measured voice. "The world as we know it is headed for collapse. If we don't take extreme action now, the results will be apocalyptic. Ms. Chase, we're at war."

"At war?"

He narrowed his eyes and snarled, "All-out war."

Chapter Thirteen

The Solstice Club in Sheffield was once the P.G. Lawrence Corset Factory. Originally built in 1916, it went out of business in 1931. It was repurposed into a bicycle factory in 1941, then shuttered in 2008. Reopened in 2011 as the Solstice Club, it was a two-story, stand-alone brick building near the border of Westport on Route 1 and was now one of the most luxurious gyms in Fairfield County. It boasted every piece of exercise equipment possible, plus the club offered spas, massages, saunas, fitness classes, a heated swimming pool, Jacuzzi, spinning sessions, yoga, dance classes, personal trainers, and a juice bar. Its website bragged that the gym supplied hot eucalyptus towels upon request.

I walked through the glass doorway into a spacious, black-and-white-tiled entry lounge area and went straight to the front counter. A buff young man in blue shorts and a black Solstice Club T-shirt wore a lanyard around his neck that told me his name was Ken. He smiled at me as I approached. "Hi, can I help you?"

"Hi, I'm Genie Chase. I was a friend of Julia Cutter."

The young man's face took on an exaggerated expression

of sorrow. "Yes, we were all so sad to hear about her and her husband." He leaned forward and whispered, "It was so tragic."

I nodded and watched as a woman with an expensive-looking leather gym bag slung over her shoulder came up beside me and waved a tag on her key chain in front of a small screen on the counter. The screen blipped, and the woman walked off in the direction of the locker room, never acknowledging my presence as I'd stood next to her. I turned my attention back to Ken and replied, "Julia was very special."

He seemed sincere when he said, "We all just adored her."

"Well, she raved about this place. Before she died, Julia told me that she worked out here almost every day. Something about how she didn't want to get old."

His face immediately changed again, and he grinned at me. He had short, spiky sand-colored hair and couldn't have been much more than twenty. The way his shoulders and biceps stretched out the fabric of his shirt, he obviously made good use of the equipment and the weights. "She was a regular, alright."

"Well, I'm thinking about joining. Can you tell me a little bit about the club?"

He turned and crooked his finger at a young woman dressed exactly like him—blue shorts, black club shirt. "Tessa, can you watch the counter? I'm going to show this nice lady our facilities."

Ken came around the counter. "Follow me." He started off but then glanced back at me as I followed. "Can I get you anything? Herbal tea? Water? Juice?"

"No, thank you."

The first thing that caught my attention was the clothing shop off to our left. It was filled with high-end shorts, shirts, yoga pants, workout shoes, sneakers, headbands, and reusable water bottles, all of them sporting the Solstice logo. I jerked my thumb in the direction of the store. "That's impressive."

"Solstice has its own line of clothing and equipment." He pointed ahead of us. "Here's cardio. When Julia started coming, she just about wore out that elliptical over there. Same machine, every afternoon. Always had *Law & Order* reruns playing on her screen."

There were twenty or so clients walking or running on the treadmills and step machines. There were six more sweating their asses off on the ellipticals. Some were watching tiny screens on their machines, some had their eyes glued to the massive television screens on the wall in front of them, and a few were openly staring at the floor-to-ceiling mirrors, watching themselves sweat.

We walked past them into the weight room where four men and two women were using the presses and the lifts, and doing bicep reps. Even though this was a high-end, expensive workout club, the rank smell of sweat permeated the gym. Grunts and moans of exertion echoed against the walls.

"Sometime around October, Julia started working out here in the weight room. I think her friend got her into it."

"Friend?"

Ken glanced away from me, seemingly flustered. He leaned in so no one else could hear. "It was none of my business, but they seemed awfully chummy. They both worked out at the same time of day, nearly every day. I hear they met working out next to each other on the ellipticals. But then he got her into working out with weights. She looked fabulous for her age, but you already know that, don't you?"

I smiled knowingly, as if I was familiar with the way Julia Cutter looked. The last time I'd seen her was in a police photo with a bullet wound in her head.

I glanced around the room. "Is Julia's friend here today?"

Ken shook his head. "Oh, no. About the same time that Julia"—he hesitated, then continued—"passed away, he stopped coming."

I lied, "Now that you mention it, I think I recall Julia telling me something about a guy she worked out with here at the club. Isn't he an ex-cop?"

"Retired, Sheffield PD. He sells real estate on the side now. Tried to interest me in a condo last fall. I just couldn't swing it on my salary here. It would've been a good investment, though."

I pretended to search my brain for a second. "What was his name? I know Julia mentioned it."

"Paul Marston?"

From my time on the crime beat at the newspaper, I knew Officer Paul Marston. He had just been getting ready to retire when I'd started working at the *Post* two years ago. He was very tall and had some beer weight around his middle. Only in his early fifties, he had a full head of brown hair, was clean-shaven, and, if you overlooked his paunch, was a good-looking guy.

I snapped my fingers. "That's it, Paul Marston. He stopped working out here after Julia died?"

Ken walked out of the weight room, and I followed him into the swimming pool area. The smell of chlorine was jarring. It reminded me of the smell in the Cutter house. "We do pool aerobics here, and of course it's available to do laps."

I had to speak up to be heard over the echoing sounds of splashing water and other conversations in the cavernous room. "This looks great. Hey, I'd love to reach out to Mr. Marston. I'm a professional therapist, and it sounds to me like he might be in some emotional distress over the loss of his friend."

I can be such a terrible liar.

Ken smiled again. "That's so sweet. Paul's passionate about working out and staying healthy. If he stopped coming to the gym, I'm sure he must be hurting." The young man seemed embarrassed again. "I think Julia and Paul were close."

I let that statement hang in the chlorine-filled air for a

moment. Then I said, "I'm sure I can find his contact information online, but it would be so much easier if you could give it to me while I'm here."

"Oh, we're not supposed to give out personal information about our clients."

Behind me, I could hear water splattering as someone climbed up an aluminum ladder, out of the pool. I attempted a warm grin. "Understandable, and I respect that. I just thought you could save me a little time, is all."

Ken glanced around him as if to see if someone was listening to our conversation. "I'm certain that they were more than just friends."

"I understand."

"And you're just trying to reach out to him to help him." The young man was trying to convince himself that it was okay to give me Paul Marston's contact information. I knew from experience that not saying anything would most likely pay off. Nature abhors a vacuum. Let the young man work it out in his head. He muttered, "I mean, you're a therapist and all."

"That's right. I just want to help him."

Five minutes later, I had Marston's address, his phone number, and how to contact him by email. Two minutes after that, I was in my Sebring, a Solstice Club application in my possession, heading up to the north side of town. The retired cop lived in a single-story, Cape Cod ranch-style home on Strawberry Hill Avenue, just off Route 1.

It was a working-class neighborhood, and while all the homes were small, they were neat and well cared for. It was a Tuesday afternoon, a workday, and only a few cars were parked in driveways up and down the street.

A Honda Accord was parked in Marston's drive. I pulled up to the curb in front of his house and shut off my engine.

Before getting out, I made a phone call to Mike Dillon.

He recognized me from caller ID. "Genie, what's up?"

"What can you tell me about a retired police officer by the name of Paul Marston?"

He paused for a heartbeat. "Why do you ask?"

"I'm just getting ready to go in and talk to him."

"Why?"

I hadn't told Nathaniel, my own boss, about the connection between the retired cop and Julia Cutter, but I was about to tell Mike Dillon. "Lisa Cutter, Morris Cutter's daughter, claims Marston was romantically involved with her mother just prior to her death. And that she'd broken off the relationship, and he hadn't taken it well. He'd threatened to tell Morris about their affair."

There was another silence on the line as Mike digested what I'd told him. When he finally said something, it was in a voice that was low and somber. "Paul was a really good cop for twenty years. Right at the end, just before he retired, his wife, Connie, left him for another man. I never asked the details, and he never told me. But it screwed with his head."

"What do you mean?"

"I'm not a psychologist, but it didn't take a genius to see that Paul wasn't himself after Connie left. He really should have talked to someone."

"You mean a shrink?"

"Someone."

"Why?"

"It did something to him. I don't know, maybe for his self-esteem. It made him angry, difficult to work with. Twice, he was accused of using excessive force. Once for a traffic stop and once while breaking up a domestic dispute."

I glanced over at the house, wondering if he was in there. "Was he forced to retire?"

"You know I can't discuss personnel issues."

"Did you ever see him after he left the force?"

He paused before he spoke again. "I stopped by to see him before Thanksgiving. He surprised me."

"How so?"

"Before Connie had left him, Paul was growing a beer gut. He confided that he thought that the weight gain might have had something to do with Connie leaving. But when I saw him standing in the doorway of his house that afternoon, he was a different man. He'd dropped thirty pounds and had a grin from ear to ear. He looked really good, healthy. He had his old confidence back."

Of course. He was working out every day.

As if reading my mind, Mike said, "Paul told me that going to the gym was like a new religion for him. He said he'd even met a woman there. Are you telling me he was having an affair with Morris Cutter's wife?"

"Yes."

"Jesus, Paul's living on a policeman's pension. Do you think that Julia Cutter would risk everything she had so she could have a roll in the hay with an ex-cop?"

I glanced at the Accord parked in front of Paul's condo. There was still snow around the tires where the sun hadn't had a chance to melt it yet. We hadn't had any snow for nearly two weeks. It told me the car hadn't been moved in a while.

"The heart wants what the heart wants, Mike. The Cutter kid told me Julia broke it off with him right before Christmas."

There was a long silence. I watched a seagull sail over the roof of the house. Mike's next questions took me by surprise. "Where are you? What are you planning to do?"

"I'm sitting in front of Paul's house. I want to talk with him."

"I don't think that's a good idea."

"Why not?"

"I already told you that he has anger management issues."

"It's not my first time at the rodeo, Mike."

"And he owns a gun."

That gave me pause. "Do you think he's capable of murder?"

"Like yours?"

"Like Morris and Julia Cutter." I studied the house again. The windows were dark; the curtains were drawn.

"Why don't you let us talk to him?" Mike suggested.

I admittedly was getting a case of the yips, and I could feel my hands go clammy. I lied, "You may be right."

I heard him exhale. "So, you'll let us handle it?"

"Ten-four."

I hit the button and ended the call. Then I got out of my car, slung my bag over my shoulder, and walked up the short sidewalk, climbing the cement steps to the front door.

No risk, no reward.

I rang the bell. No answer.

I rang again.

No answer.

I knocked on the door.

Nothing.

I knocked harder.

The curtain in the bay window to my right twitched.

Is there someone there?

I shouted at the door. "Mr. Marston, I'm just here to do a welfare check on you. Are you okay?"

His answer was muffled. "Go away."

I decided to go for broke. "Please, Mr. Marston, I'd like to talk to you about Julia Cutter."

There was more silence, then suddenly the door swung open and a tall man, muscular, hair askew, eyes red, a week's worth of stubble on his face, stood staring at me. He was wearing sweat-pants and a T-shirt. "What did you say?"

"I'd like to talk to you about Julia Cutter."

"Why? She's dead. Her husband murdered her." His words sounded bitter in his mouth.

"I know you were in love with her."

He stood motionless, his mouth slightly open, as he stared at me. Then he put both hands to his face and, shoulders heaving, began to sob uncontrollably.

Chapter Fourteen

After a few awkward moments, Paul Marston managed to compose himself, take a deep but ragged breath, and then wordlessly he waved me into the house.

The heartbreaking sorrow that permeated that household seemed palpable. The curtains were closed tightly over the windows. The only illumination came from the television on the wall, images of talking heads, two men and a woman, on a Fox News program silently grinning and chattering with each other while seated on a couch.

The living room was filled with vague scents—bacon, onions, stale beer, and the sour smell of sweat. In the silver light of the TV, I could see the room was simply furnished. A cloth couch, a vinyl recliner facing the television, and an end table. There was a small pile of newspapers next to the recliner. A half-empty glass tumbler sat on the end table.

Once we were inside the living room, Paul sighed heavily and turned toward me, gesturing toward the couch.

I unzipped my coat. The temperature seemed just a little too warm to be comfortable.

As I took a seat on the couch and he collapsed in his recliner,

I noticed something in that half-darkness that made my stomach twist into a frightened knot.

In the shadows next to the half-empty glass was a handgun.

As we situated ourselves, I tore my eyes from the weapon and took the opportunity to study his face. Handsome, full head of salt-and-pepper hair, strong chin, but his face was marred by the dark shadow of unshaven stubble and his red eyes. When I'd passed him in the doorway, I could easily see he was around six-four and still trim, even though I knew he hadn't been in a gym in over a month.

Paul leaned forward in his chair. "How do you know?"

"About Julia and you?"

He cocked his head. "Don't you work the crime beat for the newspaper?"

He recognized me from his days as a cop. "I used to."

"How did you find out about us?"

I couldn't help but notice that he didn't ask who I was working for. "Julia told her daughter. How long were you two together?"

He stared at the wall behind me and chewed slightly on his bottom lip, then answered. His voice was little more than a whisper. "Just over a year, I guess."

As my eyes adjusted to the dim interior of the house, I could see past Paul into the dark kitchen. The table was cluttered with dishes, and there were fast-food containers on the counters. Knowing that his car hadn't been moved in a while, I guessed that when Paul got hungry, he called and had takeout brought to his house. I turned my attention back to the man in the chair. "How did it start?"

His eyes narrowed as he focused his attention on me. "If you're not with the paper anymore, who are you working for?"

"I've been asked to take another look at the deaths of Julia and Morris Cutter."

His eyes grew suspicious. "Why? Police said it was a murder-suicide."

I waved it off. "The estate wants to make sure that nothing was missed." I changed the subject. "You met Julia Cutter at the Solstice Club?"

He was quiet for a moment, his breathing steady, studying me. "We were both there almost every day. I thought she was one of the most beautiful women I'd ever seen. After about two months of working out side by side, I finally got the courage to say hello. She said hello back, and we struck up a friendship."

"But it became more than that."

"Have the police reopened the case?"

Are his words slurring? Is there booze in that glass?

I glanced at the time on my cell phone. It was only twelve thirty, barely the start of the afternoon.

"No."

"Are you a private detective now?"

"No. I'm a research analyst."

Paul frowned and picked up his glass. "You mean like a scientist?" Suddenly realizing that he might be being rude, he asked, "Want something to drink?" He attempted a weak smile.

It wasn't that long ago that I might have taken him up on his offer. I glanced again at the handgun on the table and recalled Mike's warning about Marston's bursts of anger when he was on the force. "No, thank you."

He took a gulp of whatever it was in his glass. Keeping it in his hand, Paul looked like he was trying to recall something. "What was it you asked me?"

"Can you tell me more about your relationship with Julia Cutter?"

A smile crept over his lips. "She was perfect. Perfect. The

perfect woman. Smart, pretty, funny, athletic, kind. More than her prick husband ever deserved."

"So, she didn't love her husband anymore?"

He glanced down at his knees. "She said that she couldn't remember a time when she *did* love him. She said that Morris only cared about his precious company. When I met her, she was lonely, starved for real affection."

"You were lonely, too."

He looked back up at me. "Yes, so much that it hurt."

"Did the two of you ever come here?" I glanced around the unkempt living room, wondering what the rest of the house must look like.

He put the glass down on the end table and glanced down the dark hallway, remembering. Then he studied the mess in the living room. He offered up an embarrassed smile. "Yes. I really need to straighten up in here, don't I? I'm usually a better housekeeper than this."

I smiled. "But you brought her here."

He nodded. "She loved it here. It's not much. It's what I can afford on a cop's pension. But, as humble as it is, she felt safe here, like she could do or say anything she wanted."

"Did she ever talk about her husband?"

"She said he was cold and controlling. Julia said they were married in name only. They hadn't slept together for years."

Morris and Julia were both having affairs. It was likely they were having sex, just not with each other.

Paul continued, "She told me that he was a workaholic. Even in retirement, he kept going into the city to his old office. She told me he went to the office, even though he was pissed off at being forced to retire."

"Were you ever inside the Cutter house?"

He was silent for a moment, assessing my question. "Why?"

"I'd like to hear what you think about where she lived."

I want you to confirm that you've been inside their home.

"I thought it was a dark, cold place."

"Did the two of you make love there?"

I thought I could see him blush, even in the darkness of his own living room. "Yes."

"In the master bedroom?"

He held his hand up. "Oh, no. One of the guest rooms. But you're getting this all wrong. Our relationship wasn't just about sex. Hell, we're both in our fifties, not college kids. We liked each other's company, liked the intimacy that we shared. We were friends first, lovers second."

Okay.

"Obviously, there wasn't any security in the house when you visited."

He took another gulp from his drink. Licking his lips, he answered, "When Morris was working in New York, the house was empty. The security was for him, not Julia."

I snuck another look at the handgun on the table. "Why did the two of you break up?"

"I don't know. I think a lot of things changed after her grand-daughter, Amelia, was born. She spent less time in the gym and more time with her family. I think she was afraid of being found out. She'd told me that something in Morris had changed too. That being a grandfather had somehow made him more human."

"Were you angry when Julia told you she wanted to end things between the two of you?"

He eyed me with suspicion again. "I was hurt."

"Did you ever threaten to tell Morris about your affair?"

He nodded in silence and stared at the floor, ashamed.

"How did you feel about Morris Cutter? You personally, I mean, not Julia."

His chin jutted forward and his nostrils flared. "I hated him. I hated him for not being the husband that Julia deserved. I hated that he was married to her, and I wasn't. And then, after Julia broke up with me, I hated him even more."

"Did you hate him enough to want to kill him?"

Jesus, I hope that wasn't a mistake.

"Is that why you're here? You think I killed him? Do you think I'd kill Julia, too? I should have killed Morris Cutter." His words were bitter and sad at the same time. "If I had, Julia would still be alive."

The gun was like a magnet for my eyes, I couldn't stop sneaking a look at it. I took a deep breath and tried to steady my heartbeat. "Hearing about what happened to the Cutters must have come as a horrible shock."

He motioned toward the television. "I saw it on the news. At first I didn't believe it. Thought it was some kind of mistake. Then when I realized what Morris had done, it was like someone reached in and pulled my heart out of my chest."

"I understand."

"I think what happened that day..." He stopped in midsentence. "I think what happened was my fault. That in a way, I did kill them."

"What, Paul? Talk to me."

"The day before it happened, I called Julia and wished her a happy new year. I was hoping she'd see me one last time. When she told me that she couldn't, I got angry and threatened to tell her husband all about our affair. Show him pictures I took of her."

What?

"Pictures?"

He eyed me again and bit at his lower lip. "They were her idea. I kept telling her how beautiful she was."

"What kind of pictures, Paul?"

Even in the dark room, I could see him blush. "She called them boudoir photos."

"Was she naked?"

"In some of them, but they were tasteful, playful." He took a deep breath. "They were her idea. There was a point when she was so proud of her body. She loved the way she looked. She'd worked hard at it."

"You threatened to show them to her husband."

"I scared her. She must have panicked. I think Julia told Morris about us. Then in a fit of jealous rage, he shot her and then killed himself."

His hands flew back to his face, and he began to sob again.

I didn't know what to say.

He wailed, and my heart ached for him, "It's my fault she's dead. I never should have said what I said."

Paul's misery tugged at my own heart. But I had a job to do. "Paul, where were you on New Year's Day?"

His sobbing subsided. Snuffling, he asked, "What?"

I waited a moment before I asked the question again. "On New Year's Day, were you here?"

"If you're asking me if I have an alibi, I don't. I spent the day here by myself." His breathing was becoming more regular again, as anger crept across his face, slowly replacing his abject sorrow.

That's when I noticed a silver-plated, metal name tag with a familiar-looking logo sitting on the end table. It had been partially hidden by the glass of alcohol. I changed the subject of him not having an alibi. "Do you have a part-time gig?"

He nodded and glanced down at the name tag. He picked it up and studied it in the light of the television. "After I retired, I got my Realtor's license. I do it part time to make some extra money."

I couldn't quite make out the logo from where I sat. "Do you work with a realty agency?"

"Yeah, the owner is a friend of mine. We're old high school buddies. After I got my license, I asked him if I could work as an agent part time. It lists some high-end properties. You might have heard of it. The Pullman Realty Group?"

My heart did a slow roll. I was sitting in the same room as Julia's jealous, ex-lover. A man that had access to the key to and the alarm code of the house where Morris and Julia were gunned down.

A man with no alibi.

Suddenly the house felt too warm to be in anymore. The air too thick to breathe. At that moment, all I wanted was to get out of that hot, dark room and back outside to my car. "Well, I think I've taken up enough of your time."

I stood up and started to zip up my coat.

He stayed seated in his chair. His voice dropped an octave as he stared straight ahead. "I'm surprised you didn't ask me about my weapon."

An icy fist of horror clutched my chest.

Get out.

I stayed silent, unwillingly rooted to the floor where I stood.

He picked it up and studied at it as if it held historic significance. "You know, after I retired, I disassembled it and locked it up. I never wanted to have anything to do with it ever again. But the day Julia died, I cleaned it and reassembled it. Then I loaded it. It's been sitting here ever since."

"Why?"

He took his eyes off his weapon and locked them onto me. "Why do you think? Sometimes I think the pain is just too much to bear. The guilt of knowing that I caused Julia's death."

I took a short breath. "Have you talked to anyone?"

"No one to talk to."

I fought the urge to get my phone out my bag and call Mike Dillon right there and then, tell him to get over here now. "There must be someone on the force you can call for help."

He shook his head, and he stared at the gun in his hand again.

"Let me call someone, Paul. Let me call Mike Dillon."

He shook his head and put the gun back on the table. "Just get out. Get out of my house."

I wasn't going to argue. He scared me. He was a wild card. I was afraid he was either going to shoot himself or kill me. "Please let me call someone for you."

He roared at me, his voice reverberating against the walls. "Just get out!"

As I left, heart hammering, walking quickly down the driveway to the car, I kept turning to look back, expecting to either see him standing in the doorway with his gun leveled, aiming at my head. Or else I'd hear the muffled gunshot inside, knowing that he'd killed himself.

I'd left Paul's house with more questions than answers. My heart was beating wildly. I suddenly had another suspect in a double homicide—if that's what it was.

When I unlocked my car, I gave the house one brief last look, the memory still fresh of the man sitting in the dark with his guilt and a loaded weapon.

Chapter Fifteen

As I drove away, I shivered even though my heater was cranked up on high.

Hands still shaking from the tension, I pulled into the CVS store around the corner from Paul's house, parked, and called Mike Dillon. I told him about my unnerving conversation with the former cop and my fears that he would hurt himself or someone else.

"Didn't I say leave it alone?" Mike was obviously pissed off at me. "A depressed cop drinking in the middle of the day with a loaded gun? What could possibly go wrong? And then you ask him about having an alibi on the day the Cutters died? Are you fucking suicidal?"

It wasn't just anger. He was frustrated with me. It wasn't the first time I'd put myself in danger against his advice.

"I know, Mike. I'm just trying to do my job."

"You don't work for the newspaper anymore, Genie."

"That doesn't mean I'm not trying to get the truth."

"The truth is that Morris Cutter killed his wife and then killed himself. End of story. Go home and have a drink."

Ouch.

"I quit drinking, Mike."

He went silent for a moment. I heard him take a deep breath, and then he said, "I'm going to drive out there myself. I'm going to take him to see the department shrink if I have to drag his ass there."

The anger apparently had passed.

"Just be careful, Mike. Please."

"I'm always careful. It's you I worry about."

When we hung up, it gave me a chance to ponder whether Paul Marston was a viable suspect in a double homicide. Or was he the catalyst that had driven Morris Cutter to kill his adulterous wife and himself? Marston had anger issues. I knew that he worked part time for the Pullman Realty Group, and had a key and the alarm access code to the Cutter house. I knew that he'd hated Morris Cutter.

Killing him would make sense, but why kill the woman he loved?

Was it the old trope, if he couldn't have her, then nobody would?

I worked through the multiple possibilities and questions.

Did Julia have something to do with choosing the Pullman Group to sell their home? It would have given them good cover if Paul was discovered inside their home.

Was it possible that Marston could have snuck into the house, catching both Morris and Julia by surprise in the kitchen? Or had he come over on the premise that he wanted to discuss the listing and was invited into the kitchen, possibly for a cup of coffee? Had he then shot them both and placed a gun in Morris's hand to make it look like murder-suicide?

Paul had motive, he had opportunity, and he knew his way around guns.

It's possible.

Still mulling it all over, I fiddled with the radio until I found the smooth jazz station out of New York. Just as I was chilling with some David Sanborn, my cell phone rang.

Eyes on the road, I rummaged in my bag and found it. I glanced down at the screen and saw that it was a Boston number. "Hello?"

"Is this Geneva Chase?"

"It depends; who's this?"

"Colby Jones. I'm not sure if you remember me."

It was the journalist Ben told me he'd hired to take my place on the *Sheffield Post*. "Sure, you were at the *Globe* the same time I was. Congrats on the new job." I hoped that I sounded sincere. Going from the *Globe* to the *Sheffield Post* was the wrong direction on the career ladder.

"Look, I hear you're working for a detective agency now and you've reopened the investigation into the deaths of Morris and Julia Cutter."

"Detective agency, no. Lodestar Analytics is a research firm." Different states have different laws about private detectives. Most of them require some type of license. Nathaniel skirted that by calling us research analysts.

"But you're investigating the murder-suicide."

"What do you want, Colby?" I came to a stop sign, watched for traffic, and pulled onto Route 7.

"What prompted this to be reopened? I talked with the Sheffield police and they stand by their findings that it was murder-suicide."

"No comment."

"Come on, Genie. For old times' sake." I pictured him in my mind. In his fifties by now, he was nearly bald when I knew him back in Boston. He was around six feet tall and about thirty pounds overweight. Colby was blessed with bulldog jowls and watery brown eyes, and always seemed to wear clothes that were either too big for him or too small. I also recalled that he'd been married twice and, when we worked together, thought he was God's gift to women. I surmised that he didn't own a mirror.

"I don't recall where we had any old times, Colby. As a matter of fact, the sexist antics of your boys' club at the *Globe* would have qualified as harassment in this day and age."

"All in good fun, Genie. You were one of the guys. Throw me a bone here. I'm trying to impress my new boss. This kind of investigation has got to be expensive. Who's writing the checks?"

"Call my boss at Lodestar Analytics."

"I tried calling Mr. Rubin. All I got was his voicemail. Doesn't he have a secretary or something?"

He doesn't. Nathaniel works out of his apartment overlooking the East River in Manhattan. His research analysts mostly work from their own homes, their cars, or hotel rooms. There wasn't a lot of fat at Lodestar Analytics.

"I don't know what to tell you, Colby."

"I just got off the phone with Parker Lewis, VP at CP&G. He told me to go fuck myself."

It was difficult for me to visualize the avuncular Parker Lewis using such crude language. But not entirely surprising. The last thing the oil company wanted was more publicity about Morris and Julia Cutter. "They're not crazy about reporters over there."

"Look," he said, "how about I make up for what we did to you in Boston by buying you a drink? You still partial to vodka?"

Oh, he knew me from my party days. He'd even been in the newsroom the day I'd come into the office trashed and vainly tried to hammer out a story about a police sting on a city councilman. He was there when my editor fired me and threw my ass out of the building.

"Cutting back, Colby. I only drink with friends these days."

He feigned pain. "Ouch. Let me know if you change your mind. I know how to treat a girl."

Colby was good reporter, but he was a total jerk.

After breaking the connection, I called Eric Cutter. "Eric, this is Geneva Chase."

"Yes?" His voice rose with expectation. "Do you have something for me?"

I knew he was hoping I had evidence that argued against the cops' conclusion about his parents' deaths. "Right now, I have more questions than answers. But it's part of the process. Would it be possible for me to come and talk to you?"

I wished what I had to tell him, I could do over the phone. But telling someone that their mother was an adulterer was something that needed to be done face-to-face.

There was silence while he consulted his calendar. "I can meet with you, but it would have to be right now. It's the only time I have today."

I glanced at the clock on my dash. It was after one in the afternoon, and my stomach was growling at me.

"Where?"

"I'm working from home. Do you remember the address?"

"I have it. See you in about a half hour." I recalled the street number and town. A sharpened, more focused memory seemed to be a welcome byproduct of my sobriety.

I didn't have time to stop for lunch, so I swung into a drive-thru at a Dunkin' and ordered a medium black coffee and a blueberry muffin. It wasn't healthy, but I wanted something to fill the void in my tummy, and it was easy to eat as I drove. I'd get something healthier after I met with Eric.

The house where Eric and Olivia resided was less grand than his father's, of course, but nearly on the scale of his uncle's home. It was a two-story building that might have been an old farmhouse at some point. Sporting white siding, dark-green shutters, and a massive front porch, it sat on about an acre of woodlands, set back from the road, discreetly hidden from the world.

I parked my car next to a sky-blue Audi Q7. Since I knew that the Cutters also owned a high-end BMW, I guessed that this was Olivia's SUV.

I climbed up the steps to the expansive porch, rang the bell, and waited, gazing out at the sky. For me, Connecticut feels and looks gray from October to April. Winters seem like they stretch on for a frigid eternity. But on that afternoon, nature was proving me wrong. The air was clean, the cloudless sky was a deep blue, and I was ready for spring. With the temperature in the fifties, I knew that it was a false promise. It was the middle of February, and I was certain more cold weather was on its way.

Olivia, hair askew, in jeans, a short-sleeved top, and slippers, opened the door holding a screaming six-month-old Amelia. "Come in. Eric said you were coming."

Gazing at the baby, I spoke in a voice loud enough to be heard over the ear-piercing shrieks. "Somebody's cranky."

"She's ready for a nap. Follow me, and I'll show you where Eric is." Olivia's terse words sounded like she might be on her last set of nerves.

I followed her through the foyer and into the living area. The huge room was colored in accents of off-white and subtle grays, the couches were caramel-colored leather, the easy chairs were a dark brown, and the fireplace was painted the same color as the walls. All understated earth tones. The paintings on the walls were rustic farm scenes.

Down a short hall, she pointed to an open doorway. "He's expecting you."

I glanced once more at the crying child, whose fists and eyes were closed and her face a bright red. "I thought you had a nanny."

"She got a call this morning that her own daughter was sick. She had to leave to take her kid to the doctor."

"The nanny is 24/7? She lives here?"

"Yes."

"Who watches her daughter?"

Olivia shrugged. "The grandmother, I think. I've got to go put Amelia in her crib."

I watched as she hustled back up the hallway, and I thought about Olivia's disinterest in her nanny's affairs away from this house. She simply didn't care enough to ask who watched the child of the woman who watched her own. It made me sad.

When I walked in, Eric stood up behind his enormous desk. He was outlined by massive windows that looked out over his spacious backyard. Two large, wooden bookshelves were filled with trophies and awards. The walnut desktop was cluttered with piles of folders stacked on either side of his computer monitor. The walls were the same pale color as the living room, but his office was given personality by photos of Eric and Olivia on their many trips to exotic locations around the world.

We shook hands, and I asked, "Tell me again what you do for a living?"

He looked relaxed in a pair of jeans, sweatshirt, and socks, no shoes. "I own Pyxis Development. We buy, sell, and develop properties throughout the tri-state area."

"How's business?"

He gave me a restrained smile. "It's busy. We're up to our eyeballs redeveloping a hotel in midtown Manhattan."

"Impressive."

He ran his fingers through his black hair. "Anything new on the investigation?"

Rather than answer his question, I asked one of my own. "Have you ever heard of a company called Fisher, Evans, and Sinclair?"

His smile quickly vanished. "I have. Why do you ask?"

I glanced over at a small, round conference table and four upholstered chairs. "Do you mind if I sit down?"

"No, of course not. Where are my manners? Would you like a cup of coffee? Can I take your coat?"

I held up my hand. "No, thank you." Then I slipped out of my coat, folded it over the back of one of the chairs, and sat down. "The day I met with Parker Lewis at CP&G, a man by the name of Leonard Ryan who represents Fisher, Evans, and Sinclair asked me to meet him. He tried to bribe my company and me to end the investigation as quickly as possible."

Eric had been standing until he heard that, and then he dropped into one of the other chairs at the conference table.

I continued, "After the story that we've reopened the investigation hit the *New York Daily News* this morning, I got another call from Mr. Ryan doubling the offer. He told me that they wanted the investigation wrapped up by Thursday, and that we should come to the same conclusion that the police did."

Eric slowly shook his head. "I'm sure Parker and the new CEO hate the idea that the estate has reopened the investigation. They despise the publicity."

"Is that why they have their consulting firm trying to shut us down?"

He fixed me with his eyes. "Fisher, Evans, and Sinclair is much more than a consulting firm."

"How so?"

"You've heard the term 'fixer'?"

"Yeah, mostly how it relates to criminals and politicians."

"Appropriate. They also fix things for companies like CP&G. Mostly through legal means."

"Mostly?"

In answer he simply raised his eyebrows. Eric leaned in and glanced at the open doorway to make sure no one was there listening. "Look, I've only heard rumors, but the story goes that they've made witnesses in multimillion-dollar lawsuits against the company disappear."

I frowned. "Like how?"

He snapped his fingers. "Like poof, gone, vanished into thin air. Never to be heard from again."

"Seriously?"

He leaned back with a concerned expression. "It's one of the reasons why I've distanced myself from this investigation."

I sat up straight. He might have kept himself and his family distanced, but Lodestar Analytics and I were standing at ground zero.

As was Frank Mancini. I wondered if he knew what he'd gotten himself into.

"Is your sister, Lisa, still here? She stopped by to see me this morning and said she was coming here to see you and the baby."

"She was here for a short while, got a phone call, and then went back to DC."

"Did she tell you what she came to talk to me about?"

"It's bullshit," he spat. "Mom never had an affair. She'd never cheat on Dad. When Lisa told me that, I told her she was crazy. Before we got into an argument, she got the call on her cell phone, punched up an Uber ride, and was out of here."

I took a breath and wondered how to proceed. Deciding to just tell it like it is, I started. "After she left, I went to your mother's gym."

He stared at me wordlessly, his face reddening. I knew that inside he was dreading what I had to tell him.

"I tracked down the man your mother was having an affair with."

I jumped when Eric slammed his fist down on the tabletop. "Bullshit!"

I didn't say anything more for a few moments, waiting for him to calm down and my heart to slow back down to normal.

Finally, he spoke, his voice low and his words measured. "Tell me." I could see by the muscles in his cheeks that he was grinding his teeth. He stared at me, chewing over the fact that his mother had really cheated on his father.

"He's an ex-cop, retired. I'm convinced he was in love with your mother. She's the one who broke it off. He said he was so upset that he had threatened to tell your father." I didn't say anything about the nude photos Paul had taken of Eric's mother. That's the kind of thing that will send you to therapy.

"Did he?"

"He said that he didn't."

"An ex-cop." A thought suddenly occurred to him. "Do you think it's possible he killed my parents?"

I held up my hand. "I have a friend on the Sheffield PD who's going to go talk to him."

"But he's a suspect."

I sighed. "I'm not ruling it out. He sells real estate part-time for the Pullman Realty Group."

His mouth dropped open. "They have a key and know the alarm code."

"Let's not jump to conclusions. But I wanted to let you know."

Eric nearly vibrated when he said, "If that son of a bitch killed my parents…"

He didn't finish. He didn't have to. I didn't think that Eric had it in him to exact his own revenge, but rich people find a way, don't they?

———

I offered to let myself out. As I walked through the living room, I saw Olivia through sliding glass doors, out on the deck wearing a jacket, leaning on a wooden railing. Her back was turned to me as she gazed out over their manicured yard, a glass of wine rested on the railing next her, and she was obviously having a cigarette, because I could see smoke trailing up from in front of her.

I crossed the room and took the liberty of opening the sliding glass door. "Olivia, mind if I join you?"

She attempted a tired smile. "Sure, if you don't mind that I'm smoking."

I slid the door shut behind me. "Not at all. Enjoying a little quiet time?"

"Amelia finally went down for her nap. God knows how long it will last."

I came up beside her and leaned against the railing. "You have a beautiful home."

She took a short drag and exhaled. "Thank you. Would you like a glass of wine?"

"No, thank you. It's a little early in the day," I lied. I would have loved to join her in a glass of wine.

She smiled. "When you have a baby and it's naptime, you take advantage and open the wine. Was Eric helpful?"

"Yes, he was."

"Did you talk about his mother's affair?" She chewed at her lower lip after she asked the question.

"Yes. Did you know about it?"

Shaking her head, she answered, "Not until Lisa told us this morning. It doesn't surprise me, though. I don't care what Eric thinks, Morris and Julia's marriage was close to being over."

"They seemed like a solid couple."

Olivia picked up her glass of white wine and took a sip. "Are you sure I can't interest you?"

I held up my hand.

She placed the glass carefully back down on the railing. "Their marriage had been off the rails for years. I think when Amelia was born, they decided to give it another try." She glanced angrily behind her.

It was none of my business, but I couldn't help myself. "Are you and Eric okay?"

She took another drag on her cigarette. "We've had our ups and downs over the years. We succumbed to the notion that having a baby would draw us closer together. It might have had a positive effect for Morris and Julia, but let me tell you, the pressure of rearing a child on your own is deadly on a relationship."

Really, on your own? You have a freakin' live-in nanny.

"I'm guessing that Eric isn't much help?"

She rolled her eyes. "He wasn't before the baby was born, and he sure as hell isn't now. He's a workaholic just like his father was."

I had to wonder if she would have been so open with me if the nanny had been in the house, and Olivia hadn't been left with a crying child to care for.

"What's your take on Morris and Julia? Do you think it was a double homicide?"

She took another drink of her wine. "Frankly? I think all the bullshit that Morris has shoveled over the years caught up to him, and he decided to end it. I just feel bad the old son of a bitch took Julia along with him on the ride."

———

Back on the road heading south on Route 7, my cell phone went off again. It was a number I didn't recognize. "Hello?"

A woman was on the other end of the line. "Is this Miss Geneva Chase?"

"Yes. Who am I speaking to?"

"I'm Mr. Darren Reed's personal assistant. Do you have time to take a call?"

Well, la-de-da. The CEO of CP&G has a woman to make his phone calls for him. I answered, "Sure."

As I drove, the line went silent for a moment. Then a male voice came on, deep and confident. "Miss Chase?"

"Yes, hello."

"Would you have time to join me for lunch?"

"It depends on where you are?"

"I live in Greenwich, and I'm working from home today. Are you in Connecticut as well?"

I glanced at the clock on my dashboard. It was a little after two, and I was famished. "Sure, where and when?"

"Do you know where Portofino's is in Sheffield?"

While I was having my illicit fling with Frank Mancini, it had been one of our favorite restaurants. "I do. When?"

"How about thirty minutes?"

"That works. See you there."

A nosy, irritating Colby Jones calls the senior vice president of CP&G, and a short time later, I get a lunch invitation by Mr. Bigshot CEO.

Coincidence?

I don't believe in them.

———

I like going to Portofino's because it's like an expensive but comfortable pair of shoes. The colors on the walls, carpeting, and tablecloths are all tasteful earth tones. The lighting is muted without being dim. The waitstaff is attentive without being annoying, and the menu is familiar yet slightly adventurous.

Walking in with my coat on, bag over my shoulder, in a turtleneck sweater and jeans, I felt slightly underdressed as I was greeted by Massimo, the owner. "Miss Chase, what a nice surprise. It's been forever since I've seen you. Are you meeting that nice Mr. Mancini?"

I grinned at the big man. "I'm here on business. I'm meeting a gentleman by the name of Darren Reed."

He bowed slightly and waved me to follow him. We wound our way through the dining room, still busy with a well-heeled lunch crowd, some of whom would be on their third or fourth glass of wine. In the back, at a table by the window overlooking the wooded area behind the restaurant, a man and a woman were seated next to each other.

Massimo asked, "May I take your coat, Miss Chase?"

"Please." Old world gentleman that he was, Massimo helped me out of my coat, and he walked off to hang it up.

As I got closer, I saw that the man at the table was in his late forties, had brown hair that was graying at his temples, tanned skin, deep-blue eyes, and was dressed in a white shirt, red tie, and a dark-blue suit.

Even though he was working from home, Darren Reed apparently felt he needed to look the part of CEO. Unlike Eric Cutter, who was also working from home and was dressed like a fashionable slob.

The woman at the table was in her twenties, her chestnut-colored hair cut in a professional bob, and she wore a white blouse under a black jacket. Her expression was serious and made more so by the large, black frames of her glasses.

They were both talking on their cell phones, ignoring each other.

As I got closer, they quickly concluded their conversations and placed the phones on the top of the table. The man stood up, but the woman remained seated, studying me.

"Miss Chase?" He had the million-dollar grin of a politician on the stump, and his eyes drilled into my own, obviously a man who believed in eye contact. He held out his hand. "I'm Darren Reed."

We shook hands, and I noticed that his palm was moist. "Please, call me Genie."

He waited until I sat down opposite the two of them, and then he was seated. Nodding toward the woman, Darren said, "This is Nicole Collier, my assistant."

I nodded my head, and we both mumbled, "Nice to meet you."

I noticed that the woman had never cracked a smile.

A young man came to our table to take our drink orders. He'd waited on me many times over the years. Darren ordered water and lemon, and Nicole asked for a cup of tea. Our waiter turned to me, smiled, and asked, "Vodka tonic, Miss Chase?"

Busted.

Since he seemed to know me so well, I know I should have remembered his name, but I had to read it from the tag on his shirt. "No, thank you, Bobby. I'll have a glass of water and a cup of coffee."

After Bobby rushed off, Darren turned to me. His face was a mask of feigned concern. "I asked you to lunch to see if there's anything we can do to help you with your investigation."

I glanced first at him, then at Nicole. She had no expression, her eyes focused on my face. He still wore that politician's smile.

"I can't imagine what that might be. But I appreciate the sentiment."

He tapped the tabletop. "I know how expensive something like this is. Are there any resources we could supply that might move the investigation forward?"

I was hungry as hell, but sitting at that table, my appetite was beginning to fade. "That's what that nice Mr. Ryan from your consulting firm asked." The man with the lizard eyes.

He blinked at me with false sincerity. "We all want the same thing. We all want to see this wrapped up as quickly as possible. I hate the thought of dragging Morris and Julia's memory through the mud one more time."

"Well, perhaps you can help by answering a few of my questions."

He glanced at his assistant, who didn't try to hide it when she rolled her eyes.

Clearly, they're not used to having someone other than him take control of a conversation.

I started. "Was Morris Cutter forced into retirement?"

Darren looked at me condescendingly. "Going public with a family-owned company is a doubled-edged sword. You walk away with a pile of money, as did Morris. But then you're no longer working for yourself. You have a board of directors and stockholders you have to answer to. Morris Cutter was an excellent CEO for many years, but everyone reaches an end of their effectiveness. He was offered a very attractive retirement package, which he gratefully accepted."

"Do you think he might have been a little resentful?"

Nicole turned away, but I could see she was wearing a smirk on her face.

Darren answered, "He struggled with the fact that he was no longer in control of the company. He'd continued to come into the city nearly every day. He'd never even taken the opportunity to vacate his old office. The old man simply couldn't adjust to the fact that he wasn't needed there."

Ah, yes, the biggest office on that floor. The office Darren Reed coveted but couldn't move into until Morris was dead.

"Did the two of you have any discussions about that?"

"As diplomatically as possible, of course."

Nicole interjected. "But he still kept his old office."

Bobby, our waiter, brought around our drinks. "Are you ready to order?"

Without checking with either his assistant or me, Darren answered, "Yes. I'll have the veal parmesan."

Nicole ordered a cup of tomato bisque and a Tuscan kale and apple salad.

I went for a grilled chicken Caesar salad.

After the young man left, I said, "So you had a discussion with Mr. Cutter about his office."

Darren ran his hand through his hair. "I tried to explain to him that his presence was causing confusion in the office. Some of our executives were still going to him for decisions. I made it quite clear that after the holidays, he would have to start working from home."

The woman spoke up, "He claimed that he was writing a history of the company and he needed to be in the city to *use the company archives*." She wiggled her fingers in the air, making air quotes.

"That wasn't so?"

Darren answered, "No, the archives are all digital. He could have accessed them from anywhere."

Nicole sneered. "The old man just couldn't get it through his head that Mr. Reed ran the company, not him."

The CEO glanced around him for a moment to make certain no one was within listening distance. "There's one more thing you should know about Morris Cutter."

"What's that?"

He leaned in. "We think he was siphoning off money from several of the company accounts. We think he might have been doing it for years."

Nicole registered the surprise on my face, then weighed in. "He had access to those accounts, but only through our internal network. It's most likely why he was still coming into the office."

Darren shook his head sympathetically. "We think he knew we were on to him. It's possible it was a mitigating factor in the murder-suicide."

This was the first I had heard about this. "How much money are we talking about?"

It was the woman's turn to lean in. "Millions, Miss Chase."

I was confused. "He was already wealthy. Why would he embezzle money?"

Darren shrugged. "Sometimes powerful people do things just because they can." Then, he shifted gears. "How did the press find out about your investigation?"

I lied. "I don't know."

"Did Nathaniel Rubin leak it to the newspapers?"

That gave me a little shock. I recalled that Nathaniel had said something about tweaking Darren Reed by giving the story to the press. There was bad blood here. I lied again. "I would doubt that."

"Before I called you to invite you to lunch, Parker Lewis phoned me to say another annoying reporter had called our office looking to talk with me about Morris and Julia Cutter." He lost the smile, and his visage turned deadly serious. "When do you think you'll have this thing wrapped up?"

I know he wanted to hear me say something about it being done by Thursday. Instead I told him, "I don't know the answer to that. When we've gotten all the facts."

Unsmiling, Nicole spoke. "What makes you think you'll come to a conclusion that's any different than the police?"

"We may not. But you never know what an investigation will turn up."

Our conversation died when Bobby came out with our food.

Nicole put her napkin in her lap and immediately dipped her spoon into her soup.

I speared a bite-sized chunk of grilled chicken, but before I popped it into my mouth, I asked, "Why is everyone so eager to have this done before the end of the week?" I was already reasonably certain of the answer.

Darren finished chewing a bite of his veal and answered. "It's no secret. On Friday, I'm going to Capitol Hill and presenting the Ekmann Study to the Senate Committee on Energy and Natural Resources. We've had some of the best climatologists in the world working on this for over a year. It definitely shows that any kind of climate disruption is an entirely natural phenomena not influenced by carbon emissions. Once the study is presented, we'll roll out an international publicity campaign to bury this climate hoax once and for all."

I stared at him. "Do you really believe that?"

He smiled again. "Of course, I do. It's just the ammunition our friends in Congress need to keep supporting our industry."

I glanced at him and then at Nicole, who allowed the faintest of smiles to play upon her thin lips.

I lost my appetite. The world was just getting its collective head on straight about the growing climate crisis. People were clamoring to make wholesale changes, but still, there were those in power who denied the root cause of too much carbon in the atmosphere. Greedy powerbrokers refusing to lose their grip on profits provided by burning fossil fuels.

If Darren Reed gave that report to the naysayers in Washington, it would just give them the talking points they needed to keep subsidizing the oil industry.

We're so close to the tipping point already.

Darren continued, "My board of directors doesn't want your investigation clouding the issue. An investigation, by the way, the police tied up over a month ago."

He washed his veal down with a sip of water. Placing the glass back on the table, he asked, "So?"

"So?"

"Can you do it? Can you get this wrapped up by Thursday? There's a hell of a bonus in it for your company." He pointed his fork at me. "And for you, too."

Before I could answer, Nicole's phone vibrated against the tabletop. She picked it up, put it to her ear, and professionally answered, "Mr. Reed's office."

We both watched her in silence as she stared straight ahead, her eyes widening and all the blood draining away from her cheeks until she was as pale as fresh snow. Without saying a word, she handed the phone to her boss.

"Reed," he stated, frowning.

After a few moments of listening to what the caller had to say, he growled, "Son of a bitch. If I find out who's behind this, I'll hang 'em up by their balls." He cut the connection and glared at me. "The lead scientist on my research team is gone."

I didn't have a clue what he was trying to tell me. "I'm sorry?"

"Dr. Stuart Ekmann. He didn't show up for work. He's not answering his phone. He's not at his apartment. His car's gone."

Nicole, staring at Darren, tried to keep her voice steady. "Gaea?"

"Who else would it be? They're trying to fuck with the Senate presentation." He abruptly stood up and handed the phone back to his assistant.

Nicole pushed back her chair and stood as well.

Darren looked down at me. I was still seated in front of my salad, slightly stunned. His voice hummed with menace. "If I find out your boss has anything to do with this, there'll be hell to pay."

I shook my head in confusion. "What?"

He sneered when he answered, "Nathaniel Rubin. When he was with the *Times*, he did his best to drag my name through the mud. Now that he's running that shady company you work for, I wouldn't put it past him to try to fuck with me one more time."

Nicole put her hand on his arm. "We should go."

He took a breath, and when he spoke, his voice was at a more level timbre. "Finish your investigation by Thursday. Not having it wrapped up by then is not an option."

Chapter Sixteen

Those pricks stuck me with the bill.

I didn't know it at first.

After they abruptly stalked out of Portofino's, I stayed, with the intent of calling Nathaniel and finishing my salad. Before I could use my phone, Massimo, seeing that I was alone, stopped by my table. "May I sit, Miss Chase?"

I smiled at him. "Of course."

When he'd situated himself at my table, he folded his hands in front of him. "I don't see you and Mr. Mancini anymore. Is everything okay?"

I sighed. "Mr. Mancini and I split up. But I'm working with him on a project right now, and we're still friends. So, it's all good."

He put his big hand on mine. "That's good Miss Chase. You were such a nice couple."

That made me smile even more. I thought we'd made a nice couple as well.

Except for that pesky thing about him being married.

Massimo stood up, and I watched him wander slowly across the dining room, asking customers if everything was to their expectations. As he did, I thought about Frank again. I didn't miss being with him romantically, but he was a blast to be around. He was funny and knowledgeable and could speak intelligently about almost anything.

How much should I tell him about this case?

I pondered that for a moment and quickly came to the conclusion that I shouldn't be worried about Frank. I needed to talk to Nathaniel.

I ate a few more bites of my salad, and then slung my bag over my shoulder and retrieved my coat. As I started for the door, the young man who had waited on us trotted up to me with the check.

"What's this?"

"It's the tab, Miss Chase." The kid seemed a little flustered that he'd had to catch me at the door before I ran out on the bill.

I stared at the doorway for a moment, as if mentally willing the two oil cheapskates to come back and pay their share. Then I scrounged in my bag for my wallet, removed the company Visa card and handed it to the young man.

When we were square, I sat in my car in the parking lot and punched up Nathaniel's number.

"Geneva?"

"Hi, boss. I want to catch you up." I then told him about my visit from Lisa Cutter and the news that her mother had been having an affair with an ex-cop. I told him about my conversation in Paul Marston's dark house of depression, gun at the ready next to his half-empty glass of bourbon.

"Do you think he could be a suspect?"

I answered, "He's on my short list. What I haven't told you yet is that he sells real estate part-time for the same company listing the Cutter mansion. He had access to the house."

I thought I could hear him smile. "That is very interesting."

Then I told him how Morris Cutter had also been unfaithful

with Nikki Hudson, a twenty-something model who'd left her agency sometime after getting two hundred and eighty thousand dollars from Morris and his shell company. "I haven't had time to track her down yet."

"I'll locate her for you," Nathaniel offered.

Finally, I informed him of my invitation to lunch by Darren Reed and his pretty robot, Nicole Collier. "They confirmed why CP&G wants us to tie this up by Thursday."

"Is it the congressional presentation?"

"He doesn't want our investigation hanging over his head while he's on Capitol Hill."

"You've been a busy girl."

"Darren Reed also told me that CP&G suspected that Morris Cutter had embezzled millions of dollars and, knowing that he was under suspicion might have driven him to murder-suicide. Frank Mancini told me that Morris had an offshore account set up to pay off his mistress. It would be a good place to hide ill-gotten gains."

"Jesus, Genie. Is that all?"

"Yeah, well, one more thing. Reed and Collier left like their asses were on fire when they got a phone call telling them that one of the scientists who worked on the study was missing. His name is Dr. Stuart Ekmann."

I could picture him on the edge of his chair. "More and more interesting."

"The last thing he said before they left was that he thought it was the work of Gaea, an environmental activist group."

"This just keeps getting better and better."

"It gets more interesting. When he got up to leave, he spat out your name and said that you'd better not have anything to do with his missing scientist."

He gave me a hoarse chuckle. "He did, did he?"

"Bad blood there, boss."

"Like I said, I wrote a few pieces on him before he went to work at CP&G. He'd been lobbying Congress to loosen their safety regulations for offshore oil rigs. I also wrote him up when he was arrested for spousal abuse."

I knew I didn't like him.

"Did it go to trial?"

"His wife declined to press charges but agreed to go ahead with a divorce."

I asked, "You *don't* have anything to do with Dr. Ekmann's disappearance, do you?"

He laughed "I wish I had."

"Two more things. I met with Delia and Stephen Cutter. They both hated Morris with a white-hot passion. So much so, Stephen works for Gaea. There's no love lost between him and CP&G."

"The plot thickens. You said there were two things. What's the other one?"

"Reed stuck me with the bill for lunch. I put it on the company card."

"Cheap prick."

"That's what I said. Let me know when you've found Nikki Hudson."

"Good work, Geneva. You've accomplished a lot in a very small amount of time. What are you going to do now?"

I glanced at my watch. "I have a couple of free hours. I'm going to start a piece I promised Ben at the *Post* about some racist emails that have been leaked from one of the members of the school board. Then it's my turn to pick up Caroline and her friend at school. If I'm not there on time, I'll never hear the end of it."

"Godspeed, Geneva. Oh, before I let you go, I heard from John Stillwater today. He told me to tell you he's looking forward to seeing you."

I felt my heart do a tiny dance. "When is that, Nathaniel? Shana said he's been working on some project for her. She wouldn't say what it is."

"I'm sure he'll tell you all about it. He should be landing at La Guardia right about now."

His end of the line went dead at the same time my heart did a fast tattoo against my chest.

Calm down, Genie. You're too old to be crushing on a boy.

The vision of John standing in my living room wearing only black boxers popped into my head again. Toned biceps and shoulders, washboard abs, muscular legs, gun in his hand. Yum.

I shook it off and drove home to work on the freelance piece for the *Sheffield Post*.

———

"How was school?"

The girls were in the back seat of the Sebring, coats unzipped, backpacks on the floor next to their feet.

Jessica, running her fingers through her short black hair, answered, "Why are boys such jerks?"

I glanced up at the rearview mirror. Both girls were rolling their eyes. I offered, "I hate to tell you this; they don't get any better with age. Something happen today?"

Caroline stared out the car window at the stores and houses as we drove by. "Tyler was jumped in the boys' room today."

I frowned. "Tyler's the boy I met at our house the other day?" I didn't say anything about the pending date for the Valentine's Dance, just in case Caroline hadn't shared that with Jessica.

"Yeah."

"Was he hurt?"

"Bruises, bloody nose, ripped shirt, damaged pride. But they didn't knock him down."

It reminded me of the day I'd met Caroline's father so many years ago on my first day of school. Kevin and I were both just thirteen, and he got into a fight with a much larger boy. He took a real beating, but the bully never knocked him down.

I was growing to have a grudging respect for Tyler.

"What happened?"

There was a high-pitched edge in Caroline's voice. "Brandon Oliver and Justin West are both a-holes."

I gently braked as we came to a red light. It gave me a chance to study them in the mirror as they stared at their phones. "What was the fight about?"

Jessica answered while she texted someone. "They're incels because they're both jerks. They were taking it out on Tyler because he's brand new in school, and he scored a date with the hottest girl in our sophomore class."

Both girls erupted in squeals of laughter.

It took me a moment, but I realized that Jessica was talking about Caroline. My little girl was considered the hottest girl in their class? I asked, "What are incels?"

Caroline answered. "Involuntary celibates."

Dear God, now what?

"Say what?"

Jessica explained. "They're such dorks they can't get dates."

I asked, "How do you know that term, 'incels'?"

"Part of my research on school safety. A lot of active shooters hate women and suffer from a toxic masculinity. Those two dummies were textbook when they jumped Tyler today."

My adrenaline kicked in when she uttered the words "active shooter." "Are those boys dangerous?"

Jessica laughed. "Nah, just stupid."

Caroline agreed. "They need to dial back the testosterone."

Jessica added, "And it's not fair that Tyler is getting the same detention as Thing 1 and Thing 2."

"Thing 1 and Thing 2?"

"You know, like the Dr. Seuss book."

Caroline explained, "Brandon and Justin."

It occurred to me that part of the two boys' problem might be the name-calling. As much as I didn't like them for attacking Caroline's friend, I had to wonder if they were the subjects of bullying themselves. Were Caroline and Jessica becoming mean girls?

I segued. "How is that piece coming for the school newspaper?"

"Good. I did a phone interview with Assistant Chief of Police Mike Dillon."

Of course. That's where I would have started. "Was he helpful?"

"He told me about the active shooter drills the department holds. He said that the Sheffield Police Department is trained to respond to any threat in minutes."

I didn't answer her. I knew that at a recent mass shooting in the entertainment district of Dayton, Ohio, ten people were killed and twenty-seven were wounded, even though the police had arrived on the scene thirty-two seconds after the first shots were fired.

I did my best to throw off my morbid line of thought.

Glancing back up at the mirror, I smirked. "The hottest girl in the sophomore class? Really?"

Both girls erupted in laughter again.

Chapter Seventeen

After dropping Jessica Oberon off at her house, Caroline and I drove over to Poco Loco to pick up some Tex-Mex. Situated in a strip mall, the restaurant is perennially crowded and renowned for its food as well as its superb margaritas.

We waited at the front counter for our take-out burritos, giving me a chance to eyeball a waitress walking by with a couple of margaritas in frosty glasses, salt crystals encrusted around the rims.

"Are you sure I can't get you something to drink while you wait?" Don, the owner, in his fifties, dressed in a white shirt, black slacks, and a red bolero tie, knew me well. By habit, I'd stop in there once every couple of weeks to get some takeout for Caroline and me, and I'd knock back a giant-size Jose Cuervo 'rita at the bar.

I sighed. "Not today, my friend. Thank you, though."

Caroline gave me a look. "You're really serious."

"What's that?"

"Staying on the wagon."

I puffed out my cheeks and responded. "Yup."

For now.

I could hear Shana saying the word "control" in my head.

I took a deep breath and glanced around the room. To my surprise, I spotted Stephen Cutter, Morris's angry nephew, sitting at the bar, quietly eating a taco, drinking a beer, and chatting to an attractive brunette wearing a flannel shirt and jeans sitting next to him. I asked Caroline to wait for me at the front counter. Then I walked around the tables and slid up behind him.

Stephen saw me in the mirror behind the bar, turned around, and stood up. "Geneva Chase. What a coincidence. Or are you following me?"

He said it in the form of a joke, but I wasn't convinced that he didn't think it was true.

I nodded toward the spot where Caroline stood, staring at her phone. "My daughter over there and I are just picking up dinner. Thank you again for taking time to talk with me this morning."

He shrugged and gestured toward the lady still sitting on the bar stool. "This is Giselle Brossard. We work together."

She gave me a warm smile as we shook hands. Her eyes were mirthful when she said, "We're not just workmates. When he's not staying at his mother's house, we're roommates."

I wanted to ask if that meant more than sharing rent, but when Stephen blushed, it confirmed my suspicions that they were lovers.

Giselle asked, "Do you want to join us for a drink?"

Stephen winced.

I glanced back at Caroline again. "Thank you, but dinner should be coming out in a minute or two."

Still on his feet, Stephen asked, "Have you made any progress on your investigation? Am I still a suspect?"

While his words were querulous, he seemed a whole lot more mellow than when I'd met him and his mother earlier that day.

Perhaps that was due to his proximity to Giselle. Maybe it was the beer sitting on the bar.

"I had a surprise meeting today with Darren Reed, the CEO of CP&G."

His expression suddenly changed to one of eager anticipation. "Do tell."

"Well, for starters, he stuck me with the lunch tab."

Stephen shook his head. "Why am I not surprised?"

"While we were at the restaurant, he got a phone call from someone who told him that one of his scientists is missing."

He and Giselle exchanged shocked glances.

Stephen muttered, "Do you know which one?"

I ignored his question and asked my own. "How much do you know about the Ekmann Study?"

"A poorly kept secret. It's a load of crap put together by a cabal of disgraced scientists. We knew Morris Cutter was supposed to present it to Congress back in January. We were ready to counterattack with protests on that same day. But then he shot himself, and the whole thing got delayed."

Giselle spoke up. "We've heard that Darren Reed himself is giving the study to Congress this Friday."

"Will Gaea be out protesting?"

Stephen nodded, glanced at his girlfriend, and grinned enigmatically. "That and maybe we have a few other tricks up our sleeve."

"Do you think that when Reed delivers that study to Capitol Hill, it will have any effect? I mean there's overwhelming evidence that burning fossil fuels is killing the planet."

Stephen took a sip of his beer. He put the glass on the bar. "Do you have any doubt that sugary drinks like soda contribute to obesity and diabetes?"

I was taken aback by the quick change of topics. "No."

"Before that was publicly accepted, scientists had known about it for a long time. So did the soda companies. They paid millions of dollars to researchers and health professionals to seed doubt in the public's minds and to help influence Congress. For years, sodas were thought to be benign and that obesity was caused by eating fatty foods and lack of exercise. They were able to forestall the inevitable drop in soda sales. The oil industry is doing the same thing. Stalling the inevitable."

"Until it's too late."

He sighed. "It may already be too late."

"You said the report is a poorly kept secret. Why is that?"

He smirked but said nothing.

Giselle spoke up. "We have supporters everywhere, Miss Chase."

"Inside CP&G?"

She gave me an enigmatic smile.

I asked, "Then did you know about the missing researcher?"

Stephen frowned. "No, that must have just happened."

"Only a few hours ago."

"Do you know the name of the missing scientist?"

I paused for effect. "It's Dr. Stuart Ekmann."

"No shit." He chugged the rest of his beer, and Giselle got up off the bar stool. "Are you sure?" he asked.

"I heard it directly from Darren Reed."

"I'm sorry, we've got to go."

"Why?"

"We've got to find him."

"Why would you want to find him? He's working for the enemy."

He gave me a sour grin. "We've heard rumors that Ekmann was growing a conscience and had second thoughts about having his name linked to this kind of shitty science."

Giselle stared at me with a grim expression. "We have to find him before the bad guys do. We need to keep him safe."

As I watched them rush out the front door, I wondered if what the woman had said was true. Gaea had a bad reputation. Did they want to find Ekmann to keep him safe? Or did they have a more nefarious purpose?

———

"What are we doing, Genie?"

I wasn't sure. After Stephen left, I pulled out my phone and did a search for Stuart Ekmann. To my surprise, I got an address, 17 Clemmons Drive, just a few blocks from the South Sheffield train station.

With the paper bag of burritos in the back seat and the mouth-watering scents of Tex-Mex filling the rest of the car, we'd pulled up at the curb right in front of his house.

The windows were dark, the curtains were closed, and there was no car in the driveway.

Clemmons Drive was cut into a hill a few blocks from the hospital. The homes along the northern side of the street were elevated behind stone and concrete foundations. All built by the same developer in the eighties, the houses were faux Victorian with cupolas and gingerbread but on postage stamp–sized yards.

The neighborhood was a tiny step up from middle class.

As we sat at the curb, I peered up and down the dark street, trying to pick out where the eyes and ears of Fisher, Evans, and Sinclair or Gaea were waiting to see if and when Dr. Ekmann returned to his home.

"The burritos are getting cold." Caroline sounded bored.

"Sorry, sweetie." I gave the neighborhood another slow study, but couldn't pick out where the surveillance might be.

They must be very good. I know they're here.

Then I saw it, the glint of glass in the front seat of a Chevy Blazer parked in the shadows up the street. Someone maneuvering a camera into place to take our photo, a streetlight reflected off the lens.

Fear suddenly gripped me with sharp nails and icy fingers. What the hell was I thinking?

I shouldn't be here with Caroline!

I'd left the car idling, the heat circulating throughout the car. Quickly, I put it in gear and left the curb. If I continued in the direction I was headed, I was going to drive right by the surveillance vehicle, with Caroline squarely visible from the passenger's seat.

"Get down."

"What?" she asked.

"Don't ask questions, just get down."

From the corner of my eye, I saw her frown. But she did as I'd asked and leaned awkwardly across the center console.

I stared straight ahead as I pushed the gas pedal down and rushed by the dark SUV. Glancing up at my rearview mirror, I looked to see if the Blazer would pull out and follow us.

"Can I sit up now?"

I took a deep breath. They were staying put. "Yeah, sure."

"What's going on?"

"Just part of the case I'm working on."

Seeing that I was keeping an eye on what was going on behind us, she turned and peered out the back window. "You know, Google Alert lets me know when your name pops up on the internet."

"Oh, yeah?"

"Yeah, this morning a story from the *New York Daily News* showed up saying you were looking into the murder-suicide of some oil executive and his wife."

"There's no such thing as privacy anymore, is there?"

"Nope." She waved her hand behind us. "Does any of this have to do with your case?"

I wasn't sure how to answer. On the surface, it didn't. A missing scientist didn't seem to have anything to do with my investigation. Other than this bogus study kept popping up on the radar screen.

But it was intriguing and had the potential for a hell of a news story.

And I'd picked up another fact earlier that night that I hadn't known before. Stephen Cutter and Gaea had known in advance that Morris Cutter was going to present the Ekmann Study to Congress. It would have been in their best interest to stop him.

Could Stephen or Gaea have killed the Cutters?

Chapter Eighteen

We sat at the table and quietly ate our burritos, dipping our nachos in the plastic container of salsa. Tucker was noiselessly draped over my left foot, snoozing. I broke the silence by asking, "Is Tyler going to be able to go to the dance with you this Friday if he's on detention?"

She rolled her eyes. "I don't know. I wish the two dorks who jumped him would just die."

The name-calling again.

"He couldn't have just walked away?"

"According to Tyler, they had him cornered in the bathroom."

"Have those two boys been in trouble before? What are their names again?"

She reached over, picked up another nacho, and dipped it in the salsa. "Brandon and Justin. They've been outsiders since I can remember. You know, socially awkward, but physically they're big guys. Dumb as rocks but kind of imposing."

"Are they bullies?"

She popped the nacho into her mouth and thought while she crunched it into pieces. Caroline shrugged and sighed. "No, yes. I've heard kids call them names, but they do the same kind of shit. I don't know what crawled up their butts about Tyler that they attacked *him*, though. He's never done anything to them."

I scrunched up my nose and grinned at her. "Maybe it's 'cause Tyler's going to the dance with the hottest girl in your class."

Before I could say anything more, her phone went off. Caroline glanced down at the screen. "It's Tyler. Mind if I take this?"

I looked at her plate and saw that half the burrito was still on it.

I gave her a tired smile and waved toward the stairs, indicating she should take the call in her room.

She smiled back. "Hi, Tyler. Genie and I were just talking about you." Caroline, phone pressed against her ear with one hand, picked up her plate with the other. Tucker, ever hopeful that something will fall off a plate, got up and, tail wagging, followed her.

I took a sip of ice water and glanced at the screen of my own phone. Nathaniel had texted me.

Call me.

I saw that it was time stamped only fifteen minutes before.

Before I had a chance to call him, my phone vibrated and chirped. I recognized from Caller ID that it was Leonard Ryan from Fisher, Evans and Sinclair. "Yes?" I couldn't keep the annoyance out of my voice.

"Miss Chase, this is Leonard Ryan."

"I know."

"Do you know where Dr. Ekmann is?"

"Who?" I feigned ignorance.

"You know who. You're much too good at your job not to know who he is."

I almost wanted to thank him for the compliment. Of course,

I knew who he was. Once we got home, I looked up what I could on the internet before I'd eaten any of my Tex-Mex.

Dr. Stuart Ekmann was fifty-seven. He'd been an undergrad at Boston College and got his doctorate in astrophysics at Rutgers. From what I could get online, he was a better teacher than a researcher, and a complete mess when it came to marriages and finances. The internet told me he'd been married twice and had declared bankruptcy three times.

The one fact about Dr. Ekmann that interested me the most wasn't even about him. It was about his son, Donald Ekmann. He was one of three firefighters in California who had perished while battling a wildfire last September in Napa Valley. It was one of the many fires last year that were the result of the drought.

An inadvertent victim of global warming?

I continued my charade. "Why don't you tell me who this Dr. Ekmann is?"

Leonard didn't rise to the bait. "He's missing, and we're convinced he's in danger."

"Mr. Ryan, I'm curious as to why you think I'd know where your scientist is. He's not part of the investigation I'm conducting."

There was silence on his end of the phone as he thought it through. The man's final statement was terse. "If you know where he is, you'd better tell us. We want him back."

The line went dead.

I punched up Nathaniel.

"Genie?"

"You wanted me to call you?"

"Yeah, I wanted to warn you about Fisher, Evans, and Sinclair. I got a call from them asking if I knew where Dr. Stuart Ekmann is."

I smiled to myself. "Too late. I just hung up with one of their stooges. Do you?"

"Do I what?"

"Know where Ekmann is?"

He chuckled. "Not yet. But I bet I can find out. What do you know?"

"Only as much as you do. He was the lead research fellow on this bogus study by CP&G that Darren Reed's presenting on Friday. By the way, from the tone of voice from this guy from Fisher, Evans, and Sinclair, they want this Ekmann guy back in a bad way."

"Did he threaten you?"

"Not directly."

"Be careful. Hey, I have some information for you. I haven't figured out where Nikki Hudson is living these days, but I found out that she's working a booth for Empire Hot Tubs and Spas at the Home and Garden Show at the Javits Center. The show started today and runs through Saturday."

"Guess that means a trip into the city tomorrow."

"Stop by the office, and I'll make you lunch."

I eyed my own laptop set up on the counter next to the toaster. Nathaniel liked to work from his kitchen as well as the office in his living room. I also knew he was an excellent chef. Lunch at his place would *not* be a stale tuna fish sandwich. "It's a date."

His voice sounded jovial. "In the meantime, I'm getting ready to have dinner with some friends at a new French bistro in the Village."

"Enjoy. I'll see you tomorrow. Hey, is John back in New York?"

"He landed a few hours ago. I already told him you're on assignment for Lodestar. He asked if I thought you might need some help. So, I'm sure you'll be hearing from him. As a matter of fact, I'll invite him to have lunch with us."

Sexual tension fairly hummed through my body when he told me that. I tried to keep my voice steady. "Sounds like a plan. Enjoy your dinner tonight."

As I hit the End Call button, I heard Caroline slowly stamp down the steps and into the kitchen. Her face was crimson and her brows were furrowed. She'd been on the phone with Tyler, and I wondered if he'd said something to upset her. "What's wrong?"

"Brandon and Justin."

"The two boys who got into a fight with Tyler?"

"They're spreading lies about Tyler on Snapchat."

I could barely hold my own on Facebook and Twitter, and I had only recently gotten an Instagram account. "Snapchat?"

"Social media. If you're over twenty-five, you won't understand how to use it."

Thanks for the vote of confidence.

"What are these boys saying?"

"That they beat down Tyler because he's gay. They're telling everyone that Tyler begged them in the boys' room to let him..." Her voice drifted off. Usually Caroline didn't hesitate to use gutter language around me, just to see if she'd shock me. But clearly, there was something here that made her uncomfortable.

"Perform a sex act on them?" I offered.

As an answer, she simply sighed.

"What else?"

"They're threatening him. Saying that if they catch him alone again, they're going to cut off his..." Her voice trailed off again.

"His junk?"

She grinned slightly at the silly colloquialism. "Yeah, his junk."

"Want me to talk to Mike Dillon?"

Caroline shook her head. "Just two dorks talking tough."

"Toxic masculinity? Isn't that what you called it?"

"Little boys who want to be Rambo."

I smiled at her. "You know something? It doesn't get any better when they grow up."

———

I have a confession to make.

That night, I really wanted a drink. I wanted to pour myself a tumbler of straight vodka and feel the burn as it trickled down my throat. Feel the love.

Had the call from Leonard Ryan rattled me? Did knowing that Caroline would be going out on her first date worry me?

No, it was the thought of sitting down and seeing John Stillwater again.

I'd been married three times. I'd had an affair with a married man. I'd been in love with Caroline's father and ended up grieving for him. I'd had a short relationship with Mike Dillon.

Relationships…I wasn't good at them.

And now you're lusting after someone you hardly know anything about?

I wanted the drink, but I didn't.

Control.

It was almost reassuring to hear Shana's voice in my head.

I took an Ambien instead.

That was probably why I was so groggy when my phone rang at a little after two in the morning. When I was awake enough to grab the phone off the headboard, I saw that the number was Shana's. Slightly panicky at getting a call at that hour, I croaked, "Hello?"

"Genie."

"Yeah." I tried shaking the cobwebs from my brain. Why was she calling me at 2 a.m.? "Is everything okay?"

Her voice was strained. "It's Nathaniel. He's in intensive care."

Fear dug its sharp claws into my chest. "What? What happened? Where is he?"

"Bellevue. I'm here now. According to the police, they found him unconscious in an alleyway in Queens."

I repeated, "What happened? Was he mugged?"

"I talked with the cops who found him and the EMTs who brought him in. All they could tell me is that he'd been severely beaten. All the fingers in both hands have been broken, his jaw is fractured, and he's covered with bruises and cuts. He's got several broken ribs, and one of his lungs is punctured. He's still unconscious. They're checking him now for internal bleeding."

Suddenly, I was completely awake. "Did the cops call you?"

"I'm Nathaniel's emergency contact. My number is in his wallet."

I was going to have to reassess Nathaniel's relationship with Shana when all of this was over. "He told me he was having dinner with some friends at a new French bistro."

She said, "I know who he was meeting. One of them works for me. They called me when he didn't show up at the restaurant."

A man's voice, standing right next to Shana, said, "He must have gotten jumped when he left his apartment."

John Stillwater.

Shana spoke again. "John wants to talk with you."

I could hear her hand over her cell phone. "Genie, listen carefully. I need to know what you're working on."

No hello or I missed you? Right to business?

Fine, I can play that game. "Nathaniel has me investigating the murder-suicide of Morris and Julia Cutter, a retired oil exec and his wife."

He must have put his hand over the phone because I heard him saying something to Shana but couldn't make out what it was. Then he came back on the line. "Any idea why someone would want to hurt Nathaniel?"

"Could be. That same oil company, CP&G, is presenting something called the Ekmann Study to Congress on Friday. They think it will stall any kind of legislation on climate change."

John was quiet for moment, digesting what I'd just told him. "I don't see what that has to do with your case or Nathaniel."

"Dr. Stuart Ekmann, the lead researcher, is missing. The oil execs are desperate to get him back."

"I still don't see…"

I cut him off. "Nathaniel and the oil CEO have a history. When Nathaniel was still working for the *Times*, he wrote a couple of unflattering stories about him. Guy's name is Darren Reed. Yesterday, Reed told me that he suspected Nathaniel might have been involved with Ekmann's disappearance. Plus, Reed and his consulting group are putting pressure on us to wrap up our investigations by Thursday. Something about not wanting a cloud hanging over Reed's presentation of the study to Congress."

John was still doubtful. "Is that everything?"

"Not quite. An extremist climate group called Gaea also wants to get their hands on the missing scientist. One of Gaea's employees is Stephen Cutter, nephew of the dead oil exec. He's on my short list of suspects for killing the Cutters."

I heard him conferring with Shana again. Then he came back on. "Okay, concentrate on your investigation, and we'll handle Nathaniel's situation."

"I'm on my way to Bellevue. I'll see you in about an hour."

Shana was suddenly on the phone. "Genie, wait."

"Why?"

"They're not letting anyone in to see him. While he's in intensive care, they're only letting family in."

"Nathaniel has family?"

I don't know why that struck me as odd.

"Actually, he doesn't. I'm about the only family that man has. The hospital is making an exception for me. If you want to, come into town tomorrow morning. We'll all have a late breakfast in the hospital cafeteria. I'm hoping he'll be out of ICU by then."

I was about to hit the End Call button, but Shana stopped me. "Wait a minute. We don't know what we're looking at here. Make sure your doors and windows are locked, and be careful when you come into town tomorrow."

After we hung up, I pictured Nathaniel in a hospital bed.

Then I imagined what it must have been like to have someone break my fingers, one by one.

I peeked over at my bureau where the vodka was hidden in my panty drawer.

No, I didn't have a drink, even though I was wound up tighter than a cheap watch.

Yay, me.

Chapter Nineteen

I'm always wary of hospital cafeterias. Aren't hospitals where those superbugs always seem to be lurking? The ones that have developed an immunity to antibiotics. Don't you think that the basin of overcooked bacon at the buffet line would be the perfect place for those bad boys to breed? Or how about those runny scrambled eggs?

Instead of having anything to eat, I simply had a hot cup of coffee. I figured that the tongue-scalding temperature of the hot water and caffeine should have killed anything that could possibly make me sick or eat my flesh.

I paid for my coffee, then gazed out over the tables of breakfast diners, searching for a familiar face. It was an interesting crowd. Doctors in lab coats, nurses in scrubs, patrons who were there visiting sick friends and family, and well-dressed pharmaceutical salespeople visiting hospital administrators.

Nobody but me seemed to be concerned with microbes.

I spotted them in a corner across the expansive room. Shana looking relaxed in jeans, black boots, and a lavender sweater. John in a button-down blue shirt, open at the collar under a black leather coat, also wearing jeans and leather loafers.

He ran a hand through his tangle of tousled black hair as he talked with Shana and drank his coffee.

I thought I could feel my heart start to rev like the engine of a high-performance race car.

What is it about John that does that to me?

Was it the boyish good looks? Was it because I knew he could be dangerous? Was it that he had a dark past?

I've always been a sucker for bad boys.

When he noticed me coming toward the table, he cracked a shy smile. He stood up and spread his arms. "Genie, I've missed you."

Careful not to spill my coffee, he engulfed me with his strong arms, and I rested my face on his shoulder. I could smell the faint scent of his aftershave.

Letting me go, I glanced over at Shana before I sat down at their table. "How's Nathaniel?"

She gave me a cautious smile. "Better. Out of ICU and in a room of his own. You can't keep that boy down."

"Thank God. Do we know what happened yet?"

She leaned forward, glancing around her. "They wouldn't let me spend much time with him. He was still drifting in and out of consciousness, but from what he managed to mumble, I learned that as he was leaving his building to go to dinner, three guys jumped him in the street and threw him into the back of some kind of vehicle."

"Does he know who they are?"

John adjusted his glasses. "He said they were wearing ski masks."

Shana picked at a container of fruit chunks with a plastic spoon. She wasn't smiling anymore. It had been replaced by a sneer. "Whoever it was, they tortured him. They were convinced that he knew where this guy Ekmann was. They started by breaking his fingers."

John squinted at me as I sipped my hot coffee. "So, you said last night there are two competing parties who want to find Stuart Ekmann."

I was certain that by now, John knew at least as much as I did about the missing researcher. If I had to take a bet, I'd guess that John knew even more.

"The oil company who subsidized the study is one party. I know they have their attack dogs at Fisher, Evans, and Sinclair out looking for him."

I watched as John wrote the name of the consulting firm down in a notebook.

"Eric Cutter, the guy who hired us, told me that they're scary people. When I mentioned them to Nathaniel, he said the same thing. It's a company that employs mercenaries and ex-spies."

John nodded as if he'd already had his culprits.

Shana wasn't ready to run in that direction yet. "Who else wants to find Dr. Ekmann?"

"A climate activist group called Gaea."

She frowned. "Climate activists? Are they extreme enough to kidnap and torture Nathaniel?"

I shrugged. "They've shut down refineries and bombed an oil pipeline that was under construction. That put three people in the hospital. According to them, this climate crisis thing is war."

John looked up from his notebook. "And you're working on that murder-suicide investigation."

Shana's words were slow and measured. "My interest level in what happened to Morris and Julia Cutter is nonexistent. All I want right now is to find out who tortured and nearly killed a dear friend of mine."

She fixed me with a cold gaze.

I involuntarily shuddered.

John stated, "Somebody tortured him for nothing. Nathaniel doesn't have a clue where their missing doctor is."

Shana glanced at John, then back at me. "At least he *says* he doesn't."

———

We stood silently by Nathaniel's bedside. He was hooked up to an IV drip, his vitals crawled slowly across a screen on the wall, and he was blessedly asleep. His hands were wrapped in bandages, as was the left side of his face. Eyes closed, the exposed skin on his face was swollen and mottled an angry black and purple.

The room smelled like antiseptic, rubbing alcohol, and flowers. I glanced over at the shelf mounted on the wall and saw a lovely bouquet of yellow and white roses. "Who sent the flowers?"

Shana smiled. "The ladies at the Tower. They're all very fond of Nathaniel. Everyone feels horrible."

Is he a client?

Looking at him again, helpless in the hospital bed, I realized how stupid it was to even be thinking about something like that.

John cleared his throat. "What are your thoughts, Shana?"

She hesitated for a moment, then answered. "Genie is already on assignment. She's investigating the Cutter case." She gazed at John. "What are you working on at the moment?"

"I'm done with that affair in Georgia. Nathaniel isn't about to give me an assignment. So, I have free time."

She sighed. "Then how about you help me find the motherfuckers who did this?"

———

While Shana stayed with Nathaniel, John and I went out into the hall and talked.

"So that's where you were, Georgia?"

He glanced up and down the hallway, confident that no one was listening. "Yeah, sorry I didn't call you before I left. I thought I'd see you at Shana's apartment on New Year's Eve."

"I couldn't make it," I lied. I knew that if I had gone to the party, I'd end up drunk and in bed with John. In bed wasn't so bad, but I was trying like hell to stay away from the Absolut.

"Nathaniel and Shana gave me the assignment in Georgia that night at the party, and I had to leave the next morning. A sex-trafficking ring running underage girls in and out of Atlanta."

"Nobody would tell me anything."

He smiled sadly and gazed at the doorway to the hospital room. "I was undercover."

"And it was dangerous."

He shrugged.

I nodded. "I get it."

I recalled Shana's words over lunch in her apartment. How when John was on the job, he was laser-focused. How he sometimes lost sight of what was around him unless it pertained to the case.

He adjusted his glasses. "Look, I did some homework this morning after talking with you. Fisher, Evans, and Sinclair's home office is in Greenwich. I'm sure it's to stay close to the CP&G execs that live in Connecticut. Looks like I'll be spending a little time in your neck of the woods. Want to have dinner tonight?"

Suddenly, the temperature in the hallway skyrocketed, and my heart did a tango in my rib cage. Maybe John wasn't as laser-focused as Shana thought.

"Sure, call me and let me know what time."

———

Much like Grand Central Terminal, the sheer size of the Jacob Javits Center never failed to impress me. The largest convention center on the east coast, it boasted four floors and over 800,000 square feet of exhibition space. The Javits Center hosts everything from cut-flower exhibits to intimate-apparel expos to the International Car Show.

The Home and Garden Show took up only a single floor. A home show in Manhattan had never taken root, simply because most city dwellers in Manhattan didn't have gas grills or landscaping or swimming pools. Not unless their apartment buildings supplied them.

This show was geared more for the outer boroughs, where people lived in split-level ranch or Victorian-style homes with backyards. And everything on exhibit, whether it was goods or services, had a hefty price tag attached.

The booth for Empire Hot Tubs and Spas was across the cavernous exhibit hall from the main entrance. I walked past booths selling wine racks, furniture, decks, brick patios, gas grills, and high-end outdoor tables and chairs.

As I got closer, I could see that Empire was demonstrating two hot tubs that were both roiling, bubbling, steaming cauldrons. Two women in tiny bikinis sat on the sides of each with their feet dangling in the water, looking totally bored. One was a blond, one was Nikki Hudson.

A man in his thirties, with short, sandy hair and a deliberate two-day shadow of beard on his face, was clad in black slacks and a dark-blue polo shirt with the Empire logo on the chest. An event ID tag hung on a lanyard around his neck.

My attention went directly to the model with long and lustrous raven black hair trailing down to the middle of her nearly naked lower back. Her "do" was slightly different from the pub-licity photos on the internet. In the pictures, her hair was brushed back from her forehead. On that day, she had bangs that gave her a slightly exotic look.

Nikki Hudson's tiny swimsuit was the same shade of blue as the polo shirt the salesman wore. As she sat on the corner of the hot tub, her feet in the water, her green eyes met passing customers as she smiled vacuously.

When I approached, I caught the scent of chlorine wafting out of the bubbling plastic cauldrons and was reminded of the Cutter household after the cleaning crew had finished with the bloody mess in the kitchen.

"I'll bet you wish you had one of these in your backyard."

I looked in the direction of the voice and was surprised to see that the salesman was standing right next to me. Noting that he was in my personal space, I stepped back.

He persisted. "Where do you live? We deliver and install anywhere in the tri-state area. These are fun in the summer, fall, winter, and spring."

I smiled, hoping it wasn't too condescending. "I'd like a few words with this young lady." I gestured toward Nikki Hudson, who at her mention focused her attention on me with narrowed eyes.

The plastic badge around the man's neck told me his name was Jeff. He glanced at Nikki and frowned. "Well, she's kind of busy. Would you like a flyer with more information about what Empire Hot Tubs and Spas has to offer?"

"No, thank you. I just need to chat with Miss Hudson."

Upon hearing her name mentioned by a complete stranger, Nikki's head jerked. She eyed me with suspicion but said to Jeff, "My toes are getting all wrinkly, and it's almost time for my break anyway."

She swung her long legs out of the tub and came down the plastic steps, toweling off, then wrapping herself in a fluffy, cotton robe, also adorned with the Empire logo. As she stepped into a pair of flip-flops, she said, "How about you buy me a cup of tea? I don't seem to have any cash on me."

As we walked away, Jeff shouted, "Ten minutes, Nikki."

Not turning around, she raised her right fist and gave the salesman the finger.

I asked her, "Is he your boss?"

She rolled her eyes. "God, no. He's one of the sales geeks that Empire has on staff. The boss is actually a pussycat. Older man who likes to flirt with younger women. Little Jeff back there is trying to prove he has a set of balls."

We went to a café counter on the periphery of the exhibit floor. She ordered tea, and I ordered coffee. When it came, I paid, and we found a table away from any other customers.

She blew steam off the surface of her beverage. "So how about you tell me who you are and how you know my name?"

"Geneva Chase. I work for a company called Lodestar Analytics. We do research."

Nikki sipped her tea. When she put the cardboard container back on the table, she wore the hint of a smile. "Yeah? You researching me?"

"Sort of. I'm looking into the murder-suicide of Morris and Julia Cutter."

Her shoulders jerked in surprise. Then she narrowed her eyes again. "That so?"

"How long was your affair with Morris Cutter?"

Her face was stony. "I never had an affair with Morris Cutter."

"You knew him."

She nodded but said nothing.

"You met at a golf tournament."

Her tone was sarcastic. "I know. I was there."

"And Morris Cutter paid you a total of two hundred and eighty thousand dollars in three separate checks."

She sat back in her chair. Her mouth was slightly open. "Who told you that?"

It was my turn to smile. "I'm paid to know things."

"Are you a cop?"

"I'm a researcher."

"What is that, like a detective or something?"

"I do research."

She leaned forward and pointed her finger at me. "Morris never wrote me any checks. They were from the Teller Corporation."

The shell corporation that Frank Mancini had helped set up.

"What were they for?"

"None of your damned business." She looked away from me.

"Were you blackmailing Morris Cutter?"

Anger flashed fire in her eyes. Her voice was little more than a hiss. "I did not blackmail Morris."

"Why did he give you money?"

The rage on her face slowly faded, and Nikki took a deep breath. "Morris was trying to help me."

"Help you?"

"He helped me get an apartment. He didn't want me sharing a place with three other models and their creepy boyfriends. Plus, he was paying to have me go back to school. I'm going for my master's in economics."

"Pretty generous."

"I'm worth it."

I took a sip of my coffee. "Were you sleeping with him?"

She bobbed her head slightly. "Yes."

"Any idea why Morris killed his wife and then shot himself?"

She visibly shivered and put both her hands on the container of tea to warm them. She was staring at her steaming beverage when she slowly answered. "He didn't shoot anybody. He certainly didn't commit suicide."

"Why do you think that?"

She blinked her eyes, thinking. "When I first met him, Morris Cutter had a single focus in life and that was his company. He was all about the bottom line and corporate earnings. He didn't give anything else much thought. And that included his wife, his kids, and even me. I was just a passing distraction. I knew that."

"But you said he was helping you. To the tune of over a quarter of a million dollars."

"I think that somehow, he felt obliged. He said he always paid his way in life."

"Did he ever talk to you about his family?"

She scrunched up her nose. "He almost never talked about his wife. Why would he if he were trying to fuck me?"

"How about his kids?"

Nikki was thoughtful. "He didn't say much about them unless I asked. Until his granddaughter, Amelia, was born."

"What happened then?"

She stared out at the exhibition floor. "All the while I knew him, he didn't seem to be particularly close to either of his kids, although I think he liked Eric better than the girl. What's her name?"

"Lisa."

"Yeah, that's it. And his relationship with his wife didn't seem to be a good one, although an older married guy is always going to tell you that when he's trying to have sex with you, isn't he?"

How much of this adultery experience do you have?

She continued. "Anyway, when the granddaughter was born, it was like someone flipped a switch. He couldn't stop talking about her. Every time we got together, he showed me the latest photos on his phone. At first it was cute. Then it just became tiresome."

"Have you ever heard of the Ekmann Study?"

A small smile played out over her lips again. "You mean that thing he was supposed to present up on Shadow Hill? That's what he called Capitol Hill, you know."

I sat back in my chair. "So I've heard."

"Before the granddaughter was born, he was really pumped about it. About how this study was a game changer. How it would turn the tide on public and political opinion about this climate thing. The 'climate hoax' he called it. Morris said that when his scientists and researchers had finished polishing the study, he'd prove to the lawmakers in Washington that any changes in the climate were part of the natural rhythms of the earth. That burning fossil fuel has nothing to do with it."

"Is that what you think?"

"It's bullshit, pure and simple. Everyone knows the crap we're pumping into the atmosphere is fucking up the globe. Morris wanted to delay any kind of congressional action for at least another couple of years, maybe even decades."

She drummed the top of the table with her fingers. "And then he stopped talking about it once the kid was born." She gazed sadly out at the floor, like she was remembering something painful. "All I know is that he wouldn't have killed himself. And, frankly, I don't think he had it in him to shoot his wife."

I recalled the trophies in his library. "Morris was a hunter."

She gave me a sideways glance. "It's a long way from shooting deer to blowing your wife's brains out."

"Do you think someone murdered them?"

She shrugged slightly, looking tiny in the white bathrobe. "I don't know. Before he retired, he had security with him all the time because he said the climate terrorists wanted to hurt him and the company. Could be one of them. My money is on Morris's nephew, Stephen. He's one of those guys."

"Why do you think it could be Stephen?"

She waved her hand in the air. "Morris told me about the feud between him and his brother and, by extension, his brother's family. I know that Morris had been sued several times by the family over some perceived slight when the brother left the company. Morris said that after his brother passed away, Stephen's anger got worse, mostly at his mother's prodding. One night, we ran into him while we were having dinner in a nice Italian restaurant in the city. I don't know, maybe he'd been following us. But Stephen made a scene, threatening to kill Morris if he didn't do the right thing. Thank heavens Morris still had security back then. They hauled his ass out of there and threw him into the street."

That's something that Stephen hadn't bothered to tell me.

"Please don't take offense at my next question, but I have to ask."

"Where was I on the day they died? I was home alone sleeping off a hangover."

No alibi. Nathaniel said the gun that killed the Cutters was small, perfect for a woman's hand. A possible suspect?

Try as I might, I couldn't think of a motive for her to kill them.

I had one more question to ask. "Did you love Morris Cutter?"

She thought about that for a moment. Then she answered, "I had feelings for Morris Cutter. I cried when I heard that he was dead. I guess that's a kind of love, isn't it?"

Chapter Twenty

Since I was already in the city, I decided to call the offices of CP&G to see if I could line up another meeting with Darren Reed. Our talk over lunch the day before had been cut short by the news that Stuart Ekmann was missing. I had more questions for Mr. Reed.

I'd retained the number on my cell phone from when his assistant, Nicole Collier, had called me to set up the lunch at Portofino's. I hit the Call button.

Her uber-professional voice answered. "Mr. Reed's office."

I pictured her sitting on the CEO's lap taking dictation. "Is Mr. Reed in?"

"Who's calling?"

"Geneva Chase."

There was a momentary silence. "May I ask what this call is in reference to?"

Yeah, you owe me for lunch.

"I'd like a chance to finish our conversation from yesterday. Is Mr. Reed available at all today?"

The phone went silent as she conferred with her boss.

When she came back on the line, she asked, "Do you know where Dr. Ekmann is?"

That surprised the hell out of me. "No. Why would I know that?"

"Have you finished your investigation into the deaths of Morris and Julia Cutter?"

"No."

The line went silent again. Finally, she came back on the phone. "I'm afraid that Mr. Reed's schedule simply won't allow him to meet with you today. Please call back and set up an appointment for another day."

Fat chance.

"Well, if Mr. Reed's too busy to see me, how about Parker Lewis?"

When she sighed, it was as if I'd plucked at her last nerve. "I'll check."

This time the wait seemed to take forever. But then again, she wasn't sitting on Parker Lewis's lap, now was she?

Her words were brusque when she came back onto the line. "Mr. Lewis can see you, but only if you're here in the next forty-five minutes. He may be able to give you a half an hour of his time then."

"I'll be there."

Normally, I would have taken the subway, but because time was a factor, I took a cab. I felt a little guilty using the company card to pay for it, knowing that Nathaniel was in the hospital. I've been a journalist for most of my life, and I know what life is like living on a shoestring budget.

While people-watching as the taxi drove me to the CP&G offices, I wondered how John and Shana were going to track down the men who had attacked Nathaniel. There wasn't any doubt in my mind that the two of them would do it, though. Recalling Shana's session with the Israeli Special Forces trainer, I shuddered at what justice she might want to exact for the pain they put her friend through.

When I got to the CP&G offices, I noticed there was an

even bigger crowd of protestors on the sidewalk. A line of New York cops acted as a human barrier between the building and a hundred people chanting and carrying placards. Like before, I was ushered into the building by CP&G security, and when I got to the forty-third floor, another security guard buzzed me through the glass doors and into the office.

Instead of Parker Lewis coming to the lobby, his indifferent blond assistant came out and escorted me into his office. When I entered, Parker stood up and he quickly rushed over with his hand out. "Genie, so good to see you again. Can I take your coat?"

Slipping out of it, I said, "I'll just toss it on the couch."

He gestured toward his assistant in the slightly-too-short skirt, whom I could see peeking at us through the doorway. "Can Ms. Kramer get you anything to drink: coffee, tea, water?"

"No, thank you."

He waved me toward one of the two leather chairs facing his desk. "Please have a seat. How can I help you?"

If I'd been able to see the CEO, I would have asked him questions about the missing scientist. But since I was in the office of the senior VP who was a longtime friend of the family, I decided to ask about the Cutters again. "I know that the last time I was here, you filled me in a little about David Cutter and his family. What more can you tell me about Stephen?"

Parker's eyes widened behind his wireframes. "Is Stephen part of your investigation?"

"I'm just looking at as many angles as I can."

"Well, as I said before, he's grown up to be a very bitter man. I'm sure hearing the poison that his father and mother have spewed about Morris and this company over the years, well, it's no wonder he's angry."

"Angry about the money his father was cheated out of when the company went public?"

He folded his hands on the desk. "The money's part of it, for sure. But Stephen's father grew to be a raving lunatic about the environment. He blamed us for everything and anything that was wrong with the world."

"Did that include wanting to make shipping oil and drilling safer, lessening the likelihood of another *Valdez* or Deepwater Horizon?"

Parker visibly straightened in his chair and drove a finger onto the top of his desk for effect. "Genie, let me set the record straight. CP&G spends huge amounts of money for safety features for all of its ships, trucks, pipelines, and drilling equipment. What Stephen's father wanted far exceeded the federal guidelines and common sense."

"Stephen wants more than that, Parker. He told me that he thinks CP&G and all the other oil companies are poisoning the planet. I think he's determined to shut you all down."

He stared at me, processing what I'd just told him. Finally, in a measured voice, he said, "Do you know that he's employed by a terrorist organization called Gaea?"

"Yes."

"Do you know that over the last year, Gaea has hacked into our computers and shut down a number of our refineries, one of them for over a week?"

"Yes."

"And that they blew up a pipeline of ours that was under construction? Three people ended up in the hospital?"

"I heard."

He took a deep breath. "Those people are criminals, pure and simple. They should all be locked up."

"Do you know if Stephen ever visited Morris and Julia Cutter in their home?"

He blinked and cocked his head. "Why do you ask?"

"Just wondering."

He hesitated at first. Then he answered, "Yes, he has. After Amelia was born, something about Morris changed. The writing was on the wall about him retiring. He slowed down and started spending more time with his family. He confided in me that he might have been too harsh with his brother, David."

"Did he want to make amends with his nephew?"

"He actually invited both Stephen and Delia to his house for dinner early in December. Morris asked if I could be there as well. He hoped that between the two us, we could somehow find a way to placate Stephen and his mother."

"How did it go?"

"Delia declined to attend."

"But Stephen was there?"

"It was tense at first. But we all toasted Stephen's father with a glass of twenty-year-old scotch in Morris's library."

"Sounds like it went pretty well then." Why hadn't Stephen said anything about that?

Parker leaned back and stroked his mustache. "The boy was drawing us in. He was congenial all through dinner. Toward the end of the evening, Stephen took a turn and insisted on proposing a toast of his own."

My stomach twisted because I knew another shoe was about to drop. I'd met the young man twice. I was certain his hatred of Morris Cutter and CP&G had not been diminished by a glass of scotch and dinner. "What happened?"

"He started by toasting his father again but then went into a tirade where he hoped that Morris, me, and the company all rotted in hell."

"Doesn't sound like it ended well."

"No. Morris surprised me. In his day, if someone had insulted him in his own home, in front of his wife, he would have physically thrown him out the front door. Instead, Morris quietly said that he was sorry that Stephen still felt that way. Family shouldn't be at war with itself."

"Is that the only time they met face-to-face?"

"As far as I know. But both Morris and Julia said they'd welcome another chance to reconcile."

"They've been fighting for a long time."

"Morris was naive to think he could heal those wounds with a simple dinner."

"Just out of curiosity, you said he invited Stephen's mother to the dinner?"

"He did. She said she'd break bread with Morris and Julia when pigs flew out of her ass."

I shifted gears. "Tell me about Dr. Stuart Ekmann."

Parker stiffened again. "What do you want to know? I'm sure you already know he's missing."

I thought about Nathaniel lying in a hospital bed and felt a red flush of anger shade my face. I explained, "Parker, someone kidnapped and tortured my boss last night looking for information about your missing researcher. Any ideas about who might have done that?"

He put his hand to his chest. "Oh, my God, I'm so sorry to hear that. That's horrible. If I had to take bets, my money would be on those thugs at Gaea. They want to stop us from giving Ekmann's study to Congress. Yesterday, when I heard Stuart was missing, I thought for sure that they'd kidnapped him. From what you're telling me, they don't know where he is either."

"What about Fisher, Evans and Sinclair? Is it possible they're the ones who put my boss in the hospital?"

He waved his hand. "They're a consulting company, not the Mafia."

"If the report is finished and ready for Congress, why is Dr. Ekmann even relevant?"

"We simply want to make sure the man is safe. We're concerned about what Gaea or other terrorist groups will do to him if they get their hands on him."

I sat back in my chair. "What do you hope will happen when Darren Reed gives this report in DC?"

He smiled at me. "Right now, the Department of Interior and the Bureau of Ocean Energy Management are both weighing in on opening up the Atlantic and Pacific coasts to offshore oil exploration. That's been fought for years by the tree huggers who say that it will foul their pretty beaches and ruin their view of the ocean. We want to nudge that forward and start seismic testing this year."

"What else?"

He gave me a conspiratorial look. "There's a bill that's quietly moving through the House of Representatives that will do great harm to the oil industry. If passed, it will effectively shut off needed subsidies for energy companies like ours. The Harker-Stanley Bill takes those subsidies away from us and gives them to renewable energy projects. If that happens, you're going to see the price of gasoline go off the charts."

Maybe that's not a bad thing.

Parker continued, "We know for a fact that once the Ekmann Study is made public, that bill will never get to the floor. Instead of shutting us down, it will give us decades to continue making this country energy-strong and continue creating jobs."

I wanted so badly to leap up and scream at him.

But I didn't, I calmly asked, "Do you think we're heading into a climate crisis?"

He frowned. "The crisis will be if this country doesn't do everything it can to be energy independent."

I sat quietly for a moment, then asked one last question. "Over lunch yesterday, Darren Reed said that he suspected Morris of siphoning off money from some CP&G accounts."

Parker's face was grim. "I'm aware that the company has its suspicions."

"Did Morris know that he was being suspected of a crime?"

"Yes, he and I discussed it."

"Do you think it's true?"

He shook his head slightly. "I hope not. But I worry that it might have been the overlying factor that might have driven Morris to kill Julia and himself."

I tried to understand. "Morris already had a ton of money. Why embezzle from the company?"

Parker's expression was one of surrender. "Genie, I don't come from money. I've had to earn every dollar I've made. And don't take this the wrong way, Morris was my best friend. But people who come from money sometimes think they can do anything they want. It's possible that Morris, when he saw that the company was trying to push him out, decided to give one last fuck you to the board of directors. Maybe he felt entitled."

Chapter Twenty-One

As I walked through the hallway, heading back toward the lobby, I nearly collided with a group of men leaving another office. All four of them were dressed in dark-blue suits, white shirts, and red ties. They all carried black overcoats over their arms and held black briefcases. I was amused by their uniformity.

But there was an obvious disparity in ages. The man leading the pack was in his sixties, while the other three looked like they were barely out of high school.

I noted the brass nameplate on the wall next to the doorway they'd just exited. They'd come out of the office of Darren Reed, CEO.

I hesitated, standing outside the closed door, and considered barging in unannounced. But I knew that would only get me escorted out by either security or the stone-faced Nicole Collier, so I followed the four men down the hall, into the lobby, and out the glass doors. We congregated at the elevator, waiting for its arrival.

I was pleased to see that I received a few appreciative and curious glances. And not just from the older dude but the young guys as well. Just before the elevator door slid open, the older man, the tallest of them, drawled, "Do you work here at CP&G? They got some mighty pretty girls here."

He seemed familiar to me, but I couldn't place him. "I'm a researcher."

He smiled and nodded knowingly. "Did you work on that study that Darren's bringing down to Capitol Hill on Friday?"

He was about six-five, clean-shaven, and had a full head of silver hair. His brown eyes were framed by heavy eyebrows and age lines. His cheeks and nose were crosshatched with red veins from too many evenings of cigars, liquor, and hard living.

I smiled back at him and nodded. "I have an investment in that study."

He grinned. "Nice work. I particularly liked the data you folks got from ice core samples from Antarctica. What were they from, like 400,000 years ago? Y'all claim that there have been cycles of carbon dioxide spikes throughout history having nothin' to do with humans burnin' oil? And that blockbuster news that even NASA admits is true. That the earth has shifted a couple of degrees on its axis. That shit is brilliant."

I played along, not having a clue what he was talking about. "Thank you. You look familiar to me."

The elevator door opened, and he waved me in, then they all followed. He pushed the button for the lobby before he replied. "I'm Senator Hank Gottard from the great state of North Carolina. And you are?"

He held out his big hand, and I shook it.

"I'm Dr. Chase."

He attempted a seductively sage expression, complete with one raised eyebrow. "Beautiful and smart."

"Thank you." I took my hand back from his bearlike grip.

"You brainiacs even threw in some crap about cosmic rays

from the sun just for good measure." He looked around at his entourage and everyone chuckled.

I had a chance to study their faces. Just like the senator, they were clean-shaven, but they were all easily forty years younger than the congressman. All of them wore an expression with a slight squint, as if trying to exude power and being faintly sinister. If they'd been on *Saturday Night Live*, they would have been hilarious.

The senator continued as we dropped slowly down the elevator shaft. "Tell me, darlin', do any of your fellow scientists really believe any of that bullshit?"

I decided to screw with him a little. "Don't you believe it?"

He laughed quietly to himself. "I'm not that stupid, little lady. And neither are my associates up on the Hill. But you've given us a reason to sow doubt in this climate change, greenhouse gas thing. Nobody wants to stop drivin' their pickup truck. Nobody wants to stop eatin' steaks and burgers. Nobody wants to stop takin' jets to go on vacation. Green New Deal, my ass."

I must have had a puzzled expression on my face.

He explained. "Look, little lady, CP&G and the rest of the petroleum lobby work well with us. They're very generous to our campaigns, and we appreciate that, of course. In return, we keep the subsidies flowing to y'all and shut out those solar and wind people. It's in our best interest—hell, make that America's best interest—that we keep the oil industry robust and making a healthy profit."

I blinked. "Aren't you worried about what you're doing to the planet? What you're leaving your grandchildren?"

We reached the ground floor and the door slid open. I stepped out, expecting them to do the same. Senator Gottard put his hand up and held the door from closing. "We're going to the basement." He glanced out at the protesting crowd beyond the glass doors. "There's an underground passage to the garage. Look, Dr. Chase, in answer to your question, whatever bad that happens to the world, it'll be long after I'm dead and buried. In the meantime, I'll live out my life a very wealthy man and will leave much of that wealth to my children and grandchildren. From what Darren told me today, you'll be quite rich yourself. I understand CP&G is paying each one of its researchers three million dollars. He said that's to pay for any media interviews you end up doing." He fixed me with a hard stare. "My question to you, Dr. Chase, is this: Do you or any of your scientist buddies carry any of that baggage around in your conscience? Look what you're doing to the earth, darlin'. Look at *yourself* in the mirror."

———

As I walked out of the building and past the protestors, I was chilled right down to my soul. None of those congressional bastards believed in what they were doing beyond making an extra buck. Screw future generations. Screw millions of species into extinction. Screw the coral reefs. So what if millions of people die?

I reached into my bag and pulled out my phone. I saw that Eric Cutter had texted me. The message was simple: Call me.

Because of the constant din of traffic and sirens, it's almost impossible to have a phone call on the streets of New York. St. Bartholomew's Church was just up the block, so I went to it, climbed the steps, and opened the ornate doors that allowed worshippers into the massive interior. Byzantine in design, the nave was cavernous, shadows playing across the pews and walls as the light crept through the stained-glass windows. Perhaps a dozen worshippers sat in wooden benches. The inside of the church was draped in reverent silence.

Not wanting to disturb them, I hovered near the doors, punching in Eric's number.

"Geneva?"

"Yes, what's up?" I answered in a semi-whisper.

"It's my sister, she's missing. She never went back to DC."

"What do you mean?"

"Her supervisor at NASA called me. She said that Lisa never showed up for work today. She's not answering her phone. I called Lisa's partner, and she's worried, too. She says that she hasn't seen Lisa since she left yesterday morning. Has Lisa called you?" I could hear panic creeping into his voice.

First the lead researcher from CP&G vanishes, and now Lisa Cutter?

Coincidence?

I answered, "No. Has she ever done this before?"

"Never. She loves her job too much to just not show up. I'm really worried."

"No idea where she might be?"

"None."

I kept my eye on the worshippers. My growing sense of dread overshadowed the concern that I was disturbing them. "Does she have any enemies?"

He hesitated. "Dad used to tell me how much his colleagues at CP&G disliked her because of her stance on the climate."

I felt a chill when I thought of how Lisa Cutter could be a suspect in the deaths of her own parents.

Does she have something to do with the disappearance of Stuart Ekmann?

I tried to keep my words low and even. "Look, let's not panic. Let me see what I can find out. In the meantime, if you hear from her, let me know, please."

After I got off the phone, I called Shana Neese.

"Genie?"

"Hey, what's the latest on Nathaniel?"

"He's better. The doctors let me spend a few minutes alone with him. He's still a little loopy from the drugs, but he confirmed that he had just left his apartment building and was walking to the restaurant where he was supposed to meet up with some of his friends. Two men came up behind him, threw a hood over his head, and muscled him into some kind of windowless vehicle. Then they spent the next two hours or so beating the hell out of him, thinking Nathaniel knows where this missing scientist is."

"Does he?"

"He says he doesn't. If he does, he's not even telling me."

"Does he have any idea who jumped him?"

"He couldn't see anything, and they never said much more than 'Where's Dr. Ekmann?'"

"Well, while you're trying to figure out that mystery, I have a new one. Morris Cutter's daughter, Lisa, a climatologist for NASA, is missing."

There was silence on her end while she considered that. "Do you think they're related? Two missing scientists?"

"I don't know. They're on two opposite sides of the spectrum. One of them is out to prove that climate change is real, and the other is trying to prove that it's not."

"Are you going to need a place to stay in the city tonight?"

"I'm almost done here in town. I'm going to head back to Connecticut. By the way, John asked me to have dinner with him tonight."

Her voice dripped with Louisiana honey when she offered, "Have fun, sugar."

I thought I only had one more stop in New York before I caught the train back to Connecticut. I was looking forward to going home and taking a shower. After spending time at the offices of CP&G and in the elevator with Senator Gottard, even standing inside St. Bart's wasn't making me feel clean.

Chapter Twenty-Two

I sat opposite Dr. Mitchell Trentino in his tiny office on the Columbia University campus. Sitting behind his cluttered desk, he closed his laptop so that he could see me more easily.

His second-floor office was lined with bookcases full of scientific tomes and notebooks. On his wall hung three framed satellite photos, which to my untrained eye, appeared to be massive storms bearing down on the eastern seaboard.

Mitch had curly dark hair, graying at the temples. He wore a goatee and mustache that did nothing to hide his wide smile. Mitch wore eyeglasses with burgundy-colored, perfectly round frames, making him look like a mature version of Harry Potter.

"Thank you for seeing me, Dr. Trentino."

He grinned warmly, offering a dazzling show of teeth. "Anytime, Genie. And what's with the formality? It's Mitch."

I'd interviewed Mitch for the first time right after Hurricane Sandy laid waste to the coast, back when I was doing a gig at Fox News. Mitch Trentino was a professor in the school's meteorology department. His particular field of expertise was tropical cyclones, hurricanes, and climate variability and change. He's a great go-to guy for a weather interview.

He had his elbows on his desk and his fingers tented together in a steeple. "So, what are you doing now? I know you left Fox a long time ago to go to Boston."

I handed him my card. "I'm a freelance journalist these days. Right now, I'm working on a project for Lodestar Analytics."

He frowned in confusion.

I explained. "I'm doing the same thing I did for newspapers, investigative journalism."

He mulled that over. "Like a detective?"

I simply smiled. "I'm investigating the deaths of Morris and Julia Cutter. Have you heard of them?"

He looked away from me in disgust. "Their attack dogs at Fisher, Evans and Sinclair brought a lawsuit against me and the university when I wrote a piece for the *Atlantic* on how the petrochemical companies are doing everything they can to put the brakes on any kind of action that would slow the use of carbon-burning fuel sources."

I played devil's advocate. "I read where the oil companies are investing in alternative energy sources."

"Pennies. They spend more money trying to sway public opinion and influence politicians."

As if a slave to an old habit, I pulled my recorder out of my bag and set it up on his desk. "Talk to me."

He eyeballed the recorder, but it didn't stop him. He was used to them. "The five largest oil and gas firms are spending over 200 million dollars every single year to lobby against climate change policies. And that doesn't count what they're spending on social media, which is harder for us to track."

"Think it's helping them?"

"Do we have a carbon tax? Do we have cap and trade? Has the government expanded subsidies for alternative renewable energy? To show you what a great investment those lobbyists are, in 2015 the federal government gave the petrochemical companies 650 billion dollars in direct and indirect subsidies. To get an idea how much that is, in that same year, the Pentagon spent 599 billion dollars for defense."

I whistled in surprise.

He leaned forward. "Look, a quick primer in climate change: The by-product of burning coal, oil, and gas is carbon dioxide. As you pump more and more carbon into the atmosphere, it traps the heat from the sun, raising the temperature of the earth."

I felt a little like I was being condescendingly preached to. "Yeah, I get it, the greenhouse effect."

"That's right. The earth isn't warming because of solar flares or cosmic rays or any natural cycles. It's totally man-made. We're in full self-destruct mode. And what does Congress want to do? It wants to open the Arctic and the Atlantic and Pacific coastline up to more drilling. That's just freakin' brilliant."

"How bad is it?" I almost felt like I was in the doctor's office, and he'd just given me a terminal prognosis.

"Bad. You're already seeing glaciers melting at an alarming rate. The seas are warming and rising, so if you've got beachfront property, you can bet it will be underwater by the end, if not the middle, of this century. But so will Miami and New York and Baltimore and every other city on the coast. You'll see monumental droughts, and there are already severe water shortages. And if you think that the hurricanes over the past few years have been bad, they're already predicting more Category 5 storms. You remember when a Cat 5 hit the Bahamas? Total devastation."

I raised my eyebrows.

He continued. "Thousands of species of animals and plants will go extinct. You'd just better hope that humans aren't one of them."

"Can we stop it?"

His grimace didn't offer up a lot of hope. "Even if we stopped burning coal and driving cars and flying in big-ass jets, the damage would continue for decades. Eventually, it would start turning back around again. Maybe. But we're not. We're not doing a damned thing."

Suddenly, stopping Darren Reed from giving his bogus report seemed both incredibly important and insignificant at the same time.

He tipped his glasses so that they rested on the top of his head, buried in his curly hair. "So, you say you're investigating the deaths of Morris and Julia Cutter?"

"That's right."

"Does someone really think that it wasn't a murder-suicide?"

I shrugged. "Just covering all the bases."

"Well, if you think it was a double homicide, you might want to take a look at that crazy nephew. What's his name?"

"Stephen Cutter?"

Mitch snapped his fingers. "That's it."

"How do you know Stephen Cutter?"

He leaned back and clasped his hands behind his head. "Early in December, I was invited to be one of the speakers at a No Offshore Drilling Rally in Greenwich, Connecticut. Some of the most vocal attendees were from an organization called Gaea. Have you heard of them?"

"I have. I've heard them described as extremists."

He chuckled. "They're batshit crazy. One of them stood up and screamed that I wasn't doing enough. He demanded that I go to Capitol Hill on the day Morris Cutter from CP&G delivered some bogus report to Congress to dispute the findings."

"Let me guess. It was Stephen Cutter?"

Mitch nodded. "Sure was. His face was beet-red as he shouted at me. He was so upset that I could see spit coming out of his mouth."

"I've met him. He can be passionate."

"He can be a lunatic."

"Did they know the exact day Morris Cutter was supposed to address Congress?"

"Oh, yeah. Can't recall the date, but it was scheduled for a couple of days after the New Year."

"So, they knew about the report and when he was going to deliver it on Capitol Hill. That was all supposed to be pretty hush-hush."

He shrugged. "They knew."

I sat back in my chair. "How extreme is Gaea?"

"They give environmentalists a bad name. For them, the end justifies the means."

"Is there somebody running the show?"

He smiled, opened his computer back up, and punched in a web address. Then he turned the laptop to face me. On his screen was the colorful Gaea home page. The dominant image was a massive ice sheet breaking off from a glacier. Two smaller images were of an emaciated polar bear on an iceless terrain, and a massive blaze in the Amazon forest.

At the very top, a mission statement proclaimed, "Gaea is a worldwide, nongovernmental organization dedicated to shining a light on global environmental problems and fighting for their solutions."

Mitch spoke up. "They have their own public relations and communications team, their own lobbying department, and a fundraising arm. Gaea is a very organized, well-run organization." He moved his cursor and hit a button, pulling up the staff page. The photo at the top was of a man in his early thirties with a mop of jet-black hair. His ice-blue eyes were overshadowed by heavy eyebrows. He was smiling into the camera and wearing a white shirt and tie, looking every bit like an average corporate executive.

Not like a terrorist at all.

Mitch pointed to the man. "That's Warren Tarr. He comes from a blue-collar family, put himself through Harvard Business School, started a tech firm, sold it for a gazillion dollars, and now he runs Gaea."

"Have you ever met him?"

"He was at that same event where Cutter verbally attacked me."

"Did Warren Tarr say anything?"

Mitch took a breath. "Cold son of a bitch just stood in the back of the room, smiling at me. We're supposed to be on the same side."

I leaned forward. "Have you ever heard of a Dr. Stuart Ekmann?"

He frowned. "He's the lead dog on the oil company's study."

"Is he legit?"

He glanced up at the ceiling, then back at me. "Unfortunately, he is. He's got a solid reputation, but from what I hear in the rumor mill, he's up to his ass in debt and CP&G is paying him a butt-load of money to furnish them a study to give to Congress."

"He's missing."

Mitch's eyebrows shot up. "No shit."

"Do you think that Gaea is capable of kidnapping?"

He cocked his head to one side. "I wouldn't put it past them."

"How about torture?"

"I don't know."

"Murder?"

He leaned in. His face was serious. "I don't know about Gaea. But piss off Stephen Cutter enough, and I bet he could kill someone."

Chapter Twenty-Three

Before I left Mitch's office, I wrote down the address and the phone number of Gaea's home office. Taking the stairs, I got to the ground floor, stopping just inside the doorway to make the call.

I was mildly surprised when a human answered instead of a machine. A woman asked, "You've reached Gaea. How can I direct your call?"

"My name is Geneva Chase. I'm a freelance reporter working on a story about how sea-level rise might affect metropolitan New York. Might I speak to Mr. Warren Tarr?"

Without another word, Kenny G began playing as I waited, gazing out the glass door at students rushing between buildings to make their classes. Finally, a deeper voice came on the line. "Yes, this is Warren Tarr. How can I help you?"

"Mr. Tarr, my name is Geneva Chase, and I'm working on a piece about sea-level rise and what Manhattan should be doing to get ready for it."

His voice warmed as his enthusiasm level rose. "You mean other than move inland? Actually, you're working on a great story, Miss Chase. When would you like to chat?"

I really wanted to do it in person. I glanced at my watch. It was nearly two in the afternoon. "I'm at Columbia University right at the moment. I could be at your office in about twenty minutes. Would that work?"

"Of course, I'll make time. Do you know where we are?"

"According to your website, you're in the MetLife Building."

"Ninth floor. I'll tell security downstairs to expect you."

—

Compared to the offices of CP&G, Gaea could, at best, be described as modest. The organization's reception area was populated by a simple metal desk and two upholstered chairs that you might see in the waiting room of an insurance office. Obviously expecting me, a young woman with curly red hair and huge glasses came around the desk and greeted me. "Are you Geneva Chase?"

"I'm here to see Mr. Tarr."

She smiled. "Come with me, please."

She escorted me through a doorway into a large office area, filled with twenty or so cubicles. The only sounds were clattering keyboards as people typed and quiet voices on phones. Up on the walls were silent, large-screen televisions tuned to either CNN or MSNBC.

As we walked, I wondered if Stephen Cutter was in one of those cubicles.

We entered a short hallway, and the woman opened a door. She ushered me in, and I recognized Tarr right away from his photo on the website. He stood up, came to the doorway, and held out his hand. "Miss Chase, it's very nice to meet you."

He was slightly shorter than me and wore black-rimmed glasses behind which his heavy, dark eyebrows rose and fell like two caterpillars clinging to his face just above his pale blue eyes. He had on black jeans, sneakers, and a simple V-neck sweater.

We shook hands. "Thank you for taking the time, Mr. Tarr."

He held up a hand. "Call me Warren. Please, sit down."

His office wasn't much bigger than the lobby, but it did have a window that looked out over Park Avenue. The walls were adorned with framed photos of glaciers fracturing into the ocean, fires raging in Australia, a flooded street that looked like Charleston, and a raging hurricane tearing the roof off a house. On his desktop were a simple laptop, a notebook, and his cell phone. There were two chairs, similar to the ones in the lobby, in front of his desk, reserved for visitors.

A brass desk plate simply stated, "It's life or death."

I sat down, and Warren did the same.

He leaned forward. "So, you want to talk to me about sea-level rise."

I smiled at him as sweetly as I could. "Actually, I fibbed."

He sat back in his chair. "Oh?"

"I'm doing a piece on the report that CP&G is planning to give Congress on Friday. The Ekmann Study?"

His eyes narrowed. "Who are you, really?"

"I really am a freelance journalist. How much of the science in that study is flawed? It *is* flawed, isn't it?"

For a moment, I thought he was going to spit on the floor. Then he took a breath and said, "The study is all lies. What are you up to, Miss Chase?"

"Just trying to get the truth, Mr. Tarr. How much do you know about the Ekmann Study?"

"As much as I need to. There are some employees at the evil empire who are sympathetic to our cause. I know that Darren Reed is supposed to be presenting it to Congress on Friday. Hell, I knew when Morris Cutter was supposed to present it back in

January. Blowing his brains out put the brakes on that. We can only hope that Darren Reed does the same."

I could almost feel the heat of his hostility.

The slightest hint of a devious smile played across his lips. "I also know that you're not a reporter anymore, Geneva Chase." He nodded toward his laptop. "After you called, I Googled you and up popped the story in yesterday's *New York Daily News*. Someone hired you to look into the deaths of the Cutters."

Goddamned internet.

I asked, "Do you think it was a murder-suicide?"

"It doesn't matter, does it? It was justice. Justice for what he's done to the planet. He deserved to die."

"What about Julia Cutter?"

He sneered. "Collateral damage."

"Do you think someone killed them?"

Warren frowned. "That's not what the police say, is it?"

"If you had the chance, would you have killed him?" I could hear the belligerence in my own voice.

He didn't answer. Instead, he asked his own question in a voice that was thick with malevolence. "Do you know where Dr. Stuart Ekmann is?"

That was the question that Nathaniel's torturers had asked him over and over as they broke his fingers and beat the hell out of him. "I was going to ask you the same thing. Execs at CP&G think that your organization kidnapped him to stall the presentation to Congress."

"Miss Chase, you offend me. First you ask me if I could murder someone, and then, in the same breath, you accuse me of kidnapping."

I could feel my anger rise. "Someone tortured my boss because they think he knows where Dr. Ekmann is."

"Nathaniel Rubin?"

Like you didn't know.

I nodded.

"Someone tortured him?" He stopped for a moment, thinking. "I'm truly sorry to hear that. Nathaniel Rubin used to be a hell of a journalist when he was with the *Times*. Did some decent reporting on the oil industry. Now, I don't know what side he's on. I'm betting he's on the side with the most money. In the end, everyone sells out."

I glared at him. "How about you? I hear you did well when you sold your tech company."

He made a production of studying his surroundings. "Does my office look like the office of fat cat? Anything I made from the sale of my company I've plowed back into this organization."

I glanced down at the desk plate. I pointed at it. "What's that mean, 'It's life or death'?"

He clasped his hands on the top of his desk. "It means there are no second chances. Let's be clear. We're in a war where, if we lose, it will result in nothing less than the apocalypse. We don't have a backup planet. It means what it says. This is life or death."

"Any idea who busted up my boss?"

Warren ran a hand through his mop of hair, nodding. "Fascist petrochemical storm troopers."

"You know that for a fact?"

"Who else would it be?"

"I was kind of leaning toward you."

He slowly shook his head and smiled. "Not my style. Plus, I used to like Mr. Rubin." He checked his watch and held a single finger in the air. "However, if you really are looking for a story, as we speak, there's one unfolding in the offices of Continental Petroleum & Gas."

———

By the time I got back to the busy street, I'd received an alert on my phone telling me there was breaking news. I read the brief story on my screen: "CP&G offices evacuated after bomb explodes. Number of injured unknown."

Jesus Christ.

Was that what Warren Tarr had been talking about?

Only a few blocks away, I rushed to the Park Avenue address and arrived at a scene of complete chaos. The street was cordoned off, police units blocked the streets, fire trucks were in front of the building, New York cops attempted to create order out of the milling crowd, and EMTs stationed at ambulances treated the injured.

Protestors, no longer chanting, stared at the street scene from behind police tape in shocked silence.

I spotted Parker Lewis huddled with Darren Reed and two of their security people standing near one of the police cruisers. I maneuvered my way over to them.

The beefiest security guy bullied his way forward and blocked my way. Parker Lewis put his hand on the man's shoulder and motioned that I should come closer.

Honestly concerned, I asked, "Are you guys all right?"

Parker nodded but he was obviously rattled. His face was pale, and his eyes were wide. He'd left in a hurry, without even his suit coat to help ward off the damp chill in the air. His voice was shaky. "We thought it was a bomb."

Darren stared hard at me and sneered. "Police say it was a percussion grenade and a tear gas canister. They think someone managed to sneak them in past security and set them off remotely in two separate trash cans. If I ever find out that one my people helped sneak that shit into our office, I'll crucify them."

A third security guy scurried up to us with two folded blankets he'd managed to scrounge from the EMTs. Deferentially, he draped one over Darren's shoulders, then did the same with Parker, who nodded at him thankfully.

Parker stared at the scene in front of us. "Poor Mrs. Hardesty in Accounting went into cardiac arrest, and three of our staff are being treated for respiratory complications from breathing in the tear gas."

Ignoring Parker's inventory of the wounded, the CEO continued his tirade, his voice getting louder with every word. "Nobody gets in or out of our offices without a visual check from our security team. It's got to be one of our own people. Whoever it is, I'm gonna fuckin' have 'em shot."

Darren's angry outburst not only took me by surprise, but from the stunned expression on his face, I saw it did the same to Parker. He whispered something in Darren's ear, and the CEO nodded in agreement.

Probably advised him to cool down.

I thought back to only minutes ago: Warren Tarr, the executive director of Gaea, smiling and telling me there was "a story unfolding at the CP&G office."

That little prick knew exactly what was going to happen.

Looking at Parker, who seemed to be the more rational of the two, I asked, "Any idea who might have been behind this?"

He reached out from under his blanket and nervously stroked his mustache. When he spoke, his words were clipped. "Oh, it was a terrorist attack from one of those climate groups. Most likely those bastards at Gaea."

Then Darren stepped up close to me and whispered, "Have you closed your damned investigation yet?"

I shook my head slightly and stepped back.

His eyes, still red and tearing from the gas, burned into my own as he said, "I got a call from an associate of yours, John Stillwater from Lodestar Analytics. He was asking what I knew about the kidnapping and torture of Nathaniel Rubin. Know what I told him?"

"What?"

"It wasn't me or my people. Because if it had been, he'd be dead instead of lyin' in the hospital."

Chapter Twenty-Four

It was nearly six o'clock by the time my train rolled into South Sheffield, and my stomach was rumbling. Walking through the parking lot to my car, I realized that I hadn't gotten a call from John Stillwater about dinner.

Shana had warned me about how focused he was when he was on a project.

Shit, did he forget about me?

I considered calling him, but then decided that I still had my pride. Screw him. I'd get takeout for Caroline and me.

As I carried the Mediterranean quinoa salads I'd gotten from the Fresh Source Cafe into the house, Tucker bounded up to me, tongue lolling, tail whipping back and forth almost too fast to see. "Hey, buddy, is Caroline home?"

In answer, she came down the steps wearing lavender-colored sweats and her fuzzy slippers. "Hey, Genie."

"How was your day?" I put the paper bag on the counter in the kitchen, then went and hung my coat up in the hall closet. "Everything good at school?"

She opened up the bag and inspected the dinner I'd brought home. "Same old, same old." Caroline looked up at me. "Hey, this looks pretty good."

"It has grilled chicken and veggies and all kinds of healthy stuff."

She frowned. "I'll eat it anyway."

"Clown."

"I finished my piece for the *Clarion*."

"Your school newspaper?"

She sat down at the table. "Yeah, want to read it?"

"You bet."

"I'll email it to you."

I took a glass down from the cupboard and walked over to the refrigerator. "Awesome. Anything new with your boyfriend?"

Caroline blushed. "He's just a friend."

"Who's taking you out on a date?"

She changed the subject. "Anyway, Brandon and Justin are still getting on everyone's nerves."

I opened the freezer and took out a couple of ice cubes, dropping them tinkling into the glass. I turned and gave her a look, letting her know I didn't understand.

Caroline continued. "They've got this inside joke now where every time they pass by a girl in the hall, they ask her if she's a slut, bitch, or a whore. Low enough to just barely be heard. They think they're being funny."

"I'm not laughing."

"This afternoon, Tyler was walking with me to Chem Lab and he heard them say that to me. He turned around and shouted, 'What did you say?'"

This doesn't sound good.

I ran the tap and filled my glass. "What happened?"

"They kept on walking, but Brandon flipped Tyler the bird and hollered, 'You heard me, faggot.'

"Tyler started after them, but I grabbed him by the back of his shirt and held him up. After getting into a fight the other day, he didn't need any more detention."

"I'm proud of you, baby."

She smiled and puffed out her chest. "I'm not only hot, but I'm smart, too."

"Those boys sound awful."

She grinned. "Well, I won't have to worry about them for the rest of the week."

"Why not?"

Caroline leaned down and picked up Tucker, then sat back down at the table and put him on her lap. "They smarted off to our chemistry teacher, Mrs. Ripley. They've been suspended for the rest of the week."

Good. They sound like punks.

"Have you met Tyler's parents yet?"

"Just his mom. His dad's dead. Car accident." She looked away from me.

Oh, my God. That explains it.

Up until Tyler Greenwood, Caroline's interest in boys had been little more than curiosity mixed with disdain and sarcasm. But with this boy, things were different.

Caroline's father had died in a car crash when she was only thirteen. It left an awful psychological scar. Since Tyler's father had died in the same horrible way, their shared grief must have become an attraction for each other.

I studied her for a moment while her full attention was on rubbing Tucker behind the ears. I know she suffered from bouts of depression. We'd seen Dr. Tina, a therapist, off and on over the last two years. I admired Caroline's strength, but I also knew that she was only fifteen years old and, after losing both her mother and father, had seen enough tragedy to last her for a long time.

I moved on. "Does his mother work?"

Caroline glanced up at me. "She's an RN. Works at Sheffield General. A lot of long hours."

I sat down at the table and took off my shoes. After spending the day in the city, my feet were screaming at me. I rubbed them thinking about how nice a hot shower would feel. "Think we should have them over for dinner some night?"

"That would be really nice. I'm pretty sure, once you get to know him, you'll like Tyler."

As long as he stays out of your bedroom.

I was about to go upstairs and change clothes when my cell phone went off. I was surprised to see that it was John Stillwater. I heard my voice go low and sexy. "Hi, John."

Caroline shot me a quizzical expression.

John cleared his throat. "Hi, Genie. Sorry I'm calling so late. Still interested in dinner tonight?"

I glanced at the bag sitting on the counter holding two containers of salad. "Sure. When and where?"

"I'm thinking seven thirty, but you have to tell me where. I don't know the area as well as you do."

"Where are you staying?"

"The Hilton Garden Inn."

"There's a place right next door, Casa San Carlo."

"Sounds Italian. I love it. See you there."

Casa San Carlo is in a strip center on Route 7. The interior is cozy, all dark wood, Tiffany lamps, and paintings of the Italian countryside mounted on the walls. The food was always excellent, and if I remembered correctly, the waitstaff was efficient and courteous.

But I hadn't chosen the restaurant for the ambience, the service, or the cuisine.

I'd picked it because it was within walking distance of John's hotel.

———

After I apologized to Caroline for leaving her alone for dinner, I took that nice hot shower, shaved my legs, and took my time with my makeup and hair. Studying my closet, I finally decided on an off-the-shoulder white blouse. Knowing that John would most likely be wearing jeans, I chose a modest denim skirt, finishing the look with simple gold hoop earrings, rope necklace, and bracelet.

It might have been mid-February and a skirt might not have been the most practical choice, but I wanted to look nice. The off-the-shoulder blouse? Yes, I wanted to look mildly sexy.

I added the dreaded heels. After a long day in the city, they were the last thing I wanted on my feet. But when I'm wearing them, I'm positively statuesque.

I know because it's what I've been called and, hey, I own a mirror.

———

John was in the restaurant when I arrived. He was seated at a table in the corner, facing the front door, his back to the wall. Shadows from the candlelight played across his strong jaw and handsome face, giving his appearance an air of mystery. Seeing him there made my heart vibrate.

I walked across the dining area, luxuriating in the smells of warm bread, tomato sauce, rosemary, and garlic, all mingling with the vague smoky scent from the wood-fired pizza oven. I barely glanced at the other diners, who were concentrating on their plates of pasta, conducting their quiet conversations.

My attention was focused on John Stillwater.

He spotted me, adjusted his glasses, smiled, and stood up, putting his arms out. I let him envelop me and felt his warm lips kiss me gently on the cheek.

He helped me out of my coat, and I thought I could feel his eyes linger on me longer than they would have if we were just friends. It felt like hundreds of butterfly wings were fluttering in my chest.

After he hung my coat on a hook on the wall next to his leather jacket, he pulled out my chair, and then we sat down. Before we could start our conversation, a young woman in black slacks, black long-sleeved blouse, and apron, stopped at our table to take our drink order. John deferred to me.

I ordered a club soda and lemon.

Thank you for being in my head, Shana Neese.

John studied me for a moment and asked for the same.

Elbows on the table, chin in my hand, I gazed across the candlelit table at John and asked, "Have you found out who hurt Nathaniel?"

"I've still got my money on Fisher, Evans, and Sinclair. I've done a little research. It seems they have quite the reputation for behind-the-scenes blackmail, extortion, and bribery."

"They tried to bribe me."

John's eyebrows shot up.

I continued, "Offered me a half a million dollars to wind up my investigation by Thursday. They don't want it hanging over Darren Reed's presentation to Congress on Friday."

"That's a lot of money."

I frowned. "It's not the first time in my career that someone's tried to buy me off."

"That only makes me lean farther in their direction."

I gazed at him. "I wouldn't be so sure. A percussion grenade and a tear gas canister went off in the offices of CP&G today. I'm certain that Gaea was behind it. CP&G describes them as terrorists. Even Homeland Security has them on their terrorist list."

He glanced around the room, checking to see if anyone was within earshot. "Let's talk about that for a minute. Why do you suppose Gaea wants to find this Ekmann guy?"

"I don't know. Maybe to coerce him into disavowing his study?"

He took his glasses off and peered through them in the candlelight. Then he put them back on. "Possibly. Why does CP&G want him back so badly? They have the study. They really don't need the doctor anymore, do they?"

"More than once I've heard that Gaea has someone inside CP&G. There's a rumor that Ekmann might have been having second thoughts about the study."

John scowled.

I shrugged. "When I did some research on him, I found out that his son died fighting a wildfire in California last fall. Maybe Ekmann blamed climate change."

He nodded slightly. "So, you think that CP&G might want to keep him out of the limelight while they're presenting his study to Congress?"

I glanced at the bar, wondering where our club sodas were. "Could be." I changed the subject. "How's Nathaniel doing?"

"They did some real damage to him. Shana hopes that as he recovers, he'll remember more details that will help us find the scumbags."

The waitress brought our club sodas and asked if we were ready to order. John asked for a few more minutes. After she drifted off, I held my glass up. "Cheers, it's good to see you again."

We clinked glasses and John answered, "You too."

I took a sip of my club soda. "So, what's their deal?"

He took a swallow of his own and wiped his lips with his napkin. "Deal?"

"Shana and Nathaniel?"

John gave me an enigmatic smile. "Ask Shana."

I shifted gears. "Where have you been for the last month?"

"Undercover in rural Georgia. About fifty miles from Atlanta. Shana had me down there to bust up a sex trafficking operation."

I waited for more details, but I knew I'd never hear them. I took another sip of my club soda during the awkward silence.

John asked, "How is *your* investigation coming along?"

I shrugged again. "It's frustrating. A lot of circumstantial evidence and gossip. A ton of gossip."

"*Verum de rumoribus.*"

Still holding my glass, I asked, "What?"

"Truth out of gossip."

"Seriously? What is that, Latin?"

John pulled his glasses down low on his nose and gazed over the top of the rims at me. He appeared very professorial. "When I was NYPD, my first watch commander would say that when a rumor or a tip we heard out on the street turned out to be the truth."

"You could have kept me guessing. You know, smart is the new sexy."

He reached out and took my hand. I felt my face flush. John whispered, "I can pretend to be smart."

My voice got low and smoky. "Oh, honey, all I know is you don't have to pretend to be sexy."

———

We hardly got through dinner before we found ourselves in the parking lot of the restaurant. I could see his hotel just up the block. I felt my heart pounding and my blood warming.

He reached for my hand, and we leaned in and kissed, long and hard. We pulled apart for a moment, then I pressed myself against him, and we kissed again.

When we came up for air, John gazed into my eyes. "Genie, look, I think you know I'm attracted to you."

I hear a "but" in there.

"And I hope you don't take this the wrong way." His gaze was still locked onto my eyes. "But with Nathaniel in the hospital, I'm not sure I can give you my undivided attention. When we do this, I want it to be special."

I blinked.

Are you gay?

I didn't ask that. Instead I feigned empathy. "I understand. I don't want you thinking I'm some kind of slut that would sleep with a man on the first date, anyway."

He smiled. "Oh, I would never think that." Then he kissed me again, and I practically melted against his body.

Shana had warned me. She'd told me how focused John was when he was working a case.

Then he took a deep breath and whispered, "The hell with it, let's go to the hotel."

———

It was a little after ten thirty when I walked through the front door of our house and was welcomed by Caroline coming out of the kitchen. She glanced up at the clock on the wall. "Gettin' home a little late, aren't we?"

She had a slight grin on her face.

Shit, she knows what I've been doing.

"We lingered over our coffees after dinner."

"Right." Her voice wasn't convincing. "Have you had a chance to look at the piece I did for the school paper?"

I hadn't. John had been a thorough but welcome distraction. "I'll do it now."

In my bedroom, I suddenly had the urge to open my panty drawer and pour a glass of Absolut.

Instead, I took a deep breath and recalled John's lips on mine. Then his mouth exploring my body, my mouth exploring his.

Neither of us in control. Both of us lost in our lust.

I shivered at the thought of him on top of me, then me on top of him.

Control, now. No drink.

I closed my eyes and sighed. Then I opened my laptop and pulled up the email that Caroline had sent. Her piece on active shooter preparedness was about three thousand words and was well researched and concisely written. I would have expected no less from her.

But it was also heartbreaking. She talked about recent school shootings and the staggering numbers of dead students and teachers, hundreds of them, since Columbine. The list was horrifying— Sandy Hook, Marjory Stoneman Douglas High School, Santa Fe High School, Virginia Tech. The list seemed to go on and on.

Then she described what the Sheffield Police Department and the public school system were doing to prepare for that nightmare, including lockdowns, police response drills, discussions about running, hiding, and fighting.

She interviewed some of her classmates and teachers to chronicle their feelings about having to contend with the possibility that a shooting could happen at their high school.

One student said, "Every time we do a lockdown drill, my stomach hurts really bad and I can't sleep for days after."

Another described a feeling of hopelessness. "I know it's going to happen here. I just don't know when. It's the waiting that's the hardest."

A teacher told her, "We're as ready as we can be. I'm just sorry for all of you students that you even have to think about this."

I finished her piece and took a deep breath. She'd been dispassionate in her prose, evenhanded. There was no mention of gun control or background checks or outlawing semiautomatic weapons. Just an overview of the horror and the emotional toll.

I walked down the hallway, went into her room where she was already tucked into bed but still awake. Caroline was in the middle of texting someone on her cell phone. I sat down on her bed next to her.

She looked up at me. "Are you okay, Genie?"

I could feel tears burning my eyes. I leaned over and hugged her. "I love you so much."

Then she moved closer and whispered into my ear, "You smell like a man's cologne."

Chapter Twenty-Five

Since the beginning of the year, three or four mornings a week, I went for a run down to the harbor and back, roughly four miles. That Thursday morning was one of those days. I put on leggings, a sweatshirt, and running shoes. The last item of clothing I donned was a Boston Red Sox baseball cap to hide my witchy bedhead hair. There was no telling who I might bump into. Hell, John's hotel was only a few blocks from where I ran. I didn't want him looking out his window and seeing me dash by looking like I'd just rolled out of bed.

I shivered slightly at the thought of being naked and in bed with him.

That time of the morning, it was still dark and the air was crisp. A full moon was partially hidden by the horizon, and the only light came from streetlamps along the road, deserted except for the occasional parked car. I stretched and then started off at a trot. As I warmed up, I picked up my pace.

I've tried wearing earbuds and listening to music when I run but discovered that I like hearing the cadence of my running shoes against the road instead. It is like a hypnotic metronome of my own making, my body achieving its rhythm.

Along the waterfront, the sky was slowly brightening to a dull gray. The water was window-glass calm, the early morning quiet.

I was alone with my thoughts. I pictured John as he'd slowly helped me out of my clothes, then as he stripped off his own. How his warm, muscular body felt next to my own.

Reaching my halfway point, my mind shifted to Nathaniel, beaten, bandaged, and bruised, in the hospital. Somebody had wanted Ekmann bad enough to mercilessly savage the hell out of him.

I hope John finds out who did it.

Then I thought about my investigation. If Morris Cutter hadn't shot his wife and himself, who did?

Julia's ex-lover, who had access to a house key and access to the alarm code? I recalled how Paul Marston had picked up his handgun as we talked in his dark living room.

Combine anger issues with being a jilted lover?

He was on my short list.

Then I considered Stephen Cutter and thought about my meeting with Warren Tarr, the creepy executive director of Gaea. I considered how his organization had shut down refineries and blew up pipelines. And the chaotic scene outside the offices of CP&G after the tear gas had gone off.

Was Warren Tarr responsible for hurting Nathaniel? And did he have Stephen murder Morris and Julia Cutter to delay the presentation of the Ekmann Study?

Or did Stephen do it on his own? Payback for what Morris did to Stephen's father?

And then Lisa Cutter popped into my mind. She had motive—a hefty inheritance—and she'd also want to have the Ekmann Study delayed.

Then with a jolt, I realized it was Thursday. Fisher, Evans, and Sinclair, as well as Darren Reed, had made it quite clear that they wanted my investigation tied up by the end of the day. Reed was scheduled to present the Ekmann Study on Capitol Hill the next day.

Shadow Hill.

Feeling the burn in my thighs and calves, I was nearing Hawthorne Avenue, ready to turn the corner to start my run back home, when I heard tires crunching ice crystals somewhere behind me, faint at first, but growing louder and moving fast.

I glanced behind me to see an SUV bearing down on me.

Then it braked hard, skidding.

I stopped to take a look.

A man got out of the passenger's side and started to run toward me.

He was wearing a ski mask.

Adrenaline hit my bloodstream like a bomb.

Run, Genie.

My legs pumped, running hard. Behind me, pounding footsteps, closing fast.

I sprinted flat out, heart thumping, lungs sucking air.

Suddenly, hands on my back, I was pushed forward, rough. Shoved off balance, my body flying through the air, the ground rushed toward my face. I reached out to cushion my landing, scraping my hands across the cold cement, landing hard, air driven out of me.

Someone had their hands on the back of my collar, pulling me back up to my feet, jerking me back around like a puppet to face him.

"Where's Ekmann?" The man was big, over six-five, dressed in a black jacket, ski mask covering his face.

All I could do was gulp for air.

One hand held my shirt, he raised his other hand in the air, as if swearing an oath. "Where's Ekmann?"

I blinked.

When his hand hit my face, colors flashed and swirled in front of my eyes, my cheekbone went numb.

Then my face felt like it was on fire.

I struggled against the meaty fist that held the front of my shirt.

What did Shana teach you? Don't think, do.

He raised his arm again. "Where's Ekmann?"

Words caught in my throat.

Hand rushing toward me, I blocked the blow with my forearm, jerked my knee up hard into his crotch. Bringing my foot down, I raked the heel of my running shoe down the length of his shin.

He grunted, let go of my shirt, and staggered backward.

A woman's voice, off to my left, screamed from the doorway of one of the darkened houses. "Hey, are you okay? I just dialed 911."

The driver's side of the SUV opened and a man shouted, "Get back in the damned car."

The man in the ski mask backed up and limped to the SUV. When the doors were closed, the vehicle quickly turned in the middle of the street and, engine roaring, sped away.

My eyes, fuzzy from the slap to my head, couldn't read the license number, but I could make out that it was a black Lincoln Navigator.

The woman's voice shouted, "The cops are on the way. Do you need help?"

My head swam, and I knew that I was most likely feeling the effects of shock. But I didn't want the cops to slow down my day with a lot of useless questions, and I sure as hell didn't want to deal with EMTs.

I held up my hand. I managed to gasp out a couple of breathless words. "I'm fine."

I walked, gingerly at first, then faster, up the street, past the woman in the doorway who openly stared at me. Then I turned the corner, hearing the police siren in the distance.

I froze, eyes straining.

What if those two thugs were parked up ahead, waiting for me?

If I could hear the siren, then they would as well. The last thing those thugs wanted was to get stopped by the cops.

Wary, I walked the rest of the way to my house.

When I limped through the door, Caroline was in the kitchen. Hearing me come in, she called out, "Go for a run?"

"Yeah," I answered, but the fear and tension in my voice gave me away.

Caroline came out of the kitchen holding a slice of toast. "Jesus Christ, Genie. Are you okay?" She came closer and examined the right side of my face. Then she saw the red scrapes, smeared with blood, on the palms of my open hands. "What happened?"

I gently touched the bruised area under my eye with the tips of my fingers. My voice got stronger as I got angrier. "Somebody jumped me."

She covered her mouth in shock. "Oh, my God. What did he want? Are you okay? Should I call 911?"

I shook my head. "No, I'm fine. I just need to clean up."

Her voice got higher. "Did he try to rape you?"

I glanced at the worry in her eyes. I shook my head and attempted a weak smile. "Believe it or not, I beat the son of a bitch off."

"I believe it." Caroline gingerly reached out and lightly touched the darkening bruise on my face. "I think I have some makeup that might cover that."

I nodded. "I *know* I have makeup that'll do the trick." I started to go into the kitchen but stopped. I fixed her in my eyesight,

"That piece you wrote for the paper is outstanding. I'm so proud of you. Have I told you that?"

She threw her arms around me and we hugged.

I washed my hands in the kitchen sink, dried them with a paper towel, and was gratified that my hands hadn't taken any more serious damage than some scrapes. Then I gently picked up a cup of coffee and went upstairs, stripped down, and stood in front of the mirror. I was going to have a hell of a shiner, and I could see angry red and purple bruises forming on both knees where I'd come down on the road. Another bruise was darkening on my forearm where I'd blocked his hand.

Hands shaking, I wondered how far that bastard would have gone. Was it one of the same goons who worked over Nathaniel?

I was going to have to call Shana Neese and thank her for the self-defense lesson.

I took a steaming hot shower, closed my eyes, and meditated under the spray. Shana's voice was in my head. *Control your breathing. Control your mind. You're in control. Always be in control.*

Even so, I could still feel that man's hand on the front of my shirt and see his hand in the air. *"Where's Ekmann?"*

Control your breathing. Control your mind. Control your breathing.

"Where's Ekmann?"

I opened my eyes and hissed, "Fuck you."

———

John's voice was steady, but I heard concern in his words. "Do you want me to stay with you?"

I smiled and talked into my phone. I'd called him just to hear his voice. "No, but I appreciate it. I'd much rather you find out who's behind this."

"If they came at you once, they'll do it again."

"I'll be fine," I said with more bravado than I really felt.

Then he took a breath and said, "Before you go, I want to thank you for last night."

I smiled. "It's a renewable resource."

Chapter Twenty-Six

An hour later, I was going door-to-door in the Cutter neighborhood, looking for homes with video surveillance that had a view of the road leading to the cul-de-sac where Morris and Julia Cutter had lived. Nobody was home at the first three houses I went to, but I was certain that I was on camera as I stood at their front doors. Everyone in an expensive home has surveillance these days.

Hell, Amazon has made it affordable even for folks like me.

The fourth house I stopped at was where I hit pay dirt. It was only a short drive from the Cutter house. The front doorway had a clear view of the road. I could only pray that they had a camera positioned that would help me.

The tree-lined driveway was straight and relatively short. I pulled up in front of the five-car garage.

Before I got out of the car, I took out my phone and looked up the address of the five-bedroom, brick Georgian-style home to see who might own it. I saw that it had been sold five years before for a little over six million dollars to the Lancaster Corporation.

It took me another few minutes to find out that was the name of a shell company owned by Gwen Allman, the star of the 1960s hit television show *Meet the Bakers*. The photo on the Wikipedia page showed a young woman with a head of raven-colored curls, huge brown eyes, pouty lips, freckles, and a pixie smile.

I guessed that she must have been in her twenties when that photo had been taken on the set of her TV show. That would mean she was now in her seventies.

I zipped up the front of my coat when I stepped out of my Sebring. The morning chill had evolved into a sustained, icy breeze. The wind jostled the limbs of the bare trees above me.

I pushed the doorbell and waited just a few moments before a tall, slim woman wearing black slacks and a dark-blue cashmere sweater opened the door. She had the same brown eyes as in the early photo from the sixties, and her hair was still black as coal, but her face was obviously different. Her mouth seemed too wide, her lips too plump, the skin on her face too taut—almost as if she was wearing a mask.

One too many face-lifts?

Standing just behind Gwen Allman was an Asian woman, in her fifties, with graying hair, dressed in a light-blue shift and a white apron.

Gwen turned on her flats and started past the curved stairway ahead of us. Without looking back, she sang out in a loud voice, "This way."

Thoroughly confused, I walked past the woman I assumed was the maid and followed the actress. We went through the tiled foyer, into the sunken living area that was beautifully appointed with exquisite furniture, floor-to-ceiling windows, and modern art on the walls.

Then she led me down a short hallway until we arrived at our destination. The woman opened the door and gestured for me to go in.

It was a spacious man-cave complete with three big-screen

television monitors on the walls, two pinball machines with multicolored lights silently flashing on and off, a stainless-steel refrigerator, and a billiard table dominating the center of the room.

What jolted me the most was the display of four game fish mounted on one of the walls. Fishing trophies like the ones in Morris Cutter's study.

The woman sniffed the air. "This is the room I told you about. I want it gutted and redecorated the way we discussed. The two questions I need answered are how long will it take and how much will it cost?"

I turned around and looked at her as she stood behind me just inside the doorway. "I think there might be some confusion here. I'm investigating the deaths of Morris and Julia Cutter."

The haughty expression she wore fell immediately, replaced by shock and embarrassment. "Oh, my God. You're not Patti Spillane?"

I offered up a weak smile. "I'm Geneva Chase. I'm guessing you're Gwen Allman. I used to watch your show all the time." I didn't add that I'd watched it when it was in reruns when I was a little girl.

"I'm so embarrassed." She had a hand up to her face.

I saw the Asian woman behind her smirk and walk off.

Gwen took her hand away. "I thought you were the interior decorator I hired. I'd only talked to her on the phone. I've never actually met her."

I shook my head. "Sorry. I'm guessing this isn't your favorite room?"

She glanced around her. "No, this was Cochran's. He passed away a month ago. I always hated this room."

"Oh, I'm sorry to hear that. Was Cochran your husband?"

She tried to look sad but didn't quite make it work. "My

fourth. Someone once said that I'm the death of men. Since we know you're not an interior decorator, what *are* you here for?"

I repeated, "I'm investigating the deaths of Morris and Julia Cutter."

She put her hand back to her mouth again. "Why? The police ruled it a murder-suicide."

"Did you know them?"

"Julia and I were friends. I didn't know Morris well, but Cochran did." She pointed toward fish on the wall. "They used to go off fishing together."

"Where did they go fishing?"

"Morris's oil company owns a beach house in North Carolina. When they went, they'd take one of CP&G's private jets." She frowned. "I wouldn't be surprised if they didn't order up some hookers while they were down there."

I frowned. "Is that something your husband would do?"

"Please," she said sarcastically. "The worst invention ever made was Viagra. Old men thinking they're young again just because they can get their peckers hard."

"How about Morris? Was he the same way?"

"Cochran confided in me that he thought Morris had a piece on the side. Young girl he kept in an apartment someplace."

"Did Julia suspect?"

"Of course, she did. She and I talked about it. We both decided that if we didn't want them pawing at us all the time, best to keep quiet and let them have their fun with their little whores." She glanced around the room one more time. "But I'm sure you didn't come to hear me prattle on about extramarital affairs. How can I help you?"

I got right to the point. "Do you have security cameras?"

She offered me a condescending expression. "Of course, I do. Over the front and back doors, and in the garage."

"Does the camera on the front door have a view of the street?"

She thought a moment. "It wasn't meant for that. It's supposed to video anyone who comes to the door. But I supposed it does have a view of the road."

"Is it motion sensitive?"

She waved her hand in the air. "It's so sensitive that if a bird flies by, it shoots video."

"Can I see?"

"Are you with the police?"

I shook my head. "I've been hired by the Cutter estate."

"Good, I don't need the police in here." She leaned closer to me. "I have a secret stash of weed. Don't tell anyone."

"Cross my heart."

"So, you want to see the video. What are you looking for, Miss Chase?"

"Video from the day Morris and Julia died, New Year's. Specifically, that morning. Anyone going to or from the Cutter house would have had to go past your house."

"Follow me." She turned and walked back down the same hallway we'd just come through. I followed her up the curving staircase as she gracefully climbed the steps. It gave me a chance to study just how athletic this seventy-plus woman appeared.

I followed her down another hall until she opened the doorway to what must have been her office. She flicked on a light switch, and I was taken aback by how different it was from the rest of her home.

The rooms I'd seen were sparsely but tastefully furnished. Everything was beautiful and in its place.

Her office, however, was a jumble of overflowing bookshelves, stacks of old newspapers and magazines, and movie memorabilia. The walls were festooned with black-and-white photos of Gwen Allman with such celebrities as Roy Rogers and Dale Evans, Ozzie and Harriet Nelson, as well as the whole cast of *Bonanza*.

A large computer monitor sat on the desktop crowded with notebooks. She sat down at the desk, turned, and looked at me. "Don't judge me. I'm working on my memoirs. This is the one room in the house I enjoy myself in. I'm not trying to impress anyone here."

She faced the computer and brought up the video security program. Then her fingers slowly moved across the keyboard, punching in the first of January. A video appeared giving us a clear view of her front porch. If you looked hard, you could see the street.

She sighed and stood up. "Here you go. Sit down and make yourself comfortable. Would you like some coffee or tea? I can have Mai bring up a cup."

I sat down at the desk chair she'd just vacated. "No, thank you. You've already been very kind."

She started for the door, but her curiosity got the better of her. "You said you're working for the estate?"

I gave her a smile and a nod.

"What exactly are you looking for? It was a murder-suicide, wasn't it? That's what the police said. If I had to guess, Julia had finally told Morris about the gentleman she'd been sleeping with, and he couldn't handle it."

I glanced at her, slightly surprised. "She told you about that?"

"The men have their little secrets, and so do us gals."

"Did Julia ever say anything about being afraid of her man friend?"

She thought for a moment. "She said that one of the reasons she enjoyed him was he had a dark side. She said he's a retired cop."

"Did she say if he ever threatened her?"

"No." She smiled. "But she told me that he liked his sex on

the rough side. She liked it too, as long as it wasn't too rough."
Then she stopped smiling. "It was all good until she broke up
with him. She was afraid that he would tell Morris all about the
affair. She was nervous wreck over it."

I turned back to the monitor. "Thank you."

"I warned her. I told her, Julia, whatever you do, don't let your boy
toys fall in love with you. Makes it harder to kick 'em to the curb."

As she left the room, I wondered if Gwen currently had a
boy toy to play with.

The time stamp on the video had started at first light on
that morning. Annoyingly, it was activated whenever a bird or a
squirrel tripped the motion sensor. Then when the animal was
out of range, the video would stop and the next sequence would
immediately begin.

The first car that tripped the video went by Gwen's house
at a little after eight that morning. I wrote in my tiny notebook
that the car was a Lexus SUV. I knew that particular model sold
for around ninety thousand dollars. I happened to have looked
at it online a few weeks earlier when I was doing a little window
shopping for another vehicle. It was way too rich for my blood.

But it wouldn't be out of place in this neighborhood.

After five minutes of watching a pigeon linger on the front
stoop, another car drove by in the direction of the Cutter house.
This was a red Jeep Wrangler that looked like it had some hard
mileage on it. I guessed it was someone on their way to cook a
rich family's holiday breakfast.

A half an hour later, it drove by in the other direction.

Then, sometime around ten thirty, a third car drove by Gwen
Allman's house in the direction of the Cutter house. A short time
later, the video recorded it driving back.

It was a dark-blue Tesla.

The same as Stephen Cutter's.

Chapter Twenty-Seven

I drove directly from Gwen Allman's house on the exclusive shoreline of Long Island Sound to Easton, where Stephen Cutter and his mother, Delia, lived. On the way I tried to calculate the odds on whether or not the car I saw in the video might actually be Stephen's.

Before I left Gwen's office, I tried to look up how many people owned a Tesla in affluent Fairfield County. That number wasn't available, but I easily discovered that in Connecticut over three thousand people owned the expensive electric sports cars. Interestingly, there was a New England Tesla Owners Club, and there was also a club exclusively for owners in Fairfield County. But no mention of the number of members.

It shouldn't have come as any surprise that the county had its own club. The cars were pricey and trendy, just the kind of toys that the gentry in Fairfield County loved to own.

When I pulled my Sebring up in front of the house, I noticed that Stephen's car wasn't in the driveway. Getting out of my car, I zipped up my coat again. The wind was gusting and the temperature continued to fall.

I glanced at some of the landscaping on the front lawn of

the grand home. Some of the bushes had started to bud in the abnormally warm weather of the past week. I worried what a cold snap might do them.

I trudged up the stone steps onto the porch and rang the bell. The door was answered by an African American woman in her late fifties, dressed in a gray shift and orthopedic shoes. "Can I help you?"

"I'm here to see Stephen Cutter."

She appeared confused. "He's not here right now. Was he expecting you?"

I knew I should have called ahead but the excitement at possibly identifying the car clouded my judgment. "No, he wasn't. Is Delia Cutter in?"

The woman glanced behind her. "Honey, she's always in. She doesn't go anywhere these days except to see her doctors."

I saw there was a logo on the front of the woman's dress. "Are you her caregiver?"

She nodded. "One of them. Would you like to come in out of the cold?"

I stepped into the warmth of the foyer. "Are Mrs. Cutter's health issues serious?"

She glanced again in the direction of the living room. In a low voice she confided, "She's got severe emphysema and a heart condition. Can I take your coat?"

I shimmied out of it and handed it to her. "Was she a smoker?"

She frowned. "Two packs a day. Only quit a few years ago when this came over her."

Suddenly, a cackling voice cried out from the other room. "I can hear you, ya know."

Rolling her eyes, the caregiver said, "Nothin' wrong with her ears."

I walked into the living room where Delia sat in her wheelchair, the television on in front of her, tube running from a green oxygen tank hung from the back of her chair, to her nose. Her rheumy eyes looked at me with suspicion. "You know why I smoked for so long?"

"I don't."

"Sit down, Miss Chase."

I did as I was told and dropped down on the couch, more tired than I realized. Had the trauma of being attacked and assaulted that morning started taking a toll?

"Is that a black eye?"

I reached up to touch the bruise. I'd hoped that my makeup would have better disguised it. "I had an accident this morning."

She frowned. "I believed the cigarette companies, Miss Chase. They swore that smoking was safe. Even when they knew they were killing thousands of people a year. They kept lying to the public. Kept lying to their customers."

I could see the anger rising.

"Berta," she called out.

The caregiver came into the living room. "Yes, Miss Delia?"

"Please bring me some water."

When the woman disappeared, Delia continued. "The government knew. But they never made the damned things illegal. Just let us all keep smoking. Even now, all they've done is force the cigarette companies to print warnings on the packages."

I leaned forward, elbows on my knees. "Is that what the oil companies are doing? Lying about poisoning the planet?"

She slapped a bony hand against the arms of her wheelchair. "Yes, goddamn it. Only those greedy bastards are going to kill us all."

Berta came back into the room with a plastic cup of water and a straw, holding it front of Delia's thin lips so that she could sip at it. "Now, don't get yourself all worked up."

Finished drinking, she waved the woman off. "But you didn't come here to talk about my health. What do you want?"

"I want to hear a little more about your husband, David." I was lying. I wanted to talk about her son, Stephen. But I was afraid that would put her immediately on the defensive.

The hint of smile played about her thin lips. "Why?"

"I'm looking to finish my investigation, and it helps to have as much background information as possible." I set my phone on the coffee table and pressed the recording app.

"He was a good husband and a good father. Stephen adored him."

"I can tell."

"You already know that he was concerned about the environment."

"Did he belong to any conservation or environmental organizations?"

She sat back and studied me. "You mean like the crazies that Stephen works for?"

I shrugged. "Any group."

"He belonged to the Sierra Club, Oceana, and Ducks Unlimited. Maybe a few others that I can't recall."

"But not Gaea."

"I don't think that Gaea was even a thing when David was alive. He probably would have joined them, though. The end justifies the means. I think David would have liked that."

"Did David like the outdoors? You know like camping, hunting, fishing?"

She smiled again, remembering. "Some of my fondest memories are before I got so sick. We used to go hiking and camping. We hiked the Appalachian Trail together. It was autumn. The air was crisp and cool, and the trees were ablaze with color."

"How about hunting and fishing?"

She waved a tiny hand. "He's an Oklahoma boy. They grow

up hunting and fishing. Most hunters are avid conservationists. I'll bet you didn't know that, did you?"

Shaking my head, I answered, "No, I didn't."

She sighed. "One of the things he missed the most when he left CP&G was the hunting trips in the mountains. Of course they sold that lodge when Lisa went missing back when she was little. Scared Morris and Julia half to death. It was all over the news. I actually felt sorry for them."

"Did your husband pass that love of the outdoors along to Stephen?"

She blinked her eyes. "He did. But they didn't share an interest in hunting. Stephen simply doesn't like the idea of killing things."

Does that extend to Morris and Julia Cutter?

"Did your husband own a lot of guns?"

"I already told you he was an Oklahoma boy. Of course he had a lot of guns."

Berta came back into the room. "Stephen just pulled up outside."

The woman grinned. "Good."

I suddenly felt a tiny shiver of apprehension. Was I putting myself in danger by being in that house?

Not wanting to waste my opportunity, I asked, "Are the guns still in the house?"

She blinked. "What?"

"David's guns?"

"Yes, of course. They're all locked in a cabinet. I couldn't make myself get rid of them."

I wanted to ask to see them, perhaps see if there was evidence that one was missing, but Stephen had come into the living room. I could feel the chill coming off him. He had on a parka and was rubbing his hands together. "Getting really cold again out there. Hello, Miss Chase. I saw your car in the driveway."

As he came over to shake my hand, I stood up. "I hope you don't mind that I stopped by again."

He shook off his coat and sat down on one of the overstuffed chairs facing his mother and me. He squinted his eyes as he studied me. "Not at all. Why are you here?"

"I'm just getting some background information about your father." I gestured toward Delia. "She was just telling me how much your father enjoyed the outdoors."

"He loved being outside."

"What I find interesting is your father and his brother Morris grew up together hunting and fishing. Your dad became a conservationist, and Morris...well, didn't."

"It's the money, Miss Chase."

"Please, call me Genie."

"Okay, Genie. Greed corrupted Uncle Morris. In the end, Dad detested him."

"And you felt the same way."

"I still do. The fact that he's dead doesn't change how I feel about him."

Sooner or later, I had to ask the hard questions. I started with a little misdirection. "Did you hear that Gaea blew up the CP&G offices yesterday?"

He grinned. "I heard that somebody had done that. A percussion grenade and tear gas. It's hardly blowing up an office. And Gaea had nothing to do with it."

The way he sat, with his chest puffed out, he was actually proud of what had happened.

"I'm not so sure. I was in Warren Tarr's office yesterday. He tipped me off that something was about to happen at CP&G."

He played coy. "But he didn't say anything about tear gas, did he?"

"No. Have you located Dr. Ekmann?"

He shook his head. "No, but we will."

"Why do you want him? Isn't he the enemy?"

He narrowed his eyes as he stared at me. "He might not be. There's some talk that he's come to his senses about this study CP&G is giving tomorrow."

"And you'd like to have him talking to the press."

Stephen shrugged.

"See this?" I pointed to my black eye. "I got this when some thug attacked me this morning."

He stared at me with a concerned expression. "Oh, my God. Are you okay?"

"I'm good."

"Why were you attacked?"

"Someone thinks I know where Ekmann is."

He face turned grim. "Do you?"

"Was it one of Gaea's people?"

"Of course not."

He'd just lied to me about Gaea's responsibility in the attack on CP&G's office, so why wouldn't he lie about knowing who tried to beat the hell out of me?

I repositioned myself on the couch. "Stephen, where were you on New Year's Day?"

He was silent for a moment as he processed my question. I could tell he was wondering what I knew. Finally, he answered. "Are you accusing me of something?"

"Not at all. Just covering all the bases."

"Are you asking everyone else that question?"

"Yes, I am."

Delia whispered, "You don't have to answer, Stephen."

He held up a hand. "That morning, I got another call from Uncle Morris. He said he wanted to talk again. He said that he wanted to make amends with me and Mother. He asked if I'd drive out to see him before they went to brunch at Eric's house."

Delia closed her eyes. "Stephen."

I asked, "He wanted to reconcile right then?"

"He'd said that it was the New Year, a new beginning. It was time to throw out old ways of thinking and to move forward in a positive way. He said he'd do what he needed to do to make amends." Stephen was quiet for a moment, thinking. "Then he said he wanted to talk to me about the Ekmann Study and his presentation to Congress."

Delia whispered again. "Stephen."

"It's okay, Mom." He fixed me in his gaze, remembering that day. "I had to talk to him. I needed to find out more about the Ekmann Study. The more information we had, the better we could counterattack it."

He stopped for a moment, collecting himself. "It was very cold that morning, a lot like today. When I told Mom about the phone call, she told me not to waste my time, to stay here and stay warm. If Morris really wanted to make things right, he could haul his fat ass over here to do it."

Delia shook her head. "I knew it was wild goose chase."

Stephen bit his lower lip and then continued. "I had to go. Maybe find a way to stop him from making the Ekmann Study public. So, I put on my coat and drove over to their house in Sheffield." He glanced over at me. "But somehow you already knew that."

I nodded. "A neighbor's front door video recorded your Tesla driving by toward their house, then driving back a short time later. What happened when you got to their house?"

He took a breath. "Nothing. They weren't home. Or else they weren't answering the door. I stood outside and rang the bell. It was freezing, and the longer I stood out there, the more pissed off I got. So, I left."

"You never saw them."

"No."

"What time was that?"

"Around eleven thirty."

Is it possible they were already dead?

He stared down at the floor. "I never told anyone I'd been out there. If it had been a double homicide, I knew everyone would blame me. We've never been quiet about how we felt about Uncle Morris. But once it was ruled a murder-suicide, it didn't seem important whether I was out there or not."

I sat back and thought it through.

If Morris had called Stephen, asking him to come to the house on New Year's Day, that would imply that Morris didn't have suicide or murder on his mind at all. But what did he have on his mind?

On the other hand, if Stephen was lying, Morris had let him into the house, and he'd had opportunity to kill both him and Julia.

As I considered what my next question could possibly be, the room fell awkwardly silent.

Stephen narrowed his eyes at me, and his voice got ominously low. "You believe me, don't you?"

Uh-oh.

I mentally measured my distance from the front door. With him between me and the exit, I was trapped. I'd gotten lucky that morning when I surprised my attacker by fighting back. I was certain that I'd never get past Stephen if he didn't want me to leave.

I was also painfully aware that I was the only one, other than him and his mother, who knew he'd been out to the Cutter house on New Year's Day.

Would he try to hurt me in front of his mother? And certainly not in front of the caregiver.

I lied. "Why wouldn't I believe you?"

"Eric wouldn't have hired you if he didn't think his mother and father were murdered. You're looking for a killer."

I glanced at Delia and was startled to see the hatred with which she was staring back at me. Turning my attention back to Stephen, I understood what grave danger I might have just placed myself in. "The police determined it was murder-suicide." My voice was less than convincing.

Stephen stared at me.

"I'd better go."

Stephen suddenly stood up. "Yes, I think you should."

I quickly threw on my coat. "I'll show myself out."

Once I was through the front door, I breathed a sigh of relief, but I didn't slow down. I rushed to my Sebring, started the engine, and with one final glance at the Cutter house, drove off.

Stephen Cutter had just become my prime suspect.

Chapter Twenty-Eight

Driving away out of Easton and back onto Route 1, I wished that I had Nathaniel to talk to. I sorely wanted to bounce this new information about Stephen Cutter off someone.

I thought about phoning John. He could check and see if that call from Morris to Stephen on New Year's Day really happened.

I could run Stephen's story past him to see what he thought. That the Cutters were already dead by the time Stephen had gotten there.

But what if Stephen was lying? What if Morris had welcomed the young man inside? They made small talk. Perhaps Julia offered Stephen a cup of coffee. Maybe Morris had tried to make amends for the way he'd treated his brother, Stephen's father.

Parker Lewis had confirmed that was what Morris wanted to do.

For Stephen, though, there was a lifetime of hatred. It would certainly take more than a cup of coffee and an apology to assuage that kind of rage.

Plus, Morris was only days away from presenting the Ekmann Study to Congress. That surely would have pissed Stephen off.

Enough to kill?

I tried to visualize it. They were in the kitchen, Julia preparing her breakfast casserole, Morris and Stephen talking with each other, then arguing, tempers flaring, voices getting louder.

In a fit of rage, Stephen pulled out a gun from under his coat and, in a heartbeat, put a bullet in Morris's right temple and then, as Julia was turning, shot her in the head.

Whomever shot them had carried a gun into that house, making it premeditated murder.

Oh, Nathaniel, I wish I could talk to you.

I jumped when my cell phone went off. Watching traffic, I pulled the phone out of my bag and answered without looking at the screen. "Hello?"

It was Mike's voice. His voice was professional and deadly serious. "Genie, I wanted to call you before it hit the news."

His tone sent my nervous system into a panic. "What? What's wrong?"

"West Sheffield High School is on active shooter lockdown."

Oh, my God.

"Jesus Christ, Mike." My heart was pounding so hard my chest hurt.

"Look, we've already got officers on the scene. I'm on my way now."

I pushed the gas pedal down hard and passed a slow-moving SUV, just missing an oncoming Volvo. I gripped the steering wheel so tightly, my fingers felt numb. "I'll be right there."

I visualized Caroline hiding in a classroom, terrified.

"There's nothing for you to do, Genie."

"I have to be there, Mike." My voice was high, rising with panic. I could hear the fear, the hysteria in my words. In my head I saw a dark, hulking figure with a semiautomatic rifle standing in the doorway of her classroom, taking aim.

I broke every traffic law. I passed cars where it was illegal, drove with my horn blaring through red lights, ignored stop signs.

Please, God, let her be okay.

I careened around the corner on East Avenue heading for the high school, saw flashing blue and white lights from the police cruisers. Ambulances were there, too, but no sign of bodies or wounded kids being ferried out.

There were already cars parked along the street. Cops had the driveway to the school blocked off with an orange-and-white barrier. A growing crowd of parents and onlookers clustered in the middle of the street, speaking to each other in hushed tones, waiting, hoping that they wouldn't hear gunshots.

Some were praying.

Two cops stood guard to make certain no one crossed the barrier.

As I ran toward the barrier, a television news crew pulled their van up behind me.

I grabbed my cell phone from my bag and punched in Mike's number. I knew that it was wrong to call him. If there was a shooter in the school, he'd be too busy to talk to me.

Dear God, please, please let Caroline be okay.

Mike didn't answer. It went to voicemail. I didn't leave a message.

Of the two cops on the barrier, I recognized one of them from working the crime beat. "Officer Perez?" My voice betrayed my fear.

He turned. Oscar Perez usually smiled when he saw me. On that day, he was stone-faced. "Genie. I really don't have anything I can give you right now."

"I'm not here as a reporter." I nodded toward the school. It seemed unnaturally silent. The windows seemed uncharacteristically dark. "My fifteen-year-old girl's in there."

He grimaced but leaned in close and whispered. "We have

officers going from classroom to classroom, but we think the shooters were apprehended before they got into the school."

My phone twittered in my hand, and I saw it was Mike Dillon. "Is Caroline okay?"

He sounded calm and confident. "Nobody's hurt. Two sixteen-year-old boys were on some social media platform and bragged they were coming to the school to shoot it up. One of the kids in school saw the post and did what he was supposed to and called 911. He gave us the names of the two boys, and we picked them up before they'd backed out of their driveway."

I breathed in a deep lungful of air. I didn't realize just how tense my body had been. The reporter in me kicked in. "Were they armed?"

He hesitated. "This is off the record for right now. There was a loaded hunting rifle in the back seat."

Jesus Christ.

I stared down at the ground. I'm not particularly religious, but at that moment, I gave a short, silent prayer of thanks for the kid who made the call to the cops. "There were actually two boys, and they were in a car with a gun. Was it loaded?"

"Look, I can't really say anything more. We got them before they'd backed the car into the street. The principal is closing the school for the rest of the day. Caroline should be out in a minute."

We disconnected and I saw I had a text from her.

I'm OK. We're headed out now. R U in the parking lot?

I texted back, just then realizing how badly my hands were shaking.

I'm at the end of the school drive.
B right there.

A woman I recognized as being the mother of one of the students was close enough to have heard me talking with Mike. Her face was pale and her eyes were wide with terror. "What is it?"

I couldn't stop myself from smiling. "They're all okay. They got the shooters before they got to the school."

She closed her eyes and started to cry. "Thank God. Thank God. Thank God."

Yes, thank God.

———

When Caroline came out of the school with a small crowd of other students, all of them were talking quietly to each other about what had just transpired, their faces serious. No one was laughing.

She was accompanied by Jessica Oberon and Tyler Greenwood.

Seeing her, euphoria washed over me. It occurred to me that when she'd left that morning, I'd barely said goodbye.

I will never let an opportunity go by to tell her that I love her.

I waved to get their attention.

Then the man's voice whispered, close to my ear, along with a sour whiff of bourbon. "Hi, Genie. Is that your girl, there? Which one is she, the blond or the brunette?"

I turned to see the pudgy face of Colby Jones standing only inches from where I stood, grinning at me like an obscene Halloween pumpkin. "What do you want, Colby?"

"This all came out better than anyone could have hoped for, don't you think?" He moved closer to me, invading my space, making me uncomfortable.

But instead of stepping back, I stood my ground and squinted at him. "What?"

"They caught the boys before they got here with their guns, nobody got hurt, and I've got tomorrow's lead story. It's a six-column headline, for sure."

I sniffed the air. His breath smelled of booze. "You been drinking?"

He rubbed a finger under his nose. "Just a quick one to ward off this cold. You do the same, don't you, Genie?"

"No, Colby, I told you my party days are over."

"Ah, don't kid a kidder. We're one and the same. Now, I've already got my statements from the cops. I still need to talk to a school official and a student or two. Mind if I talk to your daughter?"

I couldn't believe what I was hearing. "Yes, I mind. Talk to your school officials if you want to, but Caroline and I are going home."

Out of the corner of my eye, I saw the three teenagers coming toward us.

"C'mon, Genie. I want to get in good with Ben. And I can't do it like you do."

I turned and stared at him. "Excuse me?"

"Everyone knew you were banging the editor back in Boston. It was the only way you could keep partyin' and keep your job. I'm guessing that while you were at the *Sheffield Post* you were doin' Ben."

Seething, I moved away from Colby and squeezed around the police barrier. Officer Perez didn't stop me. I rushed quickly up to the three kids and threw my arms around Caroline. Then I told all three of them, "Whatever that man over there says, ignore him, okay?"

The three teenagers eyed Colby with suspicion.

He raised his hand in a haphazard wave, and his face split into a disingenuous grin. "Hey, kids. Want to be in the newspaper?"

I shepherded them past the odious man as quickly as I could.

But before we got out earshot, I turned and hissed, "Go fuck yourself, Colby."

———

Back in our kitchen, Caroline busied herself making cocoa for everyone.

Jessica and Tyler had called their mothers to let them know they were fine and that I was keeping them at our house until they could get away from their jobs to pick them up and take them home. I had a feeling that with the emotion cranked so high from the near tragedy at the high school, neither Jessica nor Tyler would be in our kitchen for long. Their moms were most likely already on their way.

While Jessica got out the cocoa mix from the cupboard, I reheated a cup of coffee in the microwave from a pot I'd made that morning. I turned and asked the other two teenagers seated at the table, "So, do you guys want to talk about it?"

The three of them had been unusually quiet in the car ride back to our place. I thought maybe they'd feel better if they talked it out.

Caroline had just set a pan of milk on the stove. She was the first to start. "Remember I told you that Brandon and Justin had been suspended for the rest of the week? Well, that didn't mean they couldn't talk shit on Snapchat."

I shot her a look but didn't say anything.

Jessica was studying her cell phone screen when she muttered, "They're misogynist assholes."

Tyler offered me a grave expression. "They were being pretty crude, Miss Chase."

It occurred to me that I might have been unduly rough on the kid when I first met him. "You can call me Genie."

He smiled shyly.

I watched Caroline as she stirred the milk, just starting to trail steam. She was being uncharacteristically quiet.

Jessica typed a text into her phone and then looked up at me. "They were horrible to Caroline."

"Why, what were they saying?"

Jessica shook her head. "Awful things they said they were going to do to her. Beat her up, cut her, rape her."

I felt my jaw drop and my face flush with growing anger. "What? Why?"

For a moment, nobody spoke. Finally, Tyler said, "Because they know she'd never go out with either of them. They know that she's way out of their league."

Caroline growled, "All girls are out of their league." She glanced up at me. "It got pretty dark."

Jessica put her phone down on the table. "Then it was like all the kids in school got in on it. In between classes they were posting that Brandon and Justin were losers and should just shut the hell up. Sherri McMillin wrote that they should kill themselves."

Tyler sighed, "It kept getting uglier and uglier. Then it stopped. There was one final post."

My heart caught in my throat. "What was it?"

Caroline turned away from the stove, her arms crossed in front of her. "Brandon posted, 'We're on our way. We have an AR-15. You're all going to fucking die.'"

I couldn't help myself. "Oh, my God."

Caroline continued. "Tyler called 911."

I turned to him. "You're the one who called 911?"

Tyler added, "The school locked down. The cops were there in minutes."

Jessica whispered, "*See something, say something.* That's what they drill into us."

It was Tyler Greenwood who had made the phone call.

Both girls got wide-eyed when I rushed over and hugged him. "Thank you, Tyler. Thank you."

I stepped back and directed my next question to the girls. "It must have been pretty scary, huh?"

Jessica looked up at me. "When Tyler made the phone call, the police immediately contacted the school to lock down and shelter in place. The three of us were in French class. Mrs. Faraday locked and barricaded the door, while the rest of us huddled in a corner. Caroline and I held each other's hands the whole time we were waiting to hear something."

I smiled. "You're good friends."

Caroline turned from the stove for moment. "Best friends. We've known each other since we were six. We weren't going to let anything happen to each other."

Chapter Twenty-Nine

Jessica and Tyler were both picked up by their mothers before they'd had a chance to finish their hot chocolate. As they were leaving, I hugged them both again, and then their moms and I hugged it out.

I knew both of the women who were raising Jessica Oberon. I've known them for a couple of years now. But this had made us even closer, somehow.

It was the first time that I'd met Carol, Tyler's mom. She was a tiny thing, no more than five-five or so. She was wearing the scrubs she'd had on at the hospital. Carol had a sweet smile and thanked me for giving Tyler a ride.

We'd shared something, something that could have been devastatingly horrible.

I'm not the most social animal in the world, and I don't claim to have any close friends. Not something I was ever interested in.

But I had a feeling that Tyler's mom and I could be friends.

Soon after, Caroline's Aunt Ruth called, having heard about the incident on the news. I could hear her loud, high-pitched voice as Caroline held the phone away from her ear, rolling her eyes.

I kissed her on the top of her head and left the kitchen, leaving her alone to deal with her overly protective aunt.

Upstairs, closed off in my bedroom, I glanced at the time on my cell phone. It was just after three in the afternoon. I sat on the side of the bed with a hot cup of cocoa, wondering how a little vodka would taste in it. What would it be then? A cocoa-tini?

Get a grip, Genie. Control.

Closing my eyes, I tried to slow my breathing, control my thoughts, relax my sore muscles, sooth my ravaged nerves.

It had been a hell of a day. It started with being thrown to the ground and assaulted by some thug thinking I knew the whereabouts of a missing scientist.

Then there was the visit with Stephen and Delia Cutter. He'd confessed that he'd gone out to the Cutter house on the morning they were both shot to death. He denied killing them, of course.

I never should have gone in there without telling someone what I was doing.

And the cherry on the top of the stress cake was that two teenagers threatened to rape and maim Caroline, then said they were coming to her school to kill as many people as they could. What would have happened if Caroline's friend hadn't called the police?

The cops caught the two boys with a loaded gun in the car.

It gave me the shivers.

Control, Genie. Focus.

Unbidden, the image of Nathaniel lying in the hospital bed popped into my mind.

Why was someone so desperate to find Ekmann that they'd resort to torture and physical assault? Was it CP&G or Gaea, or someone I didn't know about?

Why would CP&G be looking for him? They already had the study.

They really didn't need him anymore.

Or was it that they wanted to make certain he *didn't* show up at the presentation?

And where the hell is Lisa Cutter?

Was it a coincidence that she was missing at the same time as the scientist whom she loathed?

I thought again about Caroline and how horribly those two boys had talked about her.

I took another sip of my cocoa. For a moment, the taste reminded me of cold days in my childhood when my mother would make hot chocolate for me after school. That was before dad died in the motorcycle accident and she turned bitter. His death had changed her, had altered our relationship. I'd been detained for smoking in school and Dad was on his way to talk with the principal when he had an accident riding his motorcycle on I-95 and sustained fatal injuries.

Mom blamed me until the day she died.

People change. Sometimes for the good, sometimes for the bad.

Is that why Morris Cutter was trying so hard to reconcile with his nephew?

Everyone, from Morris's son to the man they called Uncle Parker and even Morris's mistress, Nikki Hudson, had told me that the birth of his granddaughter had changed Morris. Less concerned about his business, more concerned about family.

For a moment I thought about Morris Cutter's library. A gorgeous room with hundreds of books, an ornate desk next to a floor-to-ceiling window overlooking Long Island Sound.

He'd been reading that book on the climate crisis.

Inexplicably, what Caroline said in the kitchen clicked. That she's known Jessica since she was six.

It was the same thing that Lisa Cutter had said when she talked to me about her partner. What was her name?

Janice.

Six was the age Lisa was when she vanished and her parents went nuts, thinking she was lost in the woods. All the time, it was a little girl she'd met on the lake that she had gone off with.

Could that little girl be Janice?

I opened my laptop and tried to find a news story from that time about an oil CEO's daughter going missing. It had happened too long ago to be on the internet.

But it would have been in the New York newspapers.

I called Brenda Zafiro from the *New York Daily News.*

"Zafiro."

"This is Geneva Chase."

"Hey, you're in Sheffield, aren't you?"

"Yeah."

"Was there a school shooting out your way? Looks like AP has a breaking story."

"Cops stopped it cold. Nobody got hurt. Look, I need a big favor."

Brenda took a breath. "What do I get out of it?"

"If this thing breaks, you'll get the story first."

She thought for a moment. "What do you need?"

"About twenty-five years ago, Morris Cutter's daughter, Lisa, disappeared from a hunting lodge somewhere in the Catskills. There was a huge search for her. It turns out that she'd wandered off with another little girl to a neighboring hunting lodge. Do you think you can find that story?"

"Does this have anything to do with your investigation?"

"I don't know yet."

"Gonna take a little time. I'll call you when I have it."

After an interminable fifteen minutes, she called me. "I got it. I've scanned it and I'll email it to you. What's your email address?"

I gave it to her and then asked, "Does the story give the name of the other little girl?"

"Janice Leopold."

I got a tiny thrill. Could that be the same Janice that Lisa was living with?

Seconds later, I read the story on my laptop about the little girl wandering off, calling the state police, the frantic search, and how Janice Leopold's father brought Lisa back to the CP&G hunting lodge. There was no mention of the address of either lodge in the news story.

At Morris's direction, CP&G sold theirs that same summer.

Is it possible that the Leopold family still owned their lodge?

I was filled with the excitement of the hunt. I called Eric Cutter.

"Hello?"

"Eric, it's Genie Chase. Have you heard from your sister, Lisa?"

I could hear the frustration in his voice. "No, I'm really worried. I even called Lisa's partner. She says she doesn't know anything, but she's worried, too. I'm getting ready to call the police."

"Have you ever met Lisa's partner?"

There was silence on the phone for a moment. "No. When Lisa came out as gay, Dad didn't handle it well, and frankly neither did I. I've never met her."

"I need the address of the lodge that CP&G used to own."

"CP&G hasn't had that place for twenty-five years."

"I know. Do you have the address?"

"I don't, but I think I can get it for you. I'll have to hang up and then call you right back."

He disconnected without saying goodbye, and I thought it through. Lisa Cutter, NASA climatologist, and believer that humans are responsible for the unfolding climate calamity, and Dr. Stuart Ekmann, the lead author of the Ekmann Study, a false narrative arguing just the opposite, both vanished. Both scientists disappear at the same time. Two individuals who should hate each other. Could it be possible that they were both in the same place for some reason? Hiding from CP&G and Fisher, Evans, and Sinclair, Gaea, and the rest of the world?

While I waited for Eric to call me back, I did a fast internet search and discovered that there is no hunting season in February in New York State. If the Leopolds still owned their lodge, nobody would be up there.

I jumped when the phone in my hand chirped and vibrated. "Eric?"

"I got the address. It was on Juniper Lake. I had to call Uncle Parker to get it."

After we disconnected, I looked up the directions and saw that it was in the Catskills, nearly 120 miles and a little over two hours away. I'd have to get a wiggle on if I wanted to get up there before dark.

But before I started, on Ulster County's website, I looked up who owned all the properties on Juniper Lake.

One of them belonged to Janice Leopold.

Chapter Thirty

I took Route 7 north until I got to the Taconic State Parkway and drove it for the next hour. The sun was already behind the wooded hills when I got off my exit onto Morgan Hollow Road, then to Route 12, and then onto Saw Mill Road, a dark two-lane highway that I shared with SUVs and truckers that were on their way to replenish the grocery stores and gas stations serving the tiny towns in that part of New York State.

The Catskill Mountains are more rolling hills than craggy mountains like the Rockies. That being said, there are some damned daunting inclines. My aging vehicle struggled mightily to climb them and then glided like a rocket back down again, requiring braking at treacherous twists and turns. An hour and a half into the trip, it was already darker than I'd hoped it would be, and much colder than the south shore of Connecticut.

It gave me time to consider what I was doing. Lisa Cutter, if she was in hiding at Janice Leopold's hunting lodge, was a suspect in her parents' murders. She had access to her parents' house. She knew her way around guns. She was in line to inherit millions of dollars.

And Lisa didn't want her father to present the Ekmann Study on Capitol Hill.

Shadow Hill.

In my kitchen, she'd offered the theory that her father had found out about his wife's lover and, in a fit of rage, killed Lisa's mother and then himself.

She'd wanted me to believe that.

Should I be tracking her down on my own?

I just don't think she's a killer.

I had my phone set up for GPS and, up until the last few miles, had gotten excellent directions. But then the Google Maps lady, who'd kept me company the entire trip, went silent. I picked my phone up from the cupholder and saw that I didn't have any bars. I was too far out in the middle of freakin' nowhere for a cell phone signal.

I grew up in a time without personal computers and cell phones, so not having a connection shouldn't have bothered me. But knowing that I couldn't call out in case of an emergency, I felt utterly cut off from the rest of the world. If I lost my way on those dark roads, or if I slipped off the side of one of those steep hillsides, I wouldn't be able to call for help. I'd most likely freeze to death or starve, and my body wouldn't be found until spring.

I pulled over to the side of the road when I felt it was safe and turned my overhead light on. I always like to have a secondary plan when I travel. Too many things can go wrong. Before I'd left my house, I'd printed out a set of directions. According to the tiny font on the map, I was maybe five miles from my final turn, the cutoff for Juniper Lake.

I drove on, cautiously watching for any left-hand turns, my eyes straining as I followed my headlights down the dark road. After driving for twenty more minutes, I knew I must have missed it, found a place to do a k-turn, and went back the way I came. Finally, I saw why I'd missed it the first time through. It was a four-corner intersection nearly hidden by trees, with no markings, no road sign, nothing at all that would have told me this actually led anywhere other than to the end of the world.

I took a deep breath and turned onto it. Total darkness enveloped my car as I drove slowly up a slight, paved incline, feeling my tires slipping on the slick asphalt, the car jerking when I hit patches of black ice.

A deer burst from the woods.

My heart caught in my throat at the surprise, not realizing what it was until I slammed hard on the brakes and the deer had already vanished, bounding into the darkness on the other side of the road like a fur-covered ghost.

Stopped dead, heart racing, I stared ahead as far as my headlights reached, startled to see tiny sets of red eyes reflecting light back at me from the shadows. Raccoons? Opossums? Gremlins? Trolls?

Stepping on the gas again, a slow go, watching for any animals than might want to challenge my right to be on that road, I wondered if the dark forest hid hungry bears or packs of wolves. Finally, the incline leveled out and I came to a clearing. In the moonlight, I could see the hunting lodge, hulking in the blackness of the night, every bit as dark as the forest through which I'd just come.

Janice Leopold's hunting lodge.

I pulled the car into a gravel parking area and stopped in front of a set of wooden steps leading up onto a large wraparound porch. The warm weather we'd had a few days ago must have melted most of the snow, but now, in the frigid temperatures, anything that hadn't evaporated had refrozen. In the vague light of the moon, playing hide-and-seek behind fast-moving clouds, I could see the remains of snowdrifts at the tree line.

I sat in my car for a moment, the engine running, the heater cranked high. I studied the lodge. It was constructed of fieldstone and large wooden beams. The large curtained windows were dark.

I wondered if my hunch was wrong. It didn't look like anyone was up there. It was just me and the forest animals.

Damn it, I just drove two hours for nothing?

I got out and breathed in the chilly air. I smelled the scent of the pine trees surrounding the lodge. It was so quiet that I was certain that if anyone was inside, they must have heard me crunching along the ice and gravel when I'd driven up.

Not wanting to disturb the tranquility, I closed the door as softly as I could. The quiet was stunning. No airplanes, no distant traffic sounds, no motors of any kind. Just the hiss of the wind as it moved through the bare, ice-encrusted limbs of the trees.

And then I heard it. My heart froze. Somewhere in the shadows up on the front porch. The *click-clack* racking of a shotgun shell into its chamber.

Completely dark, hidden from what moonlight there was, I couldn't even make out the trace of a shadow of someone standing up there. Hearing the fear in my own voice, I called out, "Lisa Cutter?"

I was unnerved when a man's voice came from behind me. "What do you want here?"

I turned and saw him standing in the silver moonlight, twenty feet from me. I quietly asked, "Dr. Ekmann?"

From up on the porch, a woman shouted, "Who are you and what do you want?"

I took a moment and prayed that I was right, that Lisa Cutter wasn't a killer. "You came to my house yesterday. I'm here looking for you and Dr. Ekmann. You *are* Lisa Cutter, aren't you?"

The man in the shadows shouted, "Do you know her, Lisa?"

"Yes, she's okay. But we've got to get rid of the car."

The man moved closer to me. "You have to park your car in

the barn. Get in, start it up, and I'll walk you over to show you where."

A flashlight clicked on and I saw that it was held by a man roughly my height, five-ten, but about a hundred pounds heavier. "Follow me."

I got back into the Sebring, turned on the engine and drove slowly to the point on the ground where the flashlight beam hit. As I got closer, Ekmann, dressed in a parka, jeans, and work boots, pointed the light to the wide doorway of a barn. I stopped as he got up close to the door and slid it open. Then he walked into the barn and waved the light, inviting me into the darkness.

From the dim illumination, I could see that I was parking next to an Audi Q3 SUV. They had come up here in the one car, Ekmann's. And of course, the author of the Ekmann Study would drive a gas guzzler.

As I got back out of my car again, I could smell the faint odor of oil and gasoline. I couldn't see through the shadows along the walls, but I guessed that this building housed chainsaws, lawn mowers, generators, and possibly an ATV or two.

Ekmann hissed, "Hurry."

I hustled quickly out of the barn, and he slid the door shut. Then without a word, he started at a brisk pace toward the house. We both climbed up the wooden steps to the wraparound porch. In the distance, I saw the moonlight reflecting from the surface of Juniper Lake. Across the lake, there was another hunting lodge, stark in the ghostly silver light. The lodge CP&G had owned decades ago?

Then the skidding clouds overhead abruptly obliterated what light there had been. The night was enveloped in total darkness again.

Lisa stood at one side of the front door, cradling a shotgun that looked nearly as big as she was. Her hair was pinned to the top of her head, and, like Ekmann, she wore a heavy parka, jeans, and boots. The same outfit she'd worn in my kitchen the day before. She looked at me suspiciously with her wide brown eyes. "How did you know we were here?"

"You said you've known your partner since you were six. Eric told me the story about how you were six when you wandered off with another little girl to play at her parents' lodge. I looked up who owned this place and saw that it was Janice Leopold. Your partner's name is Janice. Does she know you're up here?"

She bit her lower lip and shook her head no. "I couldn't tell her. It would put her in danger."

"Eric called her to see if she knew where you were. He said she was frightened for you."

She sighed. "It can't be helped. I'll call her tomorrow morning when I know we're safe. Let's go inside where it's warm."

I felt the heat the second I walked into the house, but no one made any effort to turn on the lights. Lisa flipped on a flashlight of her own and went to a table to light a kerosene camp lantern. Once on, the lantern's muted illumination allowed me to see that we stood in a large meeting space, the walls and floor all polished hardwood. Thick curtains were drawn across the windows. Tiffany-style lamps hung by chains from heavy beams in the ceiling. Comfortable couches, overstuffed chairs, recliners, and end tables were in random locations throughout the expansive room where visitors could gather and talk. Area rugs decorated with Native American designs were scattered about the floor.

I murmured, "Nice digs. No fire in the fireplace?"

She shook her head. "Electric heat here. No need to pump more carbon into the air than we already are."

"How big is this place?"

"Seven bedrooms, five full bathrooms, modern kitchen and dining area. Janice's parents ran the lodge up until her father passed. Her mom lost interest and gave the property to Janice. She didn't like the idea of having people up here to kill the wildlife, so she shut it down to guests, and it's been just she and I who have been using it. It's a great place to get away. I even get in a little target shooting."

I smiled. "Mind if I take my coat off?"

She leaned the shotgun against the jamb of the doorway that I guessed led to the kitchen. Lisa unzipped her parka and tossed it onto one of the chairs. "Knock yourself out."

I shed my coat and draped it over the back of a black leather couch. Sitting down, I took a breath and tried to get my jangling nerves back to normal. Hearing the pump of the shotgun had rattled the hell out of me. "So, why are you and Dr. Ekmann both up here, hiding?"

Stuart Ekmann stripped off his own coat. Under it, he was wearing a white, longsleeved shirt open at the collar. He was around six feet tall and had a husky build along with a sparse head of white hair. His facial features were soft and doughy, creating deep shadows in the light of the kerosene lamp. He gave me a shy smile. "Would you like something to drink? Maybe something to eat?"

As he asked the question, I felt my stomach rumbling. "Oh, yes, please. What do you have?"

Lisa answered. "Water, soda, beer, wine. We keep the bar stocked. What would you like?"

I really would have loved a vodka tonic. "You got any coffee?"

"Let's go into the kitchen, I'll make a pot."

The walls and floor of the kitchen were all weathered wooden planks, like the worn siding from an old barn, giving the room a rustic feel, but the stainless-steel appliances belied that. Stuart sat at the table and I remained standing while Lisa prepared the coffeemaker in the light of the hissing lantern.

There was a copper pot bubbling on the stove and the room smelled like tomato sauce, onions, and garlic. It made my mouth water.

Seeing my line of sight, Stuart offered, "I'm making spaghetti bolognese. Would you like to join us for dinner?"

"I'd love to." I knew they had electricity; the heat was on and so was the electric stove. "Why no lights?"

Lisa glanced at me. "Just in case a state cop comes up here on patrol and sees that someone is inside moving around. The lodge is supposed to be empty this time of year. We really don't want to be on anyone's radar screen."

"Who knows you and Janice have this place?"

She shook her head. "Nobody. Honestly, no one ever took an interest in who I was living with, and I never felt the need to share. Except for Mom. Mom knew."

"But nobody at CP&G."

"Nope." Lisa finished pouring water into the coffeemaker reservoir and hit the On button. "What made you think that Dr. Ekmann and I were together?"

"The fact that you both went missing at the same time was my first clue. And the fact that goons from Fisher, Evans, and Sinclair were trying so hard to locate Dr. Ekmann." I glanced over at him. "Darren Reed is presenting your study to Congress tomorrow. He really doesn't need you there, so why are they looking for you?" The question was rhetorical. I answered it myself. "And then it occurred to me that Reed might not want you there...or anywhere...at all."

Lisa nodded toward my black eye. "How did you get the shiner? Fisher, Evans, and Sinclair?"

I reached up and touched the tender flesh with two fingers. "They didn't leave a business card, but I connected the dots." I jerked my thumb toward Ekmann. "They thought I knew where you were."

Lisa held up the lantern to study the coffeemaker's progress. "You didn't think it might have been someone from Gaea? They play rough, too."

I shrugged. "No, CP&G wants to get their hands on him more than Gaea does." I shot him a look. "I'm going to guess it's because you've had a change of heart about the study, Doctor. I'm willing to bet that the two of you are heading to DC in the morning?"

Lisa grinned. "Oh, we're not taking any chances. We're having dinner, then we're leaving tonight."

"Still, CP&G is looking mighty hard for you, Doctor. Is there another reason they want you?"

He nodded and looked scared. "Not them. Just one of their executives. Back when I'd started working there, Morris Cutter and I became friends. After he retired, he kept his old office and about once a week, I'd stop by, and he'd pour me a glass of Scotch and we'd just talk. Just before Christmas, he let me in on a secret. He hadn't been coming in to his old office to write a history of the company. He was using the internal network to track down the person who was siphoning off millions of dollars from the company."

"Darren Reed told me he thought it was Morris."

"Nope."

"Who then?"

"Parker Lewis."

Chapter Thirty-One

Suddenly my interest in "Uncle" Parker grew exponentially.

"How close were you and Lisa's dad?"

Stuart went to the stove to stir the sauce. "We grew quite close after my son Patrick died."

"He died fighting a wildfire in California."

Stuart raised an eyebrow. "That's right. A wildfire that was the direct result of a drought caused by the climate crisis."

"That CP&G has a lot to do with."

He stopped stirring and stared down at the floor. "Morris and I were going through an epiphany together. Mine caused by the death of my son. Morris's was the result of the birth of his granddaughter. He worried what kind of world he was leaving behind for her. He wanted to make a difference."

"By giving your study to Congress?"

"It's all bullshit. Morris knew it. Another reason he'd kept coming into the city to his office was to keep control of the study. He wanted to be the one to present it up on the Hill. Then he and I were both going to publicly disavow it, expose it for the false narrative that it is. The press would go crazy."

Lisa spoke up. "But Dad never got the chance." She reached

up and took down two cups, then filled them both with coffee.

"Do you still think that your dad shot your mother, then killed himself?"

She brought me a cup and placed it on the table. "I don't know what to think or who to trust anymore."

"How did you and Dr. Ekmann connect?"

Stuart responded. "Morris told me that once he'd publicly disavowed my study, he was going to reach out to Lisa and see if he could repair their relationship."

I watched as Lisa chewed at her lower lip.

Stuart continued, "I think Morris sensed that he might be putting himself in danger. He gave me Lisa's cell phone number and told me to reach out to her if anything happened to him."

Lisa was trying hard not to cry. "A week after Mom and Dad died, Stuart called me. I didn't believe him, that Dad had an awakening about the climate crises. But when you told me he'd been reading the book I sent him…" Her words trailed off.

"What spooked the two of you into running?"

Stuart responded, "Darren Reed sensed I had a change of heart about the study. Gaea has a spy working in the executive offices of CP&G."

"Who?"

He shook his head. "I'm sorry, but I can't tell you that."

"Fair enough. Did the spy tell you Darren Reed suspected something was wrong?"

"Yes. The spy also told me that Parker Lewis was worried that Morris had told me that he was embezzling from the company. She said that I'd better disappear because Parker had called the thugs at Fisher, Evans, and Sinclair."

The spy is Parker's receptionist.

That's when it hit me. It had taken all this time for someone from the consulting firm to hack into Morris's laptop. Somewhere on that hard drive, Morris had left some hint or note that he'd told Stuart about Parker's crime.

I looked at Lisa, fear suddenly reaching into my chest. "Do you know what kind of car your Uncle Parker drives?"

She blinked at me. "Uncle Parker? He's had the same old car for years. It's a beat-up, old red Jeep Wrangler."

I was suddenly engulfed in a cold wave of panic. In the security video there were three cars on the road on the day the Cutters were gunned down.

One of them was a red Jeep Wrangler.

I heard the tension in my voice when I said, "This afternoon, I called Eric to get the address of CP&G's old lodge. Once I had that, it was easy for me to look up who owned what property here on Jupiter Lake. Only Eric didn't remember what the address was, so he told me he got the address from your uncle Parker." I stared at Lisa. "He's the one who killed your parents."

Her eyes widened, and she processed what I'd just told her. "Uncle Parker? I don't believe it."

I shouted, "We have to get out. We have to get away from here as fast as possible."

Lisa had an edge of fear in her voice. "There's no way he could know where we are."

"If I can figure it out, he can."

Then we all heard it. The crunching of tires against gravel and ice.

Stuart whispered, his eyes wide with terror, "We're too late."

Chapter Thirty-Two

We doused the kerosene lantern in the kitchen, then picked our way through the dark into the front meeting hall. By the time we got there, we could see moving headlights peeking through the cracks in the thick curtains.

Stuart's voice croaked, "They found us, Lisa."

I looked at her from the corner of my eye. She had the shotgun cradled in her arms. "Are there any more weapons in the house?"

She shook her head. "When we lock this place up, we always take our guns with us. This is the only one we leave here."

The headlights on the car outside darkened.

Lisa and I quietly opened the front door and crept out onto the porch, staying low behind the railing. We knelt in the shadows, and I immediately wished I'd put my coat on. I was confident that we couldn't be seen, but my heart was still beating like a jackhammer in my chest. I shivered, not knowing if it was from fear or the frigid air.

The car doors opened and three men got out. They'd arrived in an SUV, big and boxy, but I couldn't identify the model. They stood next to the vehicle, their heads slowly swiveling back and forth, gazing around them, acclimating to the darkness. Two wore business-style overcoats. One wore a parka. I didn't recognize them in the dim illumination, but when I heard them speak, I knew right away who two of them were.

Leonard Ryan was the first to say something. "I don't know, Parker. It doesn't look like there's anyone here. No cars, no lights. You sure this is the right place?"

There was a long silence. Finally, Parker answered, "Jason, go check out the barn over there. See what's inside." The man wearing the parka flipped on a flashlight and focused the beam on the barn door on the other side of the small parking area.

I leaned over and whispered into Lisa's ear, "Shit."

The man they called Jason slid the door aside and flashed the beam around the inside of the barn. He hollered, "Two cars in here. One of them is Ekmann's."

I felt more than I saw Lisa melt back into the house through the open doorway. I followed her inside, just as a flashlight beam cut through the night, probing the deck where we'd been only seconds before.

Lisa growled, "They know we're here." She reached up and flipped on a light switch on the wall next to the door.

Powerful halogen spotlights, mounted on the roof of the lodge, came alive, lighting the parking area, throwing the car and the three men into stark relief. All three froze where they were standing, hands up, shielding their eyes.

Parker's avuncular mustache curved at the sides as he offered up a sour grin. He shouted, "Lisa. Sweetie. C'mon out, darlin. All we want to do is talk."

"I'm armed, Uncle Parker."

He turned, waved at the man in the parka, and pointed to the car. Jason trotted back across the parking area, his hand still shielding his eyes from the light. He popped the back of the SUV open and took out three hunting rifles, all fitted with scopes.

Lisa stood in the open doorway and aimed the shotgun in the direction of the SUV. She screamed, "Don't anybody move."

Ignoring her, Parker called out, "Jason, bring us the rifles."

Lisa pumped the shotgun's slide. "Don't do it, Jason."

Nobody moved. Parker, his hand in front of his face, gazed in our general direction, appraising the situation. Finally, he spoke again. "Lisa, honey, I practically raised you. I watched you grow up. You wouldn't shoot your uncle."

Lisa's voice was angry. "It was you, you son of a bitch. You killed Mom and Dad. Dad was your best friend in the world. If there's anyone Dad trusted, it was you."

He stroked his mustache. "Honey, your father was a changed man. He wasn't the same Morris Cutter I've known all my life."

For the first time I spoke up. "How so, Parker?"

He moved his head, one hand still in front of his eyes, trying in vain to see me. "Geneva Chase. Yes, Eric told me you'd called to get the address of the hunting lodge."

"How had Morris changed?" I repeated.

He dropped the smile. "He wanted to do irreparable damage to the company, to the entire industry, to our nation."

"By admitting that the Ekmann Study is horseshit?" I glanced at Stuart from the corner of my eye and saw him grimace.

Parker tried smiling again. "Yes. Should I assume that Dr. Ekmann is up there with you?"

Lisa shouted, "Don't worry about Dr. Ekmann."

Parker continued, "Lisa, if your daddy did what he wanted to do, it was going to throw thousands of people out of work and cripple the energy security of our country. Not to mention it could put us out of business."

I shouted, "But that's not really why you killed them, is it?"

Parker stayed silent.

I continued, "Did Morris give you a chance to confess that you've embezzled millions of dollars from your company?"

Parker didn't answer.

"You went to their house on New Year's Day on the pretense that you were going to turn yourself in. But you really went there to kill Morris. Did you take his appointment book and laptop?"

He stared in my general direction, trying to nail down my precise location. "Yes. It took us a while to hack into Morris's laptop. But that's how we found out that Dr. Ekmann was getting ready to disavow his own study. I also discovered that Morris had told Stuart about me and the money. Obviously, someone inside our company tipped you, didn't they, Stuart? Is that why you called Lisa?"

Stuart remained silent, hiding inside the house.

I hollered down to them, "On New Year's Day, you brought a gun that you knew couldn't be traced to you."

He patted the side of his coat, indicating he was carrying a concealed weapon. "I always carry a gun with me. I told you, I'm an Oklahoma boy."

I knew we were in trouble. The three of them with weapons against the three of us with only one shotgun. Could I divide them? "Parker, aren't you afraid that the company attack dogs you brought with you will tell CP&G about the money?"

In the bright lights, I could see Parker grin. "I'm using some of that money now, Miss Chase. I'm paying these two gentlemen quite generously to work exclusively for me tonight."

"How long do you think that will last? Now that they know, whatever you've paid them won't be enough. Will it, Leonard Ryan? How long will it take you to demand more?" I needed to sow the seeds of distrust. "And then even more?"

Parker stopped smiling.

Then I wanted to hear him say it. "On New Year's Day, who did you shoot first?"

He hesitated again.

Lisa screamed, "Who did you kill first, Uncle Parker? My mother or my father?"

I saw the cloud of steam when he exhaled. "Your father."

Lisa screamed, "You bastard. You fucking bastard. You killed my parents."

"I didn't want to, Lisa."

"Fuck you, Uncle Parker."

No one moved. Parker and Leonard were positioned in front of the SUV, Jason still at the open back hatch of the SUV, cradling three rifles in his arms. As they breathed in and out, puffs of steam rose into the night. A moment locked in time, the three men were awash in the spotlights.

Finally, Parker nodded to himself, as if making a decision. His voice was sterner. "Lisa, honey, I need for you to put the gun down and all three of you come down here."

Lisa growled, "Not happening, Uncle Parker."

Switching back to a gentle, almost paternal voice, Parker answered, "Lisa, Genie, Stuart, no one's gonna get hurt."

"Get back into your car and drive away," Lisa said.

He sighed. "Jason, bring the rifles."

"I'll shoot you first, Uncle Parker."

Leonard's iguana eyes blinked and he took a step away from Parker.

Parker just stared in our direction. "Don't worry, gentlemen. Lisa might be a good shot, but she's not a killer."

Lisa, still on the edge, laughed. "Want to bet? I have a shotgun. Do you know what that can do to a man?"

Parker barked, "Jason, bring us the rifles."

Keeping an eye on the front porch, Jason came around the vehicle and handed one rifle to Leonard and one to Parker, keeping one for himself.

Lisa shouted, "Here's the deal, boys. We'll be inside the lodge waiting for you. You won't know where I am. Whomever I see first, I blow in half."

In one fluid movement, Parker took aim. We all jumped when we heard the gunshot and the sound of glass shattering. Night returned to near total darkness.

Stuart whispered, "He shot out the spotlight."

Lisa and I slid further back into the house and closed and locked the door.

Leonard, not hiding his intentions, said in a loud voice, "Jason, you're the point person. You go in first and we'll follow you."

The young man spoke for the first time. "Bullshit. You go in first. I've seen what a shotgun can do to a man."

I recognized the voice.

It's the same son of a bitch that attacked me while I was running.

Parker was apparently amused. "Gentlemen, don't worry. Lisa is a crack shot, but she's never been able to kill anything. She won't pull the trigger."

Lisa shouted, "You killed my parents. I'll be happy to put a shotgun shell in the stomach of the first man that comes through our door." She teased, "Parker, I'm hoping it's you."

There was absolute silence as the three men huddled, whispering to each other.

Finally, Parker shouted, "Lisa, Stuart, Geneva, I just told Jason to go to the barn and see if he could find any empty bottles and fill them with gasoline. If you don't come out, I'll burn you out."

Stuart answered, "If we come out, you'll kill us."

"Stuart, all I want to do is keep you out of sight until after Darren Reed gives the presentation to Congress. Then the three of you can go back to your normal lives."

Stuart leaned in close and whispered, "He's lying. We know too much. He has to kill us."

Lisa said in a soft voice, "I know."

Parker's voice sounded a little sad. "Please come out. Don't make me do this."

Stuart looked at the two of us in the dim illumination from the flashlights. "Do you think he'll really do it?"

As if in answer, through the gap in the curtain, we saw the tiny flare of a cigarette lighter. Stuart pulled the curtain aside, and the tiny flame grew into a small fire as Jason set alight the rag stuffed in the bottle filled with gasoline.

Then he disappeared around the corner of the house. Almost immediately, we heard the shattering of glass and a whooshing sound.

I sniffed the air. Gasoline and smoke.

Stuart screamed, "We're on fire!"

Chapter Thirty-Three

I tried to sound calm. "Do you have a fire extinguisher?"

Lisa's words were faint, as if she was having trouble processing the trouble we were in. "In the kitchen, I think."

"Where in the kitchen? I'll get it."

She snapped back, staring at me hard, realizing what she had to do. "No, I'll get it. I know right where it is."

Stuart was hyperventilating, standing at the window, the curtain peeled back in his fingers, giving him a view of what was happening outside. His eyes darted from the flickering bright orange light coming from one of the bedrooms down the hallway to the parking lot. "Jesus Christ, this is bad."

I could see another rag being set afire. Then, to my utter horror, it flew directly at us.

Stuart muttered, "Fuck."

I shoved him hard. "Move."

We both fell to the floor as the window shattered and the bottle flew over our heads. Behind us I heard a whoosh as fire spread from a flood of gasoline exploding from the broken bottle. The flames crawled across the wooden floor like a supernatural beast, the tongues of fire licking at the walls and curtains. Smoke muddied the air, stinging my eyes.

I turned my head and I saw Lisa standing in the kitchen doorway, caught behind the flames. She was cut off.

I screamed, "Lisa!"

"I'm okay."

I couldn't see it, but heard the hiss of a fire extinguisher as she attempted to douse the spreading fire.

Another bottle came crashing through another window. I watched the area rugs catch fire, then the curtains, then a couch.

Stuart coughed and gasped for air.

He and I were still on the floor. The smoke was becoming intolerable, the air poisonous.

Stuart grunted, "I have to get out. I can't get breathe."

He crawled in the direction of the door and then got to his feet. The door opened, and I heard his footsteps out on the wooden porch.

I waited, listening.

No gunfire.

They hadn't shot him when he went out the doorway.

I quickly weighed my chances of surviving the spreading inferno.

None. Better to take my chances outside.

I glanced back at the kitchen door but could no longer see Lisa through the smoke.

I struggled to my feet and staggered to the open doorway, rushing outside to the porch, gulping at the air, sucking it into my lungs. Moving blindly, I slipped and fell down the wooden steps, landing on the icy ground. I sat up and glanced behind me at the lodge, lit a brilliant orange and red, the flames eating away at everything inside like a hideous cancer.

In an almost surreal moment, I realized that it had started snowing. I glanced at the sky, and the moon was totally gone, replaced by low-lying snow clouds, made visible in the dancing orange and red light of the fire. Crackling, glowing embers from the fire rose and mingled with the snowflakes on their way to the ground.

Snow fell on my sweater, and I saw steam rising into the night.

"So good of you to join us."

Still seated on the ground, I saw Parker standing above me, grinning with a hunting rifle aimed at my head. Just beyond him, Leonard Ryan held Stuart prisoner, gun at his head as well.

I squeaked out, "Lisa."

Parker looked back up the steps. "Where's the last place you saw her?"

"The kitchen. In the back of the lodge."

He nodded. "Jason, get back there. If she comes out the door, try to take her alive. Remember, she's all bark and no bite." Then he looked down at me again. "Get up, please."

I struggled to stand, my legs weak from fear and the shock of almost dying in the fire. Parker leaned in, hand outstretched, and pulled me to my feet.

Leonard asked, "Where to, Parker? The ground's frozen."

My heart stopped. What did he mean, the ground's frozen? No place to bury us?

Oh God, they're going to kill us.

He signaled with his chin. "There's a ravine not far from here."

"How will Jason find us?"

Parker chuckled, glancing around him, surrounded by falling snowflakes. "He's not the brightest bulb on the tree, but even he can follow our tracks in the snow." He moved the barrel of the rifle up and down. "Geneva, please, that way."

I glanced back at the house—a raging, crackling, inferno. I didn't know how anyone could still be in that house and be alive.

Feeling the muzzle of the rifle on my back, I moved forward, my legs moving independently of my body. One reluctant step in front of the other, knowing I was stumbling to my death. I was immersed in alternating waves of terror and exhaustion. Images of Caroline and Tucker floated in and out of my head.

I'll never see them again. They'll never know what happened to me.

We got to the edge of the parking area, and I stopped.

Parker pointed with the gun. "That trail right there. After you, Geneva."

Barely through a dark opening in the dense forest and thickets of brush, difficult to see in the falling snow, I started trudging, one heavy foot in front of the other, across and over exposed roots and downed limbs, my hands and feet numb from cold and terror.

We weren't more than a dozen steps in when we all heard the shotgun blast, an explosion echoing through the night air. We all turned and stared behind us at the orange glow coming through the trees as the house continued to burn.

We waited.

One heartbeat, two heartbeats.

Stuart whispered, close in my ear. "Lisa got him. She shot the bastard."

Just as a small bubble of hope rose in my chest, we heard another gunshot.

This one from a hunting rifle.

Parker turned to Leonard, smiling slightly. "I told you Lisa couldn't shoot someone."

Leonard muttered, "But Jason's never had a problem."

I puzzled it out in my head. Lisa must have waited in the burning house as long as she could. The she made a break for it out the kitchen doorway. Seeing Jason standing in the flickering light of the flames, Lisa most likely pointed in his general direction and pulled the trigger.

But she couldn't kill bring herself to kill him, even at the expense of her own life.

Then Jason took his time and killed her.

My utter despair was complete.

Parker ordered, "Let's keep walking."

My feet felt like lead, my legs had no strength. But somehow, by sheer will, I trod slowly forward down the snowy trail, every so often prodded by the barrel of Parker's rifle.

Finally, we came to the edge of a steep ravine. It was an inky black maw, a grinning abyss. Over the sound of the blazing lodge behind us, I heard the tinkling babble of a creek somewhere below.

Parker muttered, "Stop."

I gazed around me at the dark woods. Then back down into the darkness just a step beyond.

My grave?

Mustering what little strength and courage I had left, I turned and faced my killer. I was going to make that fucker look me in the eye when he shot me.

Stuart stood next to me, and when he saw me turn, he did the same.

Leonard sighed, blinking, and said, "Really? You want to see this?"

I wanted to answer, but I couldn't find my voice. I wanted to say something clever, my last words. But instead, I stood in silence waiting for death.

A gun went off.

Leonard bucked forward and fell to his knees. He shoulder had exploded, blood, bone, skin tissue exposed through a ragged hole in his coat. His eyes were wide in surprise, his mouth open but not saying anything.

Parker stared at him, his eyes unbelieving.

Seeing the opportunity, Stuart leaped at Parker, grabbing the barrel of the rifle in his hands, shoving it, aiming it at the woods.

They struggled, Stuart pushing and pulling with both hands on the barrel of the gun, Parker jerking at the gunstock, finger still on the trigger, unable to aim.

Don't think. Do.

I stepped close, closed my fist, and punched him hard in the center of his throat, then landed a flurry of punches to his face.

He couldn't defend himself while he held the gun with both hands.

He stumbled, his body angled out over the ravine. He tried to catch his balance, letting the rifle go.

His arms wheeled in the air, his eyes wide with terror.

He was gone.

Stuart and I heard the sound of rocks and brush as he slid down the ravine. Then it stopped.

I looked at Stuart. He smiled. He was holding the rifle.

I glanced down into the darkness.

From behind me, Leonard moaned in pain and shock.

I saw the muzzle flash before I heard the gunshot. Like a high-powered mosquito, the bullet flew by my head, missing me by only inches.

He always carries a concealed handgun.

Stuart's grin vanished when we heard Parker starting to climb back up the ravine.

Lisa called out from somewhere behind us. "Let's go."

I heard Parker's mad scrambling. Climbing like a deadly spider up the steep incline of the ravine.

Again, I was struck by terror.

I turned, fixing Leonard Ryan in my sight as he struggled to get back onto his feet, using his rifle as a crutch.

I growled, "Bastard," and kicked him in the side of his head. Then I reached down and tried to snatch the gun away from him.

He held onto it like grim death.

What is it with these guys and their guns?

The two of us struggled until Lisa screamed, "Leave him. Let's go."

As if he'd awakened from a nightmare, Stuart started sprinting back down the trail, toward the lodge, heading in the direction of the roaring fire. He held Parker's rifle in one hand. I wondered if he knew how to use it.

I didn't.

I followed, my legs pumping hard, jumping over roots and limbs in our way.

Glancing back, I was horrified to see through the falling snow that Parker had crested the ravine and was kneeling next to Leonard.

We caught up to where Lisa had taken the shot that hit Leonard Ryan. She turned and ran, just ahead of us. We got to the clearing and she slowed down. "Do you have your car keys? We need to take your car; you're blocking Stuart's."

Racing past her, I grunted, "Got 'em."

We dashed to the barn. The door was already open. We jumped into the Sebring, Lisa in the passenger's seat, Stuart throwing himself into the back.

"What did you do to Jason?" I yelled, putting the keys in the ignition.

"Asshole believed Parker and let me get the drop on him. After I gut-shot him, I took his rifle and shot him once in the head."

Tough lady.

The engine growled to life.

I threw the car into reverse, punching the gas pedal. We bolted out of the barn, and the back window shattered in an explosion of shattered glass.

Stuart shouted, "Jesus Christ, they're shooting at us."

From the corner of my eye, I saw Parker with Leonard's rifle up to his shoulder, sighting our car, ready to take a second shot.

I quickly pulled the lever down to Drive and slammed on the gas, throwing stones and ice behind us, feeling the bullet as it thudded into the trunk. We tore back down the icy road, now slick with a layer of fresh snow. My eyes alternated between peering out the windshield and glancing up at the rearview mirror.

My veins turned to ice again when I saw them.

Headlights.

I pushed the Sebring harder, knowing that my car couldn't outrun their SUV.

At that speed, the road was treacherous. The snow had hidden the sides of the road, and the headlights glared into the blowing, hypnotic swarms of snowflakes.

I glanced back up at my mirror.

Damn it.

The headlights were brighter. They were closing the distance between us at a frightening speed. I couldn't go much faster and still safely negotiate the snowy road.

Like something out of a nightmare, the headlights relentlessly bore down on us.

Our heads jerked back when the SUV rammed into our backside.

Lisa turned around and rested the rifle she'd taken from Jason on the seat back. "Stuart, lie down."

She aimed through the broken back window and pulled the trigger. The sound of the gunshot exploded inside my car. Barely daring to take my eyes off the road for even a split second, I glanced up to see the SUV drop back, slowing slightly.

We were almost at the bottom of the hill, the two-lane road below us glistening dimly in my headlights. I was going to hit it at a high rate of speed. I was going to have thread the needle carefully, braking just enough to take the turn, without losing control, but staying ahead of Parker and Leonard.

The SUV hit us again.

I slammed on the brakes. My tires couldn't find purchase, couldn't get traction on the slippery surface.

They were shoving our car forward. We were out of control.

The intersection ahead of us was suddenly awash in light. I realized in horror that a vehicle must be approaching our turnoff.

I pushed hard on my brakes again and again.

We kept accelerating forward.

I caught a glimpse from the corner of my eye of the oncoming vehicle.

A truck.

I pumped the brakes.

No good.

I slammed down on the gas pedal and we pulled away from the SUV.

Headlights just outside my window.

A horn blared and brakes squealed.

Too late?

Wild-eyed, holding my breath, I twisted the wheel, and we slid, going sideways toward the other side of the road, flying into a ditch, hitting it hard.

I heard it before I saw it, the truck smashing into the SUV, pushing it sideways down the icy road, sparks flying, metal screaming.

When they finally stopped moving, the driver of the truck jumped out of his cab and ran, sprinting through the falling snow as if his life depended on it.

Stuart muttered, "Jesus, it's a fuel tanker."

I saw the flames coming from under the truck, then spreading across the road as gasoline spilled from the storage tank. My eyes ached while I stared at the wreckage, waiting for Parker to crawl out.

Lisa whispered. "We've got to get him."

Before anyone moved, the SUV was engulfed in flames.

The explosion lit up the night.

We crawled out of my wrecked, sideways-in-the-ditch Sebring and climbed up onto the road, watching the fire burn. My heart beating wildly, hands shaking, I feebly asked, "Everyone okay?"

Stuart muttered, "Holy Christ."

Lisa answered, "I'm good."

I steadied myself by putting both hands on the top of my car.

I heard Stuart say something and shake his head.

Still staring at the fire, I asked, "What did you say?"

He twisted his head to look at me, his eyes wild, his lips vacillating between a crazy grin and a grimace. He snarled, "It's a goddamned gas truck."

Chapter Thirty-Four

"Do you know what you want to buy yet?" Caroline sat at the kitchen table, scrolling through her laptop, looking at cars. "What do you think about a nice Mustang?"

I laughed. "I don't have the settlement from the insurance people yet. I don't think I'm going to get enough from my poor Sebring to pay for a new Mustang."

"You like the rental?"

It was a Mazda CX-30, a cross between an SUV and a hatchback sedan. Sporty-looking yet functional, I liked the metallic burgundy color and the responsiveness. "You like it? You wouldn't be ashamed to be driven to school in it?"

She chuckled and rolled her eyes. "It's not like you're dropping me off at school in your beat-up Sebring."

At its mention, I winced. It's strange how we can become attached to a machine. In our minds, it becomes more than what it is. It becomes a friend moving you through troubled times, rainstorms, and even bad relationships.

And on that fateful night in the Catskills, it saved my life.

I gave the bare bones information to Brenda Zafiro as I promised. She broke the story in her newspaper. But I wrote the definitive freelance piece for the *New York Times*, starting with our investigation and ending with the destruction in the Catskills. The irony of how Parker Lewis and Leonard Ryan died wasn't lost in the story. True, the fuel tanker wasn't owned by CP&G, but still…

I also wrote about Dr. Stuart Ekmann, who disavowed his study, calling it "bad science and hokum." Over the last few weeks, he's been a staple on the Sunday morning talk shows.

Missing, however, was Darren Reed, former CEO of the international energy company, CP&G. The presentation he was supposed to give to Congress had been delayed when Parker Lewis's death was made public. When my story hit and was picked up by most of the other media outlets in the country, a number of senators on the Hill decried the oil company's attempt to hoodwink the nation. The CP&G board of directors fired Darren Reed.

My piece in the *Times* also prompted a congressional investigation into Fisher, Evans and Sinclair. I had little faith in how that would end up, but at least the "consulting" firm was under the glare of a public spotlight.

Nathaniel returned to work, although he had to hire an intern to help him. His hands were going to take some time to heal. Most likely his psyche as well. But, knowing Nathaniel, I guessed that he'd bounce back pretty quickly.

Meeting with Eric and Olivia Cutter was both gratifying and sad. I'd brought the investigation to a successful conclusion, but when Eric heard that it had been "Uncle" Parker who had murdered his parents, he broke down and sobbed.

I was happy that his sister, Lisa, had been in the meeting to help console him.

The investigation being successfully completed, Frank Mancini sent the final check and bonus to Lodestar Analytics.

Nathaniel had his intern make out a check to me in the amount of seventy thousand dollars .

Sure, I could have walked away with a lot more than that if I'd taken the bribes that Leonard Ryan had offered. But still, holding that check, it was the most money I've ever had at any one time.

And I could look at myself in the mirror.

Valentine's Day came and went. I drove Caroline and Tyler to the dance, and then picked them up when the event was over. If I'd been worried about the two of them, I shouldn't have been.

They talked occasionally on the phone, but it appeared that the fledgling relationship had gone chilly.

When I asked Caroline why, she reluctantly told me, "He kisses funny."

John and I had another dinner together, and another torrid night in a hotel, but then Nathaniel gave him an assignment that took him to Los Angeles. He wasn't sure when his investigation would wrap up and when he'd be back.

And, just as Shana had warned me, he didn't call me while he was on assignment.

The world continues to slowly wake up to the existential danger as a result of the climate crisis. But there is still too little being done.

I sipped my coffee and watched Caroline studying her laptop screen, searching for cars she'd like me to buy. I worried what kind of world I was leaving for her…and her children.

I worried that I wasn't doing enough.

Then she brightened and turned the computer around so I could see the screen. She asked, "How about a Tesla?"

Read on for an excerpt from

RANDOM
ROAD

the first Geneva Chase Crime Reporter Mystery,

**rereleased in April 2021
with a new introduction by the author.**

*"Creativity is the ability to introduce order
into the randomness of nature."*
– ERIC HOFFER

Chapter One

"Last night Hieronymus Bosch met the rich and famous."

That was the lead sentence of the story I filed later that night with the *Sheffield Post*. My editor spiked it, saying, "Nobody who reads this newspaper knows who Hieronymus Bosch is."

Instead, the story began:

"Six people were found brutally murdered, their nude bodies mutilated, in the exclusive gated Sheffield community of Connor's Landing."

My name's been on the byline of hundreds of stories over the last twenty years, in four newspapers, three magazines, a half dozen websites, and, for a very short, shame-filled stint, Fox News. I've honestly lost count of how many crime scenes and murders I've covered—drug deals gone bad, jealous lovers, random shootings, bar fights, gang hits.

This one was different. It felt surreal.

These murders happened in the wrong place. They weren't supposed to happen there.

The three-story turret of the 1898 Queen Anne home stood like a guard tower looming over a two-acre carpet of manicured landscaping perched on the shoreline of Long Island Sound. Wicker chairs and glass tables rested on a massive wraparound porch, waiting for crystal glasses of Pinot Grigio and plates of warm brie. Antique panes of leaded glass overlooked the harbor where schooners once docked. A gentle sea breeze rustled the leaves of hundred-year-old oak trees.

Connor's Landing, a small island community named for a nineteenth-century whaling captain, is separated from the mainland by saltwater tidal pools and connected by an old wooden bridge.

Even in the dark of night, I could see how beautiful it was. A haven of sprawling grounds overlooking the water, houses the size of small hotels, yachts worth more than some small corporations, lifestyles of the rich and the super-rich. All owned by people who, even in this economy, continued to manufacture money.

This particular estate was fabulous. The crime, however, was horrifying.

The cops wouldn't let me beyond the yellow tape and into the crime scene itself, so I waited in the suffocating, hot July darkness until I could get enough information and at least one official quote. Then I'd rush back to my desk and put together a story before press-time.

Leaning against my ten-year-old Sebring, I felt the heat and humidity frizzing up my hair. Whining mosquitoes kept trying to zip into my ears. Sweat trailed slowly out from under my bra and down my ribcage. Every so often I'd glance up at the sky where stars poked glimmering holes in the darkness and the moon hung like a pale sliver in the night.

While I absently fingered my smartphone and squinted

through the darkness at scribbles I kept in a tiny notebook, police officers were coming and going throughout the house with regularity. Lights were on inside. Windows showed me cops moving slowly around, the flashes of cameras recording the scene.

So far, I was the only member of the Fourth Estate who had shown up. My competition was the local TV cable station, WTOC, and another local newspaper, the *Bridgeport Times*. I chalked up my good fortune to someone else's tough luck. The police scanner app on my phone had said that there was a jackknifed tractor trailer on I-95 and traffic in both directions was stopped dead.

Any other reporters in the vicinity were frustrated behind their steering wheels, covering a traffic accident instead of a multiple homicide.

I'd been waiting in the driveway behind the yellow tape for nearly an hour when Mike Dillon, the deputy chief, finally came out of the house. He's about forty, tall and lean, with brown eyes and an angular face that looks cunning to me, wolf-like. He was wearing a summer uniform with short sleeves but no hat. The sheen of sweat below his receding hairline glistened in the staccato red and blue lights of the police cruisers. Mike walked deliberately toward me, acknowledging my presence with a grim expression and a nod.

"Hey, Mike."

"Hey, Genie." His voice sounded a little more somber than usual, for good reason.

"I've been listening to the chatter. Sounds pretty bad in there." I nodded toward a small cluster of paramedics who'd been called earlier that evening, but weren't needed. Like me, they'd been standing outside in the oppressive heat and wishing they were in an air-conditioned bar back in town. They were waiting, not to take the injured to the hospital, but to take the dead to the morgue.

"I hear you've got six bodies." It was more a statement than a question.

Mike came up beside me and crossed his arms. He took a deep breath, using the moment to compose his thoughts. Mike Dillon was accustomed to talking to the media. He hated to be misquoted; he hated it when anyone took cheap shots at him or the police department; and he hated pushy reporters.

But it was pretty evident that he liked me. And it isn't because I'm not pushy, because I am, or that I don't take the occasional cheap shot, because I do.

Mike liked me because, even though I'm a few months shy of forty, time has been kind to me. Men in bars still tell me I'm pretty, and I haven't had to resort to Botox yet, although I've thought about it. The treadmill has kept my weight in check, and I've still got great legs.

I know that it isn't PC to admit this, but Mike thinks I'm hot, simple as that. With men, it always amazes and amuses me how much concession that'll buy.

Taking a long breath, he answered, "Yeah, six bodies, all homicides."

"How'd they die?" I had my notebook ready.

"Hacked to death. Blood and body parts everywhere."

I glanced up. He was looking away from me, staring into the darkness toward Long Island Sound. He wasn't seeing the water, though; his mind was still visualizing what he saw in that house, something unspeakable.

"Hacked to death?" I repeated, stunned.

He answered in little more than a whisper. "They were cut to pieces."

It took me a second to process what he'd just told me. I've covered a lot of murders, and this was surprisingly gruesome.

"Jesus Christ."

"I've never seen so much blood."

"What was the murder weapon? Machete?"

"Don't know yet."

"Got a motive?"

"Don't know yet."

"Robbery gone bad?"

"Not ruling it out."

"Does it look like it could be some kind of ritual?" I was fishing.

Mike glanced back at me to see if I was pulling his leg. He frowned. "No pentagram on the wall, if that's what you're asking."

I thought a moment. "Who found the bodies?"

"We did. We got an anonymous call."

I nodded. "Time of death?"

Mike took a moment to frame his reply. "Coroner thinks sometime around one o'clock this morning."

They'd been lying dead in that house for over eighteen hours.

"Ready to release the victims' names?"

He shook his head. "Can't."

"Can't or won't?" The police liked to contact the next of kin before releasing names to the press. "I already know that this house belongs to George and Lynette Chadwick." I held up my smartphone to show him how I'd uncovered that fact. "Are they two of the victims?"

He didn't answer.

"Who are the rest?"

"We don't have positive IDs yet."

"No?"

Mike cocked his head. "The victims are all naked. Bodies are all stacked up in a pile. The killer or killers took all the wallets and purses with them. None of the victims have any identification."

"Did you say the victims are naked? Were they naked when they were killed?"

He nodded slowly in the affirmative.

I glanced back up toward the house. In the circular driveway, past the police cruisers and the ambulances, there were three SUVs and a Mercedes E350. "I'll bet the victims belong to some of those, and I'll bet you've already run the plates, Mike."

While the cop shrugged, his eyes stared into my own. "Look, Genie, I've got to notify families before I can give you names, you know that. And I also know that you'll be running those plates yourself once you get back to your office. Unless you've already done it." He pointed to my phone.

I had, of course, but before I could print the names, I'd need confirmation from the cops. Two of the SUVs belonged to the Chadwicks. The third, an Escalade, belonged to John and Martha Singewald. The Mercedes was the property of Kit and Kathy Webster.

None of the names meant anything to me. Not yet.

"Any idea on who might have done it?"

Mike gave the stock answer. "Yeah, we've got some solid leads, and we expect to make progress on this case over the next few days."

That was the deputy chief's way of saying they didn't having any suspects. If he did, he would have said that he expected to make an arrest.

Instead, he'd said that he expected to make progress.

Big difference.

That meant that the cops didn't have a whole lot to work with yet. But I couldn't write that because that wasn't what Mike said.

"Well, there's not a lot of story here, Mike."

"What? Are you kidding me? You got naked, and you got hacked up bodies stacked up like cordwood. Makes a hell of a front page." Even though Mike likes me, he sounded disgusted.

I held up my hands. "Sarcasm, Mike. It was sarcasm."

He was right, of course. This was a big story. Six naked people cut up into pieces in one of the most exclusive neighborhoods on the Gold Coast of Connecticut. And right at that moment, the story was entirely mine. On the one hand, I was repulsed to my very soul that six people died like this. The final moments they endured must have been absolute hell. Nobody deserves that kind of ending.

But on the other hand, I was at a low point in my life, bottomed out. If I didn't screw it up, this could be the catalyst to put my career back on track. I desperately needed to get it right.

I tucked my phone and notebook into my oversized handbag. "So, how's Phil doing?"

I was referring to Officer Phil Gilmartin, twelve-year veteran of the Sheffield Police Department.

"He's okay. Still a little sore."

"I didn't hit him that hard."

"You gave him a black eye."

"Tell him again that I'm sorry, okay?"

"Genie, I like you. But don't hit any more cops. It really pisses them off."

I shrugged and raised my hands. "I'm payin' for it, Mike. You know that. I'm on probation and attending AA meetings for the next six months."

"You humiliated him."

"So next time he'll remember to keep his guard up."

"Not funny."

I pointed to the house with the six naked bodies still inside. "Call me if there's a break in the case?"

"You know I will." Mike spoke the words, but I was almost sure he didn't mean it. Knowing Mike, he'd call me when it was good for Mike.

———

Twenty minutes later, I was at my desk watching my editor chew on the stale corner of an old tuna fish sandwich. He stared intently at his computer screen, silently editing my story on the Connor's Landing murders.

Earlier in the day, the ancient air-conditioning system in the building had gone belly-up, and even that late in the evening, the internal office temperature hung in the low nineties. As he looked over my story, Casper Wells took out his handkerchief and absently wiped away the beads of sweat trickling down from his graying scalp and pooling in his bushy, overgrown eyebrows.

Finally, blessedly, Casper hit the Send button, looked up, nodded, and gave me a sour grin.

Time for this girl to go.

I took a look around the building. This was when I enjoyed the office best. It was quiet. Most everyone in the editorial office had gone home for the night. The ubiquitous chatter of the police scanner was silent as were the computer keyboards. The screensavers' ghostly, silver glow threw odd shadows over the chaos of the newsroom. Random piles of newspapers and manila folders were strewn around the floor next to ancient metal desks, littered with more folders and dirty coffee cups.

The office, like the business itself, was showing her age.

With a sigh, I picked up a couple of file folders from my desk, shoved them into my bag, waved at Casper, said good night to the pre-press guys, and walked out.

Glancing at my watch, I had to make choice. I could head over to the Paradise Lounge for a vodka tonic or go to AA.

ABOUT THE AUTHOR

Allie Miller Photography

Thomas Kies lives and writes on a barrier island on the coast of North Carolina with his wife, Cindy, and Lilly, their shih tzu. He has had a long career working for newspapers and magazines, primarily in New England and New York, and is currently working on his next novel.